BENEVOLENT

Book Three of the Sirona Cycle

Hartley James

Benevolent © 2020 Anthony H. James

This edition © 2021

This is a work of fiction. Any resemblance to persons living or dead is purely coincidental.

Cover image courtesy NASA/JPL-Caltech

For Mimi

Chapter One

Belshore

How do you deal with something that is just so vast, so alien, so obviously powerful, but just so *other?* There wasn't any alternative word that she could apply. In the end descriptions simply failed her, just as they had since the vast ship had first appeared. The question kept running through Mahra Kaitan's head all the way back to base, so much so that she could barely even focus on the navigation. She wondered briefly if the other navigators on the other ships that comprised their fleet had heard what she had heard too, the voice that was not a voice, concepts that turned themselves into words echoing inside her head and beyond and through. Hearing wasn't quite right, because whatever it was had manifested *inside* her head, nowhere else. At least she didn't think there had been sound. And then it had blossomed out, absorbing her with its power. In a way, it was remeniscent of the connection that she had had with Aleyin so long ago. But no, it was different from that too. Briefly, she thought back to that first time she had become aware of his words…no, that was not quite right either…his *thoughts* inside her head.

Shortly after the fall of The Cradle, both of them had found themselves transported on that mercenary ship, very much against their wills. Aleyin had gripped her hand and spoken to her in a low whisper so that none of the others could hear.

"I want to show you something," he'd said. "It's just a little trick, but I want you to know it in case we get separated. It might help you. It might end up helping us both."

Mahra had given him a puzzled look but waited to see what he might have to offer. Aleyin had continued in the same low whisper giving her a series of simple instructions. She'd complied, closing her eyes, and trying to form an image of Aleyin's face. Back then, she had found it difficult to concentrate, particularly riding in the hold of a beaten-up mercenary vessel and her thoughts had flitted all over the place, cluttered with unwanted images, stray associations that sprang into being and then leapt away, carrying her focus with them. After a few moments, she'd given up and opened her eyes. Aleyin had urged her to keep at it. She had tried again, closing her eyes, attempting to calm her skittish thoughts. Finally, she was able to draw a picture of Aleyin's pale face in her head. She concentrated on filling in the detail, making the image clearer and clear. She had held the image tightly, concentrating on nothing else. It had been so difficult to summon the will to keep her mind clear of the other thoughts that clamoured for attention.

A few moments later, and she had finally noticed that new sensation inside her head. It was like a buzzing, but broken up, fuzzy but regular. She tried to keep focused on the image of Aleyin's face but the more she tried, the more the buzzing grew. It became regular and repetitive, following the same cadences over and over. Slowly it became more distinct.

Benevolent

Then, in an instant, it was as if she could make out words in the regular pattern of sounds.

Mahra, can you hear me? Mahra, can you hear me?

Her eyes had flown open with shock. Aleyin was peering intently at her face.

"B-but ... " she managed to stammer.

"No," he whispered quietly, holding a finger to his lips. "Now, try it again. Don't say anything. Just close your eyes and try it again."

Doing as she was told, she closed her eyes and attempted to conjure the image of Aleyin's face once more. It was more difficult this time, her mind still reacting to the shock, tumbling with thoughts of what had just happened. With some effort, she was able to frame Aleyin's face in her mind's eye. The buzzing grew in the back of her head and started to take shape.

Mahra. Mahra. You can hear me now. Nod your head once slowly to show me. That's it. Now it's your turn. Start with my name. When I have it, I'll squeeze your hand. Concentrate. Direct the words at my image.

"Mahra, are you still with us?"

That was Timon Pellis. Apparently he still hadn't moved past their little confrontation, because that hint of brusqueness remained.

"Any time now...," his voice came once more over the com.

"Yes, yes," she couldn't help but snapping back at him. "We're not there yet."

"What the hell *was* that?" said Jayeer quietly, as much to himself as two his other two crewmembers.

It took Mahra a moment or two to realise that Jayeer was referring to what they'd just experienced, and actually not the interchange between Timon and herself.

Jayeer was right. That was the question.

How do you deal with something that is just so vast, so alien, so obviously powerful, but no...just so other.

That thought rolled through her head again.

By comparison, the Sirona were models of humanity, though they were not human either, but they were far more like humans than whatever it was that they had just encountered. Mahra could barely bring herself to imagine what these newcomers might look like. If that monstrosity of a thing that she assumed was meant to be a ship was anything to go by....but then, perhaps, she was just letting her fear prejudice her assumptions, and she didn't mind admitting, even if only to herself, that whatever these beings were, they scared the hell out of her.

"Mahra..." It was Timon again.

"Yes, I'm here, Timon."

She quickly checked the patterns in her mind's eye. Those geometries that told of their destination, of their entry and exit points into jump space, those tell-tale signs that only she, or the others who carried the same neural and other biological augmentations could sense. They were close; only a second or two remained.

"Timon, bring her up a fraction. Yes, good. Jayeer, steady...and...wait...now!"

Jayeer Sind, their slightly portly engineer and lead scientist stabbed at the drive controls on her command and they shimmered into existence in another place, albeit this time, somewhere vastly recognisable. They hung above the familiar grey blue globe that was Belshore. All around them,

Benevolent

other ships winked into existence. The sheer number was impressive enough, but it was nothing next to the vastness that they had just left behind, that thing that had appeared out of nowhere, without the slightest shred of warning at all. They had been there to take on the Sirona, to send a message, and then…in an that portent-laden instant, the Sirona no longer seemed to matter.

At last they were back home again, and only now that they were, could she allow herself to take a deep shuddering breath. It almost felt as if she had neglected to take the slightest breath of air into her lungs since that great ship had appeared and those impossible words had echoed inside her head, absorbing all else.

Slowly, Mahra let the air ease from her chest and she caught her bottom lip between her teeth before drawing in another shallower breath, let her senses still, forcing herself to calm and her breathing to regularity. Around her, the ship noises, the creaks, the pings, the unexplained sounds continued on in background, the barely noticable hum of the power and the drives, the chatter from Belshore control coming over the com, as well as the voices from the other ships. There was a taint to the air, a sourness she noticed as she took her next breath, steadier now. She needed a shower. Adrenaline, fear, reaction, it seeped from the pores. She wrinkled her nose. From Timon and Jayeer, there was nothing, no words at all. She could almost see them staring blankly into the void before them, processing what had happened. Mahra looked out at the other ships, the combined forces that they had managed to muster, and here they were, at the tail end of a retreat. Beaten by a concept. Beaten by a voice inside her mind. She shook her head. It had been all too easy. They hadn't even put up any real sort of fight.

Despite that, she had no doubt what the outcome would have been if they had. Not a one of them would be here to think about it.

Even Chutzpah, her zimonette companion, perched on the back of her flight couch, made no move, which was unusual enough. This close to home, he would normally be starting to become a little agitated, but not now, after everything that had happened, not this time. All she sensed was a steady calmness. Once again, she wished that she could read his actual thoughts, something like the connection she'd had with Aleyin back then, rather than the mere impressions provided by the bond that they shared. Somehow, it was something more akin to empathy, their link. Sometimes she suspected that Chutz could actually read her thoughts even if it was not possible the other way round, but she had no way of proving it and it remained little more than a suspicion.

Once more, the image of that vast ship swam into her inner vision and she caught her breath. How could she even be thinking of anything else? It had to be simple displacement on her part, a means of coping with that vastness. That immensity did, however, seem to challenge the imagination.

She ran the sequence of events through her mind once more. They'd been ready to engage, when the Sirona had simply disappeared. She'd been ready for a new many-pronged attack as soon as she had felt the new signs of emergence, but this time it had been different. It was like some enormous vibration that had begun pushing through into normal space. And in the next instant, it was simply there where nothing had been before, a huge physical presence covered in bronze and swirling green and milky

Benevolent

opalescent protruberances like blisters stacked one upon the other, some small, some large. The sheer size of the craft had made it almost impossible to take in, even to conceptualise, but there it had been, dominating their field of view, obscuring everything behind it, like a wall. Thankfully no one had fired. The voice that was not a voice had appeared inside her head, telling them to leave. When they hadn't complied promptly, without warning, four of their ships had fallen apart. She could only think of it that way. There was no detonation, no explosion. From one moment to the next, the ships, two large and two smaller, had fallen into what ammounted to collections of floating junk. It had been far too far away to see the details, but the thought of what might have happened to their crews was enough. Even if they had not been shaken apart like the ships they flew in, it would have been instant exposure to space and then…well there wasn't anything good after that. Mahra swallowed as the image played out in her head. She'd seen that happen more than once. They hadn't needed another warning, and together, the fleet had made a reactive jump back to their safe staging area, the agricultural world of Falvius. After a quick conference amongst the fleet commanders, it was decided to make a retreat to their separate worlds of origin. Harder for the Sleeth, for so they called themselves, to pick them off en masse, or at least they hoped. They would then decide what they were going to do. Although Mahra failed to see any reasonable response available at the moment. She shook her head. That would be up to someone else to decide anyway.

Despite the thoughts absorbing her mind, there was something else still worrying her, something nagging at the edges, ever since that all too recent uncomfortable confrontation with their flamboyant pilot. Timon had as much as accused her of being self-serving and insensitive. Ever since that day, she'd had more than a little time wondering if he might not in fact be right. She'd never really had anyone to teach her otherwise, and all throughout her life, it was more often than not her own choices that meant the difference between survival and something else, or at least a very different sort of survival than it had ended up being in most instances. Not that that was any real excuse. They were her team members. She thought of them as a team, as a unit. She should be thinking about them, considering them as well, including them in the choices that she made. She just wasn't very good at it. She never had been. It had always been just Chutzpah and Mahra, and before Chutz, just Mahra and Mahra alone. And that's the way it had been ever since that catastrophe back on The Cradle, the invasion that had started her on the path to what she was today.

Perhaps none of that would matter anyway. Perhaps none of them would be around to worry about such trivialities. For all she knew, they might be facing real annihalation. That vast alien presence might have the capability to make entire worlds fall apart just like those ships, there one instant and scattered pieces the next. But that was just mere speculation. Not she, none of them, had any real way of knowing. The way the Sirona had scattered, the way those ships had been taken apart, neither of those things augured very well.

Chapter Two

New Helvetica

Valdor Carr stood in his accustomed spot, the space he felt comfortable in when he was deep within his musings. It was the same place he had stood when, what seemed so long ago, the Sirona had interrupted him that very first time. He felt tempted to turn, check the room for any uninvited presence, but he knew that was just a nonsense. There was no reason for the Sirona to visit him now. Not since Marina's revelations about the links between The Benevolent and the Sirona, the way they worked, their purpose. He sucked in one cheek and then reached for the crystal tumbler resting on the stone sill, pausing to let the aroma waft over his senses before he took a healthy mouthful of the amber fluid, and closed his eyes as the warmth and the burn filled his mouth and then throat as he swallowed. He allowed himself the briefest of grimaces. The liquid hit his belly and he felt it, bringing another slight grimace. Once upon a time, and not too long ago, he had owned a sizeable portion of the city that stretched out below this penthouse window. His gaze roved over the buildings, the districts, the old-style structures hiding corporate and technological machineries throughout. Many of them had been his, though not visibly. Series of shell companies, holdings, surrogates, worked in his stead. Sometimes his main factotum would act for him. All that had been taken away after the Sirona came. All that had simply disappeared with barely a struggle. Valdor Carr had simply folded and he was less than proud. Circumstance had worked to bring him back, nothing else. He had faced up to that, and the knowledge worked like a thorn in his guts. He tilted the glass from side to side and then took another sip. At least now he was back, and he was starting to regain some of that ownership. Valdor Carr was very rarely one to give up. He always had a series of options in reserve, and this time was no different. Marina and The Benevolent had their plans, but so too did Valdor, but for the moment, he would certainly be keeping those plans to himself.

Back when this was just beginning, Valdor had decided to push his endeavours in the biocomp direction. The same thing that he'd been trying to accomplish with the ILGC merger, but now, with what he knew, he'd added a couple of twists, changed his chosen outcomes, and then sat back to watch. The whole neural implant equation that had entered centre stage with Mahra Kaitan's appearance had altered the playing field substantially. He'd seen what the combination of the two had done. He'd been surprised, but just with the fact that it was a direction that had never entered his thinking. Once or twice, when he'd been discussing the broad brushstrokes of the thing with Marina, she had pushed for the use of human subjects, insisted that they could be expendable, but Valdor had not been comfortable. He didn't much like that idea at all. He'd tried explaining that it rather defeated the purpose of what he was trying to achieve, i.e. the removal of the human element altogether, but she was having none of it. Back then, he'd believed that perhaps he had been expecting too much of her. He'd taken another run at it, pointing out the advantage of not having to rely on surgically enhanced individuals rather than faster, more reliable biotechnology, but

Benevolent

again, she wouldn't accept it. It was as if she was seeking another, different outcome altogether and she wouldn't be budged. In the end, he had simply given up. It was funny, when he thought about it; at one stage Marina would have been one person he would have trusted with his life. Not anymore. He knew so much about her now than he had back then. Still, however, despite all that, he wasn't sure how much Marina was nothing more than a mouthpiece. He would have liked to believe otherwise…he'd known her for a long time…and she'd been wily enough to mask the truth of her involvement with The Benevolent from him, but all the same, one did not necessarily equal the other. Nonetheless, he was complying with The Benevolent's desires. That didn't stop him diversifying into other areas at the same time. He nodded, took another swallow of the brandy, and then turned back to his desk.

He settled himself in the large wing-backed chair that sat behind his desk—still an affection, but it continued to serve multiple purposes, statement of power relationship, status symbol, shield against intrusion, a bit of luxurious indulgence, so he kept it. It enforced the subconscious power relationship with any who sat opposite, prompting the unconscious archetypical symbols of authority and position. Its wings enveloped him when he wished to be alone with his thoughts. Sometimes, after a particularly long session, or even in the middle of one, he could sink back into the padded comfort to doze, but mainly he used it to cut distractions. He was a little surprised that Marina had not chosen to get rid of it during her interim tenure. He could be thankful for that much, at least. In fact, she had not changed too much in his apartments and offices. It was if she knew she was going to be little more than an interim caretaker.

Hartley James

Placing his palm on the recessed panel cut into the desktop's black expanse, he tapped out the boot sequence with his fingers. The comp was keyed to both his palm and a precise pattern only he knew and yet Marina and her people had seemed to have little trouble bypassing it. Of course, he'd changed everything once he was back in play, but he was still nervous about how secure everything might be. Did The Benevolent maintain some sort of watching routine embedded deep within his systems? There was no way of knowing for sure. He'd engaged security professionals to check everything out, but they'd come up clean. He was tempted to use a fresh set of contractors to run the checks again, someone he'd never used before, but some of his people went way back and they had always served him very well.

The screen irised into existence above the desk. Lightly, he tapped the end of his middle finger into a faintly edged depression on the desk surface to initiate the update sequence. Colours, graphs, figures, and notes sprang immediately into existence, scrolling rapidly across the screen and he leaned forward. His practised eye scanned the sequences, skimming the surface of the information, finger poised, ready to hit pause if anything that might warrant his attention.

The displays showed the usual assorted details: power bases, shares, holdings, profit and loss, mergers, acquisitions. Nothing really there that would beg for special attention. A couple of his newer forays into virgin territory could do with a bit of tweaking. Patchy performance here and there, but there was nothing that couldn't wait

He tapped his finger and the rapid information march halted. Everything was going to plan. Perhaps not entirely to The Benevolent's plan, but most certainly to his own, and that would do for now.

Benevolent

"We call ourselves The Benevolent," she'd said.

"The what?"

"We are a group of people interested in seeing that humanity is pointed in the right direction."

"Oh, come on."

"No, I'm deadly serious, lover. Will you just sit down again? For me? This may take a little time."

"You first," said Valdor.

She had sighed and nodded and then pulled out a chair again and sat. Reluctantly, Valdor had moved slowly to his own chair, frowning as he took a sip and then sat.

"What did you say you call yourselves, whoever yourselves happen to be?"

"The Benevolent."

"And why?"

"Because we have humanity's best interests at heart."

He'd stared at her disbelievingly. It clearly showed on his face.

No, listen to me Valdor," she had said lifting one hand. "Since the expansion of our species, the advances in technology, we have entered a new stage, one where we have taken halting, clumsy steps against aliens, against species with technologies and advancements far greater than ours. We are mere toddlers on that stage. For the most part, humanity is greedy, self-obsessed, interested primarily in power and acquisition. You should know that position very well, lover."

He had snorted at that, but once more Marina had lifted her hand and waved his protest away to forestall any interruption.

"Well, it may surprise you, but some of those races out there are interested in the very same things, power and acquisition. Faced with the challenge that presents, humanity, as a whole, is woefully ill-equipped to deal with the necessities of what is surely to come. We don't know from which quarter, which race, which direction any of it may arrive, but it will come. Of that there is no doubt."

Valdor shook his head then.

"Wait. Hear me out. We, The Benevolent, have been carefully steering events, power structures, outcomes, in directions that we believe will result in our own survival and in fact, the ascension of our species to a much better place. Mostly, the rest of us, those of our kind are too busy staring at themselves in the mirror and wondering how easily they might get the advantage over the person sitting next to them. For the most part, they don't even see the other races, the species out there. Oh, they might be aware of them, certainly, but it doesn't mean that they see them as the threat that they really are. And that threat is to our survival as a race as a species. The fact that everyone doesn't see it is a factor of our other endearing characteristic as a species—our hubris. That may sound alarmist, but you think about it. What are we equipped for other than winding up as the lackeys of some overlord race? Humanity needs guidance, lover."

"And what makes you…this so-called Benevolent, the chosen ones to deliver this guidance?" he'd asked.

"We are," she said simply. "As simple as that, lover. We are."

And that had been that. There had been no further explanation or justification.

If he was honest with himself, he was starting to question how altruistic the ultimate aims of The Benevolent might be, or whether, instead, it was more like a case of enlightened

Benevolent

self-interest. They could claim noble ideals, but with some of the things that they had probably caused to happen…well…. In Valdor's experience, smart, rich people rarely acted in anyone's interest except their own. Oh, they could put up a fine enough front, but scratch the surface and it usually revealed something else entirely.

Chapter Three

Belshore

As *The Pilgrim* and other ships cruised into landing, the chatter picked up, not only from traffic control, but from the surrounding fleet members. Now, here, back home, away from the sight of that vast presence, there was relief and something more. Speculation ran throughout the fleet. It soon became evident that none of the other navigators had heard, or, no, still she was struggling to express it, perhaps sensed, what she had from the vast alien mind. She presumed that the consciousness behind those thoughts was as great as the ship. To it, or them, she didn't know which, they, the assembled forces of humanity were nothing more than tiny creatures. She listened to some of the discussion and then took the decision that she needed to be sure once and for all, and she broke into the conversation.

"This is Mahra Kaitan, talking to all the other navigators. Did any of you, anyone at all, hear anything back there, any sort of message or voice?"

The answers started to bounce back in, all in the negative.

"Mahra, do you think that's a clever idea?" asked Jayeer over the secure channel.

"Why not, Jay? We need to work out what happened."

"So why did you all break off?" asked Mahra.

"Tell us," came a semi-familiar voice. "You were the one who gave the order, weren't you?"

Benevolent

Mahra recognised her now. It was Larissa. Always quick on the biting retort that one. Too little patience. Maybe she herself could be accused of that as well.

"All right," she said. "I get it. Thanks, all. I just needed to know."

The next she addressed only to Timon and Jayeer. "I wasn't the only one though," she said. "Chutz clearly heard or felt it as well."

"Are you sure he was not just reacting to what you were experiencing?" asked Jayeer.

She paused, considering that possibility. "No, it was more than that." She reached up to stroke him, but he barely reacted to her touch. "And right now, he's not exactly acting like himself. Whatever it was has definitely affected him. I'm not sure if he's spooked or what, but it seems, I don't know, as if he's entered some sort of calm, meditative state. I don't think I've read anywhere that zimonette's hibernate, but he's being uncharacteristically sluggish."

"Well, we can worry about that after we get down," said Timon. "We don't even know if they're a threat, these whatever it is they call themselves. They seemed to chase the Sirona off pretty damned fast and that much suits me fine, thank you very much. You know, the enemy of my enemy and all that...."

"Hum," said Jayeer, but nothing else.

"Come on, Jay. Surely, you've got something to add," said Timon in response.

"No, that's all right," he said. "That's all right," the last trailing off thoughtfully.

Timon was right though; they didn't know. All they had to go on right now was a set of loosely cobbled together assumptions based upon the briefest of impressions before their joint mass panic. She ran the sequence through her head again, looking for any clues, but there was nothing. They'd travelled out to engage the Sirona in what they believed was their home system. The Sirona had disappeared. That huge vessel structure had emerged. An alien presence had appeared in Mahra's head telling them to go home. As they hesitated, the aliens made short work of four of their ships, and in the next moment, they had all beat a pretty hasty retreat. That was it. Of course, if she thought about that more, it just left her with additional questions to add to the list that was already growing in her mind. How had they known that they were going to comply? Could they sense the jump drives? If they could sense the drives, could they also track them, just in the same way she had been able to track the Sirona ships? Were they likely to follow, and if so, what were the consequences then? That thought prompted a sudden chill and she reached out with her senses, checking if there was any sign of pursuit. So far nothing, and she relaxed a fraction. And what of the Sirona anyway? Where were they? Why had they taken off so rapidly? Had they met these creatures in their staggeringly large ship before? Were they simply afraid, just like she was, or was there some sort of animosity between the two races? Too many questions. Way too many.

Of course, she had no way of answering any of them. Maybe they wouldn't even get the chance.

As they cruised slowly down to the surface—even though the fleet was somewhat diminished, there were still too many ships for traffic control to co-ordinate and contend with—the chatter continued, speculation, sheer awe, fear, wonder, but all of it simply washed over her. All she could think of was that presence in her head, how she could *feel* the difference. How had it, or they, even known that she, Mahra, in fact anyone, could react and respond to their presence? That thought made her swallow. Was she like some sort of beacon shining there invisibly in the blackness, simply radiating her existence? She suddenly thrust out her senses again, seeking any sign that the vast alien vessel might indeed be following, but again there was nothing.

"I supposed we will need to report to Garavenah once we get down there." Timon's voice.

"Either that or Aegis," said Jayeer.

"Not that there's much to tell really." Timon again.

"Perhaps we should go back and try to track the Sirona ships. What about that, Mahra?" asked Jayeer.

It took her a couple of moments before she could actually form the words to answer him.

"Are you completely out of your mind, Jayeer Sind? Or were you just not with us?"

"No, of course," he said. "But we did have a mission. Aren't you in the least a little bit interested in where they might have gone? As fascinating as it is, for all we know, that…thing…is probably not there anymore. We don't even know what it was doing there. And, really, it can hardly see us as a threat. As I said before, we did have a mission after all. I suggest we stop worrying about them, or it, and get back to being concerned about why we were there in the first place."

Mahra frowned, trying to make sense of what he was telling them. Sometimes Jayeer became a little obtuse, it was true, and overly *focussed,* but this was something else entirely.

"Didn't you see what happened to those ships?" she said. "Really?"

"Yes, of course," he responded. "But we expected at least some casualties, didn't we? They just happened to come from an unexpected direction."

"Um, Jayeer…." Timon's voice was urging caution, and well he might be.

"I was merely putting it out there," said Jayeer. "As a possibility, you know. We have the chance before we're down. It wouldn't take much to jump back. And we all know how keen you have been to get at the Sirona, Mahra."

"Garavenah would have our guts…," muttered Timon.

"No, Jay. No," said Mahra after a moment. "This is something completely different. We can't do that. We can't."

"Let's just land, get through the debrief and then work out what we are going to do then," said Timon."

"I agree," she said.

"Fine," said Jayeer. "As I said, I was only putting it out there. Testing the water, as it were…."

Mahra shook her head slowly, her lips tightly pressed together. She reached up to give Chutz a reassuring scratch, but he barely moved in response. It was really quite unlike him. Something else to worry about on top of images of the enormous shape that would be haunting her for some time to come.

The Pilgrim was about tenth in line to set down and as she felt the ship ease into position, she was already fumbling with her restraints, eager to get out of the pod and back onto land, just any other environment, really. With her com no longer attached, already resting snugly in its cradle, the back and forths of the other ships and traffic control were absent, and Jay and Timon's voices came as muffled mumbles from the direction of the bridge. There were creaks and other noises as *The Pilgrim* settled back into the strain of proper gravity. Reaching up behind herself, she caught Chutz and steered him onto her shoulder at his familiar perch.

Benevolent

"You okay, Chutz?" she asked quietly, worried, but he merely tilted his head at her face in response, which in turn brought a little frown to her brow.

"You need something, Mahra?" asked Timon from almost directly below. He was already making his way out towards the lock.

"No, no, Timon. It's alright. Just talking to Chutz."

"Okay, then. Jay's right behind me," he called up. "I'd like us to get moving, if you're okay. Face the music sooner rather than later.

"Yes. Got it, Timon," she said. "I'm on my way."

By the time she'd climbed down from the pod, Timon's and Jayeer's backs were already blocking the outer airlock. She grimaced, realising that she didn't have her blade with her. There was nothing for it. Reaching up to steady Chutz in his current state, she hurried to catch them up. She could come back and retrieve the blade later. She didn't think that she'd be likely to need it where they were going. The smell of the port wafted in through the open lock, fuel, lubricants, a hint of rain on the air. Despite the gust of non-recycled air and the smells that went with it, her own stink still accompanied her all the same. She needed to do something about that. All around the voices and sounds of crews disembarking washed in with the scents as well as the sound of other ships still landing. All of it was a confusion of noise and she wasn't even in a position to see it all yet.

Here, back on Belshore, there were other things to trouble her as well. She still hadn't recovered from the whole Jacinda incident. There was nothing she would have liked more than to disappear up to Jacinda's place, regroup, assess her options away from all of this noise and the taste of defeat that tainted it all. In an ideal world.... She gave herself a wry smile and a small shake of her head. Jacinda was long gone and Mahra didn't even have any idea where she had gone. That thought brought a wave of bitterness washing through her anew. How could she have been so stupid? Or perhaps she hadn't been stupid. She simply didn't know the truth of it. Jacinda's disappearance had left her with so many unanswered questions. Perhaps something had happened to her. Perhaps there was nothing that Mahra had done. Perhaps. Despite the enormity of what they were facing now, those nagging thoughts were still there, fading a little now, but still present, whispering in her ear when she was least expecting it. She shook her head again, this time with a grimace and stepped out into a cold drizzle and crowds of crewmembers heading into the buildings in front of them.

Quickening her pace, Mahra caught up with Timon and Jay, drifting into the tail end of their conversation.

"I don't like it, Jay, I don't mind telling you."

"Still, there is an opportunity. Think what they might offer."

"Always the optimist, Jay. Do you really think we're in a any position to negotiate with that...that...thing, whatever it was?"

Mahra caught the tone in Timon's voice.

"Did you feel something, Timon?" she asked.

He glanced back over his shoulder marking her presence.

"Ah, there you are. How do you mean, Mahra?"

"Well, sure, that ship was huge and strange, but there's something in the way it seems to have affected you. You're not exactly sounding like the Timon we know and fear."

"Ha."

Benevolent

He seemed to consider as they reached the door, and he paused, one hand upon the frame, looking down at the ground, a trace of a frown on his brow.

"Perhaps you're right, Mahra." He shook his head. "Strange. No time to think about that now though," he said, scratching under his chin and then smoothing his moustache as he stepped through the door. "We need to get going."

He was right. Jayeer had said nothing, simply watching the brief exchange and blinking behind his thick lenses. Timon strode off down the corridor with Mahra following and Jayeer bringing up the rear.

Garavenah met them before they were even half the way to her offices. She stood, hands on hips, blocking the corridor, as usual radiating a presence despite her small stature.

"I should think so too," she said. "What the hell happened up there? We got something from the feeds, but nothing is very clear. What was that? And Mahra, you had something?"

"Should we be discussing it here?" said Timon. "Where's Aegis?"

"Elsewhere," said Garavenah. "Never mind that, Timon, I need to know what's going on. What of the Sirona?"

"No idea," he said. "They simply vanished."

"Talk while we walk," said Garavenah, turning, walking up to the next junction in the corridor and turning, not in the direction of her offices, but towards one of the large hangers that they often used as an assembly and briefing space. "So, these new ones…. called…."

"Sleeth," offered Mahra.

"The Sleeth?" said Garavenah, glancing back for confirmation.

"Sleeth, the Sleeth, I don't know. The word isn't quite enough."

"What are they? Who are they?"

"We don't even know if it's a they," said Timon. "That ship was strange. Like nothing we've ever seen. Not what I'd expect a ship to look like."

"Well, that much was clear from what we could see and hear," answered Garavenah.

They emerged together into the open hangar space. There was no one there, just a single ship. Garavenah glanced around and then nodded to herself wandering slowly over in the ship's direction. There was something different about it. Not the normal CoCee configuration at all as far as Mahra could see. Jayeer was looking at it quizzically as they approached, scanning it from tip to tail, seemingly far more interested in the craft than the conversation.

Garavenah stopped and turned to face them all.

"So, what are we going to do about it?" she said.

Timon frowned, blinked, and then looked at Jayeer, then at Mahra.

"Sorry, Gara, I…."

Garavenah nodded. "The truth is, we are about to get into a mire of debriefing, posturing, and planning. Personally, I feel that's probably going to be the last thing that we need at the moment. We have no idea what's happening, who or what these Sleeth are, what happened to the Sirona, none of it. All we know is some vast newcomer made short work of some of our ships and sent you all running home. Well, that's not us, is it?"

Timon cocked his head a little, his eyes narrowed.

"Yes, I know, Timon. I know. Whatever happened out there, we were clearly outmatched, but we need to do something. And, as usual, when we need to do something that's not necessarily got the backing of the entire Council. We need to, well…."

"…rely on old Timon Pellis to do the job. Is that it Gara?"

Garavenah raised her eyebrows and gave a quick toss of her head, her lips pressed firmly together.

Timon gave a short laugh, which echoed around the hollow space, but it wasn't a sound of amusement and nor was the expression on Garavenah's face.

"And to that end…." Garavenah turned and gestured at the ship behind her.

With Garavenah's action, Mahra turned her attention to examine the ship in more detail. It had some of the earmarks of the CoCee current fleet, but the lines were different. It was more compact, sleek. She suddenly realised what it was that had been throwing her off. There was no visible pod. In fact, at least from this angle, she couldn't see any evidence of weaponry. That gave her pause. She quickly stepped around the nose to get a view from the other side, which simply served to confirm that suspicion. She moved back around again. This ship was unlike any of the fleet she'd seen. A little puzzled, she stepped back around to join the others again. Timon was holding himself back, she could tell, but his jaw muscles were visible, not a good sign. Finally, unable to control himself, he spoke.

"Are you telling me that you are about to do this to me again? Isn't once enough?"

"What are you talking about, Timon?" said Garavenah, clearly a little taken aback by his reaction.

"First you take away my pride and joy, the love of my life, adulterate her, bring her back with a different name, and now, from what I can see here, you're about to take her away altogether. Am I right? Tell me I'm not."

Garavenah sighed and closed her eyes, lowered her head and took a deep breath before looking up at Timon again.

"You and your beloved ships, Timon Pellis…."

"One ship, Garavenah. One ship. Not *ships*. No matter how much you managed to abuse her."

"Yes, yes, I get it."

"Well?" he spread his hands wide.

Garavenah sighed again. "Yes, you're right," she said.

Timon growled and looked at the ceiling giving a slight shake of his head and a bigger exhalation of breath.

"We've been working on this for some time. Of course, completely under wraps. We knew that there would likely come a time when we needed to be a little more discreet about our activities. Hence, what you see here."

"But there's no weaponry," said Mahra.

Timon was only half paying attention, his lips firmly pressed together, and his eyes narrowed, still pointing somewhere above rather than on Garavenah or the ship. She almost expected him to cross his arms and pout, the way he was going on about it.

"Yes, so it would seem," Garavenah answered. "But it has its complement. There is no need for a pod. We are not foreseeing the need for visual."

"But what if the systems get knocked out?"

"Yes, there is that. But for you that shouldn't be a problem, should it Mez Kaitan? And that's something we've been considering. Up until now, we've only been considering your abilities in the context of navigation. A few among us have been thinking about potential broader applications of what you can do. From everything that we've learned, we are assuming that you probably don't need to actually see a ship

Benevolent

either with or without instruments, to be able to pinpoint and shoot at it. Or perhaps I'm wrong."

Mahra frowned, thinking about that for a moment. She supposed Garavenah was right, not that she had had any chance to test the assumption, but she supposed it made sense. She gave a brief nod of confirmation. They were taking a hell of a lot for granted though and she couldn't help a brief frown as that suspicion took shape. Garavenah caught it, clearly.

"But…. I am hoping that you are not going to be in a position where you need to shoot at anything at all," she said. "So, what I am going to ask you to do, for the moment, is off the books as well. With the confusion of the debrief, and with everything that's happened, the returning crews, sorting out conflicting stories, it's the perfect opportunity for you three…um four…," she said glancing at Chutzpah, "to slip away. It would take me an age to get approval for this. I can see the debates dragging on for days and nights."

"Slip away where?" said Timon, finally deigning to speak.

"I need you to go back. See what you can find out. See what information we can gather. I need you to stay alive in the process. This ship…," she said, gesturing behind without turning, "I believe represents the best opportunity for us to try to achieve just that. It has new stealth alloys as part of the outer hull. It doesn't exactly stand out against the backdrop of space. You should appreciate that, Timon. You've always had that ancient pirate gene running through you, haven't you?"

Mahra heard Jayeer whisper a single word to himself.

"Yessss."

Mahra shook her head, narrowed her eyes at him. Sometimes too smart for his own good, Jayeer. Then, when he didn't even look at her, glanced back at the ship again.

Garavenah was right, it was matt blue-black, deep, and dark like the empty spaces. There were no identifying signatures on it anywhere. The hull appeared mostly unbroken by ports or windows, although there was a space where she presumed the bridge lay. She imagined with whatever tech it had fitted, it would be quite capable of keeping itself hidden, at least from casual observation. She wasn't so sure, however, how that might fare against the Sleeth. They had no idea if these beings used conventional technology as they understood it at all. Once more, the thought rose. They were most certainly taking a lot for granted.

"Aren't we going to be missed?" asked Mahra.

"Oh, yes. Most certainly," said Garavenah.

"And no doubt you've got some story cooked up to cover that," said Timon, rocking back and forth on his heels, peering suspiciously at the ship.

"At least in the interim," she said.

He nodded.

"Well, does she at a least have a name?"

"Not yet. For now, there is just a designation. I suppose naming rights fall to you."

He looked at her, held her gaze. "Oh, I've got a name all right," he said.

"And what's that?"

"She'll be *The Nameless.* Nothing to get attached to. No significance. If she's to float around in the shadows, then that's what she'll be…nameless."

Jayeer glanced up at him, a slight smile on his lips. Mahra could see his reasoning, even if there was something a little petulant about it in the end.

Garavenah, paused before nodding. "So be it," she said, glancing back at the ship.

Benevolent

Jayeer cleared his throat. "Even though I didn't know about it, Garavenah, I am sure that there are others who undoubtedly do. Its existence must be known. And, on top of that, no matter how stealthed it may be out in the reaches, someone, probably more than someone is going to notice our departure."

"Yes, of course you're right, Jayeer," said Garavenah "But...those in the know are in the know for a very good reason. All the same, we have a story about test flights and experimental ship all cooked up and ready for consumption."

"It's strange timing to be embarking on test flights," said Mahra.

"Again, right," said Garavenah. "But generally, the people around here know enough not to ask too many questions beyond the first answer they get. Anything else, we can deal with easily enough."

"So, let's see what she's got," said Timon.

Garavenah nodded. "Certainly, but we will need to be quick. I'm going to have to make an appearance pretty soon." She turned and started walking back towards the main building. "I'm going to have to trust in you to work out some of what she's got on your own, circumstances being what they are. I'm sorry for that, but I don't think there's much of a choice. There aren't exactly manuals."

"Um, just one thing...," said Mahra.

Garavenah stopped and turned. "Yes?"

"How do you know you're not sending us straight to our end?"

"I don't," said Garavenah as she turned back towards the doorway and resumed crossing the broad echoing space away from them.

Mahra stood there, staring at her retreating back.

"Well, that's just great," she said quietly to Chutz, shook her head and then moved to follow the others inside *The Nameless*. If they really were going to do this, she needed to know a couple of things about this ship and what it might be capable of.

Benevolent

Chapter Four

Sirona Space

The giant red globe painted darkness with plumes of crimson and red black. Where before, clusters of silver ships sat around its periphery there were none. Nor did a single vast vessel dominate the nearby space. There was movement, however. Small globes, gold and green, swirling with other almost-seen colours, like oil upon water, swept, arced, dipped performing an uncoordinated dance. Occasionally, they came together, merging, becoming one, or merely joined, like cells dividing and then splitting. One moment, conjoined twins or triplets, and then individuals, swooping away again, then returning to touch briefly.

Of the Sirona, there was no sign.

It appeared that what the CoCee strike force had assumed was the Sirona home system, had been overtaken by another, or several others. It was hard to be sure.

For a while, the globular shapes continued their dance, flitting here and there throughout the system's space, seeming to delight in the dim redness that reflected from their metallic, fluid surfaces. After a while, the movements became less pronounced, gradually slowing as one by one, the bubbles merged, drawing together into clumps and then groups that, in turn, coalesced to form a much larger whole, consuming the space with its vastness. Gradually, the few stragglers also merged, till there was only the one shape, silhouetted against the dark blood-hued orb.

For a few moments, there was nothing, no movement, no trace of activity, a still-life in the blackness, and in the next instant, that vast ship, that one made of many, was simply no longer there. It blinked out of existence leaving nothing in its wake apart from the great red star, standing alone and deserted in the void.

It was unclear where they had come from, but it had not been their first visit. They remembered it, as they remembered everything, but so too did the Sirona. The echoes of that first arrival had lasted for generations. The Sirona would not soon forget, especially not now, since the vast entity's return. Even the Sirona were unsure whether it was properly *entity* or *entities.* In the end, it didn't matter. The Sirona were creatures of business. There was no good business to be had when that *thing* was anywhere nearby.

Chapter Five

New Helvetica

Valdor was back at his desk once more, toying with a particularly complex set of acquisitions that he was running through a series of well masked shell companies. He glanced up in annoyance as his com alerted him to an incoming call. There was no indicator whom it was from, and he grimaced, briefly considered ignoring it and then thought the better of it. With a brief shake of his head, doing his best to compose his features and mask the annoyance, he palmed the connection into life.

In a sharp white suit, hair arranged just so, the image of Marina Samaris took form above the desk. With a sigh, he also invoked visual.

"What, lover? Was that a sigh I heard? Not pleased to see me?"

"Of course, it's a pleasure to see you, Marina. I was just in the middle of something."

"Well, at least that sounds promising. I hope it's something to do with our mutual interests…."

"When is it ever not? Like I have a choice."

"Of course, there's a choice darling. But, as we both know, choices have consequences."

"Yes, yes." He gave a little shake of his head and pressed his lips into a tight line..

"What can I do for you, Marina? I'm a little busy here."

"Be that as it may, lover, we need you to come in."

He frowned. "Didn't you hear me? I'm busy."

Marina's voice grew firmer. "And we need you to come in."

This time, he gave a proper sigh. "Fine," he said and palmed the connection closed.

And that was the problem right there. At the moment, he was nothing more than a tool of The Benevolent. He had only regained his place here, on New Helvetica, because of The Benevolent's actions. Although, if he thought about it, he'd probably lost it in the first place because of them. And it was that knowledge that kept him in check, at least on the surface. He had no desire to end up back on Kalany in the family villa in the middle of steadily but slowly repropagating farmlands. The wanton acts of destruction that had devastated so much of the kahveh fields had not been total. Enough vines survived to take cuttings, regrow some of what had been lost, but the finest crops came from the oldest vines, and there was no replacing that. The knowledge that in the end, what had happened on Kalany had been at the behest of The Benevolent didn't make his current position any the more palatable, especially knowing that much of his personal status came by dint of his family and they in turn, rode on the backs of the now devastated kahveh crops.

Fine, they wanted him in, he'd come in.

He shut down his system, stood and checked himself in the full-length mirror that stood next to the concealed elevator door that would take him down to the street. He leaned in closer to the mirror, brushing his fingers through the hair on one side. It was getting a little unruly and he'd need to attend to it soon. He checked what he was wearing. It would do, he supposed. The cloth flowed, dark, midnight blue, almost black. A ruffled grey shirt exposed at the neck, and a simple steel pin attached at the shoulder. Yes, it would do. He chewed at the inside of his cheek, studying his reflection, considering if he might change it, but then thought the better of it. This outfit

Benevolent

gave him presence. He wasn't going to make any particular impact on Marina—they'd known each other too long—or at least, he'd thought they'd known each other. But it wasn't Marina that he was concerned about with the subconscious cues. It was anyone else she might be in company with when he finally arrived. He glanced around his office space once more. Too early for a brandy really. He paused then. He was forgetting something, he was sure. Then he had it.

Stepping quickly back to his desk, he triggered the concealed drawer and reached for the small hand weapon that lay cushioned within. He briefly considered the options, and then opted for tranq needles. In most cases, on New Helvetica, they were more than adequate. The New Helvetian rules and regulations had become a part of the social norm, almost programmed into the psyche of the locals, but, just now and again, in the right quarters, there were those who took advantage of that. And, there were always offworlders, especially in the quarters Valdor was wont to spend time in during the early hours. Yes, the small hand piece was likely to be confiscated at his destination, but he felt better having it than without it. He slipped it into his pocket and pushed the drawer shut again. He spun and crossed back to the elevator, unable to resist another confirming check in the mirror, but his image was the same as it had been a few moments ago. At least the overall climate on New Helvetica allowed for the heavier fabrics and the fir trimmings that suited him so well. Giving a little shrug, he reached forward, activated the elevator, and stepped inside, clasping his hands behind his back as the door slid to a shut behind him.

Valdor walked everywhere in New Helvetica city. By comparison with a lot of the other major capitals scattered on the various worlds, it was tiny. Because of the world's investment in tech, bio and military, the place was not only very well off compared to a number of other places, but it had a certain level of exclusivity. He paused on the street, noting the slick damp, the touch of fog. There would be clouded halos around the streetlamps later and that moist chill presence in the air that crept into the bones. He could smell it in the air already. Right now, it was off season; the true snows that brought the resort set hadn't really started yet, though there was always snow somewhere on New Helvetica. Pretty soon they would start to see the influx of the snow seekers, all decked out in their iridescent therm-wear. If Valdor had his way, he'd ban the lot of them. The problem was, they were just as much a part of what made New Helvetica what it was as the history and the parks and the old stone buildings lining the very street upon which he stood. Sucking air through his teeth at the thought, he turned and started a leisurely walk towards the street's end, wondering what it was that had suddenly prompted Marina to request his presence in the offices. He didn't particularly like going in, preferring instead to be sequestered away in his own inner sanctum. Besides, there were things about this particular destination that rankled.

Along the way, he passed a few tourists, in the bar district, a few of the locals, nodding to couple of them, but it was mid-afternoon, and trade had not really started yet. There were a few business types, all decked out in their formal conservative suits, pale greys with the high collars that were in fashion amongst that set at the moment. At least he wasn't constrained by the dictates that applied there. He wouldn't be seen dead in those outfits. In the end, he reached the ILGC building without incident and stood for a few moments on the other side of the street, looking at the scrolling holos on either side of the large glass doors, the name display above and letting his gaze rove upwards, the one at the very top. The irony of being called in like a lackey to the very place that he had been responsible for creating didn't pass him by, and he took a deep slow breath, then let it slowly out through his nose before pressing his lips together firmly and crossing the street to enter. As he had expected, they picked up his weapon on the

Benevolent

scans as soon as he entered the building, and he was politely ushered to one side, where they relieved him of its weight in his pocket, just as politely informing him that he could have it back when he left. It didn't matter who he was, and he was fairly sure that they were aware of exactly who he was. It didn't matter. On New Helvetica, procedure ruled just as it always had.

"You are expected, Mezzer Carr," the receptionist told him with a deferential inclination of the head and an outstretched hand indicating the way. "Please make your way to the elevators. They will take you to where you need to go."

He nodded, and without saying anything headed straight for the elevator bank in the foyer's centre. As if he needed directions…. He stepped inside and the doors closed. There was no indicator, no panel of buttons or a touch display, no voice control that he could see, not that he knew where he was supposed to go for the meeting anyway. There must be something that registered for actual employees, but he wasn't aware of it. Clearly there'd been some upgrades since he'd last left the building. He didn't have long to spend in speculation though, for moments later, the door whisked open, revealing a white reception area. Low leather couches and chairs, a glass table in the middle. What looked like reading displays were set in the chair arms. There was some minimalist art on the walls and some sort of glass sculpture in the corner. The floor was smooth, shiny, some sort of hard polymer in a dark-flecked grey. The room had no windows. The unfamiliarity of the décor and the lack of windows gave him no clue as to where exactly in the building he might be, but he tried to project its location in his mind's eye with reference to where he'd joined the elevators. It was somewhere right in the heart, up high. Marina sat in the middle on the couch, her arms spread out across the back. In another of the chairs sat a young woman, one that he didn't recognise.

"Valdor, darling, so glad that you finally deigned to join

us."

"Nice to see you too, Marina."

"Sit, yourself, Valdor. We have some things to discuss."

He paused, looked around the room. There didn't seem to be a door apart from the elevator. Either it didn't have one, or it was very well concealed. He wondered what else might be hidden. With one eye on the room's other occupant, he lowered himself into one of the vacant chairs, rubbed his hands along the arms before swinging his gaze to meet Marina's. He was hardly likely to be discussing anything, unless he knew to whom he was talking.

"So, you appear to have brought along a little friend." he said, tilting his head in the other woman's direction.

"Oh, this is Tsinda," Marina said in response.

"Okay." He turned his attention to the young woman.

"Tsinda works for me. I asked her along to observe."

Valdor studied the room's other occupant.

This Tsinda had a roundish, slightly oval face, large dark eyes, perhaps a little larger than suited his taste, but it was attractive in the way the feeds were. If the bobbed blonde straight hair had been dynamically sculpted tresses, then the picture would have been complete. Not exactly to his taste, but…. She had a full mouth, narrow chin, and a short nose. She met his scrutiny unabashedly, giving as good as she got. He could see a sharp intelligence and a speculation working behind those eyes. She sat back, crossed her legs, and then looked away as if dismissing him. Valdor narrowed his eyes in response.

"I see," he said to Marina without breaking his gaze. There wasn't even a flicker from Tsinda.

Okay, he thought, as he turned back to Marina. "So, what is it you want to discuss?"

"We've had word, lover, about some things that have been going on in the CoCee." She sat forward. "Apparently their little expeditionary force hasn't delivered the result they

Benevolent

were after. They seem to have met some sort of setback, though what exactly happened isn't quite clear. It's hard to tell, as we haven't heard from our other friends at all."

Valdor frowned.

"Your short friends, I suppose you mean."

"Oh, don't worry," said Marina, leaning back and waving her hand. "Tsinda knows all about the Sirona."

Valdor turned to look at her again. She was studying him, her gaze not even faltering as he met her eyes. He thought he caught the slightest quirk of her lips, but he could have been imagining it. He turned back to Marina. But as he did so, he glanced quickly back to see if Tsinda's expression might reveal something when she thought she might relax. There was nothing. He turned his attention to Marina fully.

"Okay, so…."

"We need to come up with something and soon. I know you've been resistant to the whole idea of using actual live test subjects, but I'm afraid we are getting beyond that now. What we predicted, what The Benevolent predicted, has come to pass. There is clearly a new player in the game, and we need to prepare ourselves, Valdor. You have a role in that, but I fear that what we're anticipating is not going to happen. At least not with the way things are going at the moment." She sat forward, looking at him intently. "Darling, I'd love to be able to trust you, but I think I know you better than that. We *have* known each other a long time, after all."

Valdor gave a quick derisive snort. "Yes, well, I thought I knew you for a long time, Marina. None so blind as those that won't see. Turned out it was quite something else altogether, didn't it?" The knowledge still stuck in his throat.

Marina just waved the barb away.

"Be that as it may, lover…anyway, I am still me and you are still you, but there's a bigger consideration on the table."

"Yes, yes, I get that, Marina. Or so you say."

The reality was that Valdor had little interest in The

Benevolent's agenda at all. He wasn't at all concerned with humanity's place on the interstellar stage unless it had the side-effect of bolstering his own position, and thereby, his income stream. The relative comforts that came with that were simply a bonus. But for now, it suited him to play along.

"So, what is it that you're proposing."

Marina held his gaze for a few moments before speaking. "I know you've been resistant, and I think I understand the reasoning, but I am not really sure whether it is altruism on your part or something else. Regardless, politics and weaponry are not enough; that much is clear. We need to do something to give humanity a push, and with some of the advances that have been made in ILGC, we have the chance. Call it evolution, call it what you like, but we have a chance here. A real chance. Humanity's next step. We've seen what can be done. Or at least some of it, but we need to get past the necessity to rely upon bioengineering to achieve what we need. We need to get to the core, to push our species further into something that can be passed on, generation to generation. We thought that engineering enough of a crisis, giving humanity a common foe would be enough to let them see the need and act together united."

Valdor shook his head. "Don't you think that's a bit naïve?" he said. "I appreciate your idealism, but people aren't as clever as you might give them credit for. Yes, they see the threat, but they don't see the solution. They never do until it's thrust right under their noses, and even then…. And I'm not sure that I see the same solution that you and your people, this *Benevolent* do, Marina. Not at all."

"Whether you do or not, lover. The time is right. In fact, the time is necessary. We have the means, and you can be a part of making that happen, or…." She left the last word hanging.

He blinked a couple of times in response. There was more than a little of the zealot in her words, something he'd never

Benevolent

expected from her. He had never actually taken Marina for a fanatic. But then he supposed, in the end, he'd never really known who she was after all. Nor had he ever imagined himself sitting here receiving less than veiled threats from the woman he had taken as his confidante for so long. Despite himself, he let out a sigh.

"What?" said Marina.

"No, nothing," he said. "Nothing that matters anyway. All right then. I'll play."

"Good boy. I knew you'd see sense. Think about it, lover," she said. "In the end, you don't really have much of a choice."

Chapter Six

Belshore

Despite Garavenah's trite assurances, there was no way Mahra was going to be able to get used to being inside a box with no clear sight of what was going on outside except from displays or her extended senses. There were narrow viewports in her station, but nothing that gave her a clear view of the expanse of space around her. This was a design flaw to her mind. Her extended senses helped but they weren't really like seeing anyway. It was more like some sort of semi-transparent overlay on everything she was already seeing. Oh, certainly, she could sense things, feel their presence, but that wasn't seeing was it? And in the end, human beings were visual creatures. So much of their lives was spent watching in one form or another, seeking clues, looking for patterns. She screwed up her mouth as she looked around the featureless space. Like *The Pilgrim* there were instruments that would blossom into life with the slightest command, but unlike the weapons pod in *The Pilgrim* she couldn't see out. And there was that other thing; you were far more likely to trust your own eyes, no matter how wrong they might be. Notwithstanding the fact that in certain states of consciousness, they were likely to be the most unreliable source of input altogether, it still remained a fundamental. She grumbled to herself as she strapped in, ready for their little expedition. She could hear Timon also grumbling from the bridge, with Jayeer throwing in the occasional mollifying couple of words, but that

Benevolent

was just Timon being Timon, bitching about his precious ship. She wondered briefly whether he would come to regret that petulant act of naming. Nevertheless, here they were aboard *The Nameless* and that's how it would stay. It was bad luck to indulge in renaming a ship. She had no idea where the superstition had come from, but she wondered if it had any foundation. Perhaps there was nothing in it after all. *The Dark Falcon* had become *The Pilgrim*, again at Garavenah's behest, and it didn't seem to have heaped any particular misfortune upon its crew. Maybe she just wasn't seeing it. Misfortune was something that you didn't necessarily know was dogging you. That was part of its particular charm.

"All set up here," she said over the com. "Wherever up here is," she added as an afterthought.

"I hear that," said Timon.

"Argh, will you two stop it?" said Jay. "From what I've seen so far, she's a beauty. You'll change your mind as soon as we're underway, Timon."

"Maybe. Maybe. Anyway, enough chatter from all of us. So, let's do this, shall we?"

"What about traffic control?" asked Mahra.

"Garavenah said we've been cleared. Keep it quiet," he said. "Whatever Garavenah says. You know." That hint of petulance was still in his voice. Mahra wasn't sure that it boded well for the ongoing tension that lay between them, still unresolved. They really had to do something about that.

"Right."

Despite Mahra's discomfort, Chutz seemed right at home, content to perch up on the back of her flight couch, looking at the flowing displays, chittering quietly to himself, though for some reason, she felt that he still seemed a little subdued. She wondered what he was thinking, what he'd made of that vast alien vessel. As the ship rolled smoothly out of the hangar space and out onto the apron, she checked what she was seeing on the holos. There didn't seem to be any vast improvement there, apart from the fact that each of the images were joined seamlessly, making her feel like she was suspended in a bubble floating along of her own volition. It was actually a little but unsettling and she thought it would probably take a little bit of getting used to. The visual display showed the tall walls rolling past, the floor sliding away beneath them, above them the roof, then the archway of the hanger doors and then open sky, a few pale wispy clouds. Up ahead there were lines of ships, a couple of people in coveralls going about their duties attending to those ships, pausing to stare curiously at the passing vessel. If they were ship mechs, then they'd know right away that this was an unfamiliar design. It wasn't any wonder that they'd be curious. She closed her eyes, shutting out the visuals and reached out with her senses, probing to see what she was perceiving matched with what she had been seeing. Someday soon, if there was going to be a someday soon after the little expedition, she wanted to do some work on trying to hone those senses, sharpen the perceptions. Apart from the signatures and shapes in jump space, and the actual energy signature of the ships, emerging, departing, and history, there was no real way she could 'see' in the way Garavenah had alluded to, Up till now, everything that she perceived had been pretty much trial and error. At least it had started that way, but she had no tangible way of knowing if what she perceived currently was the extent of it, whether she'd be able to refine it even more, or whether this was as good as it got. She needed the space to work on it, and it needed to be out there, away from any distractions. There simply wasn't the chance though. Everything seemed to be happening too quickly now.

"Here we go," said Timon, and *The Nameless* rose smoothly into the sky. Mahra opened her eyes and watched as the port grew smaller, dwindling below and behind them. The acceleration pushed against her and Chutzpah rumbled something, more to himself than to her, she could tell. She

Benevolent

switched her attention to the space above. Pretty soon, they'd be asking for directions.

"Right," said Timon eventually.

Mahra reached out feeling for the points, knowing instinctively where it was that they were going. She started guiding him towards their position.

"Fire, she's fast," said Timon. "Responsive too."

"See," said Jayeer. "It may not be all that bad after all. Perhaps you can stop shedding tears into your tiny drink now."

"Hmph. And that'd be enough out of you, Jayeer Sind," he responded.

Despite the fact of what they were about to do, the fact that they might not even be coming back…after all, they'd had a pretty clear warning…the banter continued unabated. She would have expected nothing less from the pair.

She could feel their point approaching and she readied herself to give the command. There really had to be a better way to do this. She knew instinctively now where there destination lay, but what happened after she'd made a hundred jumps, a thousand. Would she be able to retain all of that awareness inside her head? What about more? It was going to be a long time before they reached that point though. Perhaps it didn't matter at all. This might be the last jump she was ever going to make. Chutz chittered at her ear, giving her a gentle nip and she brought her attention back into focus.

"Right," she said quietly. "Jay. Steady. Steady. *Now.*"

As she gave the command, her heart was in her throat. She expected nothing less than to emerge and have *The Nameless* instantly torn apart by that vast alien intelligence floating ahead of them in their impossible ship.

The system was empty, at least what she could see on the displays said it was. That great red orb hung alone in space apart from the slowly drifting debris that marked where their own ships had been before. The fragments were further apart now, but you could still see that were they to be pushed back together, they'd form ships. She swallowed, hesitating to think which of those pieces might once have been crew members. Not trusting the displays, she reached out with her senses once more, but of the alien ship there was no sign. Not a trace of the Sirona either. Nor was there any trace of Sirona wreckage as far as she could tell. Had they reacted that promptly? If so, something had really scared them off.

"They're gone," said Jayeer unnecessarily.

"Right."

"Are we sure about that, Mahra?" asked Timon.

"As sure as I can be."

"But are you *sure?*"

"What do you want me to say?"

"Can you tell where they went?" asked Jayeer, cutting in.

"It's confused. I can't really…."

"Well, can you try again?" said Timon.

Mahra clamped her teeth together and shook her head.

"I'll try," she said after a moment.

Once more, she reached out with her senses. The traces of where the Sirona had been, scattering in all directions were still there, but merely echoes now. Of the larger, other alien vessel, there was nothing, no trace, not even a remnant.

"No, I'm sorry."

"Shit," said Timon. She could almost picture him gritting his teeth. "We need to know where that damned thing has gone."

"Do we?" said Mahra. "Do we really? They were here. They told us to go away. We went away. Now they're gone. We don't know where they've gone and really, Timon, I'm really wondering if we should care. We may never see them again. From the impression I got, we were pretty insignificant in the scheme of things. They dealt with us as you might deal with an annoying insect. Shouldn't we be more worried about the Sirona?"

"How do you mean? Aren't these new ones, the Sleeth or

whatever they're called more of a concern? Don't you think they're the bigger threat?"

"Weren't we here for the Sirona in the first place? Isn't this supposed to be their home system, or that's what we thought. I'm beginning to doubt that now. We formed a fleet to take them on. The entire CoCee backed the action. We have no way of knowing if what happened here was simply an unlucky turn of events. We don't even know if this system is nothing more than a staging area for them. I think we should still be concerned about the Sirona, don't you? For a long time, everyone was convinced that they were inscrutable little creatures intent on their own particular version of business transactions. Well, I for one never believed that. Now, after Kalany, I'm not the only one. It was about time some other people saw what they were capable of for themselves. I really think we should be worried about what the Sirona are going to do next. We should worry about the Sleeth if and *when* it becomes an issue, not before."

"She has a point, Timon."

"And don't you think that might be a little coloured by her history? I'm sorry Mahra, but we need to consider the bigger picture."

"I think I am, Timon." She bit her lip, closed her eyes, and took a breath before continuing. "Yes, I can see you have a point, but if you think about it so do I. I've seen what those creatures can do. Yes, we've seen what the Sleeth can do, but really, think about it. They swatted at us. That's all. If they'd wanted to, they could have taken out the entire fleet. At least I believe they could have. They appeared from nowhere, they disappeared leaving not a trace of where they went, and they seem to be able to shake apart ships with their thoughts. Unless you have some idea of how we are supposed to face up to that, or if we'd even want to, I think maybe we need to concentrate on the threat that we might just be able to deal with. But hey, that's just me."

"You're sure there's no sign?" was his only response.

She gave a sigh of exasperation. "As sure as I can be, Timon. Have you even been listening to me?"

"Yes, I've been listening. We don't get to decide though. Whether I agree with you or not, it's not up to us."

"And Mahra, now Timon has a point too," said Jayeer quietly.

And he did. She knew it. Things had been so much easier in a way before the CoCee, before the fleet and Garavenah and Aegis. When she had to answer to no one but herself and whomever her current employer happened to be. Of course, not so long ago, to all intents and purposes that had actually been Timon, but that had been before she knew the whole nature of Timon Pellis and Jayeer Sind and what the pair of them did and for whom. She reached up and stroked Chutzpah's back absentmindedly. If she didn't feel that it was so important, she might just be tempted to cut her losses and go somewhere else, try to sign on with a rogue hauler or something like that. She wasn't sure that she'd be given that choice anymore. She closed her eyes and bowed her head.

"Fine," she said. "Where to now, Commander?"

"I think it's back to Belshore. Lick our wounds," said Timon, ignoring Mahra's pointed use of his title.

"What wounds?" said Jayeer.

"Our pride, Jay. Our pride."

They had reached a dead end, or so it seemed for now.

They made the journey back in silence, apart from the necessities of navigation and ship operations, each of them reflecting on what had happened and what they might do next, or at least Mahra assumed that's what the others were doing. She certainly was. As they made the jump and Belshore shimmered into existence before them, Timon started *The Nameless* on the slow glide down towards ground and the dock. She watched the displays with only half a mind. Her part was done. She had other things to think about now. This

Benevolent

tension between herself and Timon was starting to grate, and she needed to do something to resolve it. No, scratch that. They both needed to do something to resolve it. Jayeer, as usual was keeping himself well out of it, letting it play out as it might, and in the end, that wasn't really helpful. Though, to be honest, she didn't know how it might develop if he started to take sides. She thought that they all could do with a little bit of breathing space, but with the speed that things were happening, she didn't think that any of them were likely to have that luxury any time soon.

Chapter Seven

New Helvetica

At first, Valdor wasn't quite sure what it was that Marina wanted from him. He was even less sure what this woman…no, he thought, more girl…. had to do with anything and why Marina had insisted on having her there.

"Come with me, Valdor," Marina said and stood. This Tsinda stood at exactly the same moment, not needing to be prompted. With the barest of frowns, Valdor got to his feet. The girl was still watching him.

"I'm fairly sure that you're familiar with the manufacturing facilities, and we've no need at this particular point to travel out to the site, but in the meantime, I think you should have a look at some of the work that's been going on here in the research wing."

Valdor's frown only got deeper. "What work?"

"Come, you'll see."

On the surface of things, Valdor still owned ILGC. The company holdings belonged to him. The board was still, at least on the surface, under his control, although a couple of the newer board members didn't exactly belong to him. Still, he ought to be aware of any undertakings that went on within the building, regardless of the reality. He normally had ways of making sure nothing slipped beneath his overall scrutiny. That something clearly seemed to have done so now, concerned him. In fact, there was more about this relationship that was starting to concern him.

Benevolent

"Come, this way, lover."

Marina wandered over to one of the rear walls and without doing anything, a section withdrew, revealing a broad hallway beyond. It was as he had suspected. Tsinda seemed to be waiting for him to move, so he did just that, following Marina's lead, making sure that on the face of things, to all intents and purposes he would continue to appear unruffled by what was happening. This room with its hidden doorways, however, was not something he remembered from the building, though it could easily have been the sort of thing he would have had installed himself. He had a rough knowledge of the building's layout, being more familiar with some areas than others. There were parts of the head office operation that he had never had the need to visit. He had other people to do those things for him. He could feel Tsinda's presence behind him, but he wasn't going to turn or even acknowledge it right now.

Marina led them down a corridor to an area in one of the sections more familiar to him. This part was reserved for parts of the bureaucracy that were necessitated by any sort of corporate venture. Though he had a love for the more technical aspects of his undertakings, offices were something he could understand. Regardless, they only held a vague familiarity for him. It had been months since he had even set foot within the building. She led them to an elevator bank, stood back and motioned him inside. Tsinda followed and then Marina joined, palming the controls. The walls were mirrored, and as they descended, even though he kept his gaze firmly fixed ahead, he was aware of Tsinda standing beside and slightly behind him, studying him in the mirror. He allowed himself a little glance in her direction, meeting her eyes, and thought he caught the vaguest trace of a smile before he looked away again. He wasn't quite sure what was going on there at all. He glanced at Marina, but she seemed focussed either on her own thoughts or on where they were headed. As the doors slid open, she stepped out, and without hesitating or even looking back, headed off down a passageway to the right. He knew where he was now, and giving himself a quick nod of confirmation, he started down after her. All along the long corridor were broad windows running from waist height to the ceiling, allowing a view of wide lab spaces below with banks of equipment, storage facilities, fume chambers, other technical equipment that he could probably work out the use for if he spent some time, but a lot of it not immediately recognisable. Various people moved around their business, involved in diverse tasks, some of them in discussion, a small group in front of a display board drawing diagrams and formulae, he noted them and passed by, only to find another similar grouping followed by another. When they reached the end of the corridor and came to the last set of windows, Marina paused, put one hand up against the pane, gazed fixed on what lay below.

"And here it is," she said. She didn't even look at Valdor to see his reaction, seemingly fascinated with the room's contents.

What lay below was nothing Valdor remembered. How long had it taken them to equip a room like this? They must have started shortly after his exit from New Helvetica back to Kalany. Well before his return in any case. Large floor to ceiling cases lay in rows, tilted slightly back, made of a grey-green metallic substance, probably some sort of metal. Each of them had a semi-translucent cover, which looked as if they could be open, and if he was not mistaken, every one of them contained what looked like a human form. From the sides and top of every chamber, for that's what they were, like some sort of diving, or decompression chamber, ran thick tubes and conduits. He started counting, and then stopped. It didn't matter how many there were. All that mattered was that they were here, and that they seemed to contain people. He had a suspicion what this might be, and he'd been very clear to steer a path away from this direction in his earlier dealing with The

Benevolent

Benevolent. Since that time, the topic simply hadn't arisen.

"What is this, Marina? Are those people?"

She turned to look at him and smiled. "You might say that," she said. "And then you might not. It depends on your perspective."

"And what do you mean by that?" he said, turning to look down into the large lab room below,

"Well, when does the *homo* cease to be *sapiens?* Where's the dividing line? I don't think any of us know the answer to that. We're at a point now where it doesn't really matter. The trials are showing satisfactory results. The mortality rate is dropping. It's time to move to the next stage."

"Mortality rate?"

"Of course. Progress is not without sacrifice, lover. You know that."

He turned to look at her slowly. He'd been afraid of this.

"But these are people. They're human beings…."

"And that's just the point isn't it. You, me, all of us, we're a lesser species. Stupid, clumsy, stumbling *homo sapiens.* This here, what we're doing, this is the future. This is *our* future."

He gave a short unamused laugh and turned to look back down at what was going on in the room below.

"Come on, Marina."

"You think I'm not serious, Valdor? I can assure you that we're deadly serious about what we're doing here. The work that you initiated with the biocomp platform gave us the springboard for further work. That, in combination with the progress you've made with your own team's efforts have led us to this point." She paused, moving her hand slowly up and down on the glass and catching her bottom lip between her teeth, then she took in a deep breath, then let it out slowly and nodded just as slowly, as if to herself.

"The CoCee navigators, the neural implants, all those were merely stepping-stones."

"Stepping-stones to what, Marina? I don't understand

what you're doing here."

"What *we're* doing here, lover."

He waved her statement away in annoyance. "No, what you're doing here, Marina. What is it precisely that *you're* doing here?"

"If you want to be like that. Engineering the next generation of humanity's future."

"Do they know what's being done to them?"

"Of course, lover. All of them are volunteers. They are happy to serve the future. They're even happier to be that future."

He shook his head. "How can you know?"

"How can we know what, Valdor? What the results will be? We can't. We have some initial indicators, but that work with the Kaitan woman, the resultant outcomes with the CoCee navigation fleet, all those are just tasters of what's possible. Who knows? But if we continue on this path, I don't think it matters. What we think will merely become a footnote in history."

"And what about the authorities."

She laughed then. "Oh, Valdor, when has that sort of thing ever concerned you? Anyway, governments, the CoCee, all of it…all that's merely window-dressing. Everything that happens occurs as it will, a lot of it with a gentle guiding hand in the background. Those bodies are merely the public face of acceptability. We count a number of those key figures as members of our ranks. Now and again they need to steer things in certain directions, but for much of it, they hardly matter. If there's a threat to our progress, that threat gets dealt with and the public are none the wiser. It doesn't matter anyway. We have their best interests at heart, and mostly, they're too stupid or simply too naïve to know what's good for them. For the most part, the vast majority of them wouldn't even care. You, Valdor. You in particular should be above all that. You understand how things work. I'm surprised you would even

Benevolent

ask." She stepped forward and placed a hand on his shoulder. "Really, lover."

He shook his head and pursed his lips. He turned back to the window, extricating himself from her touch.

"So what now?"

He could still feel Tsinda's scrutiny, but still she had said not a word. He glanced over at her as Marina answered.

"We need to take this forward, but we need to do this as an advancement under the umbrella of ILGC activities. The Benevolent must not be seen to be involved. That would present too many complications at the moment. What with the CoCee fleet activities, and the apparent defeat, now is the ideal time, we feel, for happy circumstance to play its hand. ILGC has always been your operation, Valdor, on the face of things, and even more so ever since you've returned. If this breakthrough comes from ILGC, it is all the better. It gives us, The Benevolent, further time to strategize and set things in place."

He stared down at the chambers, at the lines of apparent volunteers and chewed his lip. He thought about saying something, and then changed his mind.

"I have to say, I'm not exactly comfortable with this, Marina."

"You don't have to be comfortable, darling. You just have to play your part. Even if it's not for the same reasons, it will be worth your while in the long run."

This time, he turned to look at Tsinda directly. "And what's her part?"

"Oh, Tsinda will be right by your side, lover. Your helping hand."

He looked at Marina and narrowed his eyes.

"Again, you don't really have a choice."

"I thought you might say that."

He looked back at Tsinda. She seemed to be barely suppressing a smile, or rather, perhaps it was the trace of a smirk.

"All right," said Marina. "Let's show you what we've been up to. I'm sure that you have questions."

He did. Too many. But he wasn't sure that he wanted to ask some of them, at least not yet.

"Come on then, this way."

She led them down to the end of the corridor and down a staircase that led to another shadowed hallway below. As they reached the end, Marina glanced up and nodded, and a door opened in front of them. Clearly, they were being monitored the entire time. She stepped through and led them into the middle of the wide, long room that they had seen from above. There were about half a dozen people in there, some of whom hadn't been in evidence when he'd been watching before. They all turned and stopped what they were doing as they noticed the new arrivals. It was difficult for Valdor to assign a gender to any of them as they each wore the same sort of shapeless pale-blue smock, some form of breathing mask and caps.

"Go back to what you're doing," Marina told them. "I'll let you know if we need anything." Her authority amongst these people was clearly recognised. They returned to their tasks paying barely a mind to the visitors.

Valdor let his gaze rove around the room before crossing to stand in front of one of the large cylinders. He stepped forward to peer at it more closely, reaching out with one hand and letting his palm rest against the side. It was slightly cool. Whatever the grey-green material was, it didn't feel like metal, more like some sort of polymer. The not-quite transparent cover seemed to be somehow lit from within and he could make out the human shape quite clearly. This one appeared to be female, though the features and edges were indistinct, slightly blurry. He stepped around to the side to look at the attachments, following the thick tubes that disappeared behind the container. For the most part, they were dark grey, but here

Benevolent

and there were thinner, white tubes and a couple of blue. He could only imagine what their function might be. Satisfied, for the moment, he stepped out in front of the next one. This too contained what appeared to be a female form. He glanced along the row. There were, in all probably twenty on this side. Looking behind him, he confirmed an equal number.

"And you say these are volunteers. Where from?"

"They come from a group of elite forces that serve in various capacities throughout the known worlds. They are no strangers to conflict, nor to space travel. As you can see, or assume, I would suppose that none of them are particularly old. All of them are still of breeding age, and we expect them to do just that eventually. Whether naturally or artificially, it doesn't matter. Frankly though, they are more useful if the offspring are not carried to term, but rather extracted and accelerated if they go that route."

Valdor turned to face her. "So what you're trying to do is to raise elite soldiers."

She shook her head. "No, you shouldn't jump to conclusions, lover. That's just where they come from for the most part. They tend to be in good physical condition, and in the areas we recruit from, they also tend to be smart. Smart is a distinct advantage. We want them at their peak in every respect. Some of these people are chemists, physicists, engineers."

"I don't hear you say psychologists, or sociologists or medical researchers."

"Again, Valdor," she said with a little sigh. "You are colouring things with what you want to hear. That's not what it is at all. We really do want the best for humanity as a race, as a species. Our technology, our science, the level of where we are makes the racial imperative lazy. Without struggle, there is no need to advance. All we are doing it is giving it a little push."

Valdor turned away from her then. The idealism in her words was becoming just a little too much for him. If he could believe that she herself truly believed half of what she was saying, then it was not only a surprise to him from Marina, but altogether a vast leap away from his own set of driving motivations. The only thing he cared about the advancement of was one Valdor Carr, and Valdor Carr's imperative had never been lazy when it came to Valdor Carr. Right now, whatever The Benevolent were up to, it suited him to play along.

"Do you know anything?"

"What do you mean?"

"Well," he looked sidelong in her direction. "The outcomes I mean."

"Perception is one," she said. "But we knew that much was achievable from the other work. What other abilities fall out remain to be seen. At the moment, we believe it's reproduceable. Most of the work is at the genetic level. Quite frankly, it's beyond me. Once we've moved on from here, we'll be looking for volunteer subjects in our more accomplished people. If we are going to perform a sea change in the future of humankind, it's going to take more than a handful. We need to steepen the curve, and that's going to take numbers."

For some reason, he thought that the source was likely to be expanding in some directions and not in others. He doubted very much that they'd be looking among the farmers and labourers or the miners across the various worlds. That was something that was growing like a thorn. Regardless of his own selfish needs, the thought that the future of humankind might involve only certain sections of that entire population did not sit comfortably with him.

"And you, Marina?"

"Ha," she said. "I just wouldn't make the cut, lover. And besides, you don't seem to appreciate the fact that I am not doing this for what I can get out of it. So, no, I'm not an immediate candidate. You, on the other hand…." She turned to look at the girl. "Tsinda…." She let the implication dangle

Benevolent

there before turning back to look at him.

"Anyway, that's for later thought. Right now, we need to move on to our next phases."

"And where do I come in?"

"Well, as I said before, it needs to come from the right quarter. The time is right. We need to progress with fitting out some of our installations, first here and then elsewhere. Here, because on New Helvetica we can do that discretely. We will start to use our people to discuss the possibilities with key members of the CoCee, planting the seed as it were, and then meanwhile, the work will be underway. By the time you need to come out and bring it into the light, it will be too far advanced.

"And what of the Sirona?"

"The Sirona will stay out of the way for a little while, giving the CoCee and other parties time to take a breath and consider what has just happened. We want it to well and truly sink in, let them understand how limited their options are. This new alien appearance, well, that was a little unexpected…."

"New appearance?"

"Oh, of course. You don't know. How could you? There appears to be another alien player in the picture."

Valdor felt his guts go cold.

Marina looked at him as if he were a slow child. "We've been warning you about this for a long time, lover. All of you."

"You, meaning The Benevolent."

"Of course. Anyway. We are there now. This arrival has changed the landscape. What it means to us remains to be seen, but they seem to be much larger and more powerful than we could have imagined. It makes our mission so much more important. But come, we have things to plan. Have you seen enough?"

He had. He nodded slowly in assent.

"Good."

Tsinda chose that moment to step forward and hold out

one hand ready to touch fingers as was common local custom by way of greeting. Not really thinking about it, he lifted a hand and touched the end of her fingers to his.

"It's a pleasure to meet you, Valdor Carr. I think I am going to enjoy our working together."

"Hum, yes."

Her voice was rich and confident, nothing young girl about it. The way her gaze lingered on his, the scrutiny before, it all hinted at something, though he wasn't sure what it was yet. If Marina was to have her way, he guessed he'd have time to find out. All the same, she was making him feel a little uncomfortable. He looked away, ostensibly to watch the room's other participants going about their duties. It was then that he realised that there was something else that had been making him uncomfortable since they'd entered, something that had drifted just below the surface of his conscious awareness; it was the smell. The place smelled like a hospital. Of course it did. He wrinkled his nose. He didn't particularly like hospitals, preferring instead the sanctity of private clinics. Just one more thing to add to the list of things that was making him less than happy at the moment.

He shot a quick glance back at Tsinda. As far as Valdor was concerned, the jury was still out with that one.

Benevolent

Chapter Eight

New Helvetica

Marina Samaris sat, waiting for the other commlink parties to join. She looked down at her nails, curling the fingers on each hand to study them, angling each one slightly one way then the other. She had been thinking about the introduction with Valdor, running it over in her head, and yes, she believed in what they were doing, but from time to time, doubt crept in. If there was one thing Marina was good at though, it was maintaining a front. She pursed her lips and shifted her attention to a spot on the floor. Tsinda was gone. She'd left with Valdor to travel out to one of the production plants, ostensibly to help him oversee the start of refitting operations, but really to keep an eye on him and whatever else she might happen to get up to that would help encourage him to stay with the program. Tsinda was good at what she did too, and Marina knew well that Valdor was not impervious. Every little bit helped, after all. The relatively free and open space afforded by their meeting room nestled within the ILGC complex was ideal for the distant casts. There was enough room, and the furniture looked like it was designed to keep the place uncluttered. Of course, the high-level shielding managed their requirements for security and privacy for discussions with the core membership.

An image shimmered into view. Dareth Garin. He was high up in the government on one of the ag worlds. He adjusted his sleeves and nodded as he looked over at her, or at least at her own projected image in the room where he sat, his severe features set. Garin was never one to show the slightest trace of warmth, not that this medium was very good for the nuances of anything else than straightforward communication. Marina actually preferred to meet in person. Sometimes, it was all about the chemistry in the room.

"Dareth, how are you?"

"Hmph," he responded. "It's early."

That was the other problem with this form of meeting; there was no good time for them to happen. It was always early in the morning or late at night at someone's location. Perhaps the jump drive would do something to make those sorts of problems less of an issue, but they weren't there yet, and somehow, she doubted it. In-person meetings involved travel, and each of them had things to do. They were not really the sorts of individuals who had a lot of time on their hands. Just at that moment, Eleni Kraus also joined, her column of light appearing opposite Garin. Kraus was an older woman, her dark skin patterned with gold as was the fashion on her homeworld currently. Her hair sat coiled high upon the top of her head. She looked at both of them, nodded to each in turn.

"Good day to you both."

There was a grunt from Garin at that.

"Where are the others?" he said a moment later. "If you don't mind, I need kahveh."

He stood without seeking anyone's permission and disappeared from view. Marina sighed quietly to herself. The others were late. It was always like this, trying to coordinate, especially at short notice. Garin returned a minute or so later, bearing a small cup with him and resumed his seat. He took a tentative sip of the hot liquid and then lowering the cup, spoke again.

"I don't see why we need to meet anyway. Wouldn't a simple communication have sufficed?"

"Let's wait for the others to show up. I'll explain then," said Marina.

Benevolent

"Well, they're taking their own sweet time," said Garin, giving a grimace and then lifting his cup for another cautious sip. No sooner were the words out of his mouth than the other three that they were expecting all turned up almost at once.

First came Larit Fren. It was always difficult to assign a particular gender to Fren. Marina tended to think of Fren as her, but she was cautious when assigning pronouns when they were in conversation. Fren wore a long flowing robe, as was in accordance with her status as one of the elders in the Kytos Cluster main religion and the trappings that went along with it. Mostly they got called a religion, but as with Fren's fluidity, it wasn't clear whether it was a religion or more a life philosophy. Within the Kytos Cluster alone, the Altans ran to millions. When you added those scattered throughout the other worlds, it was a lot more. There was no doubt they were a significant force, and one not to be discounted, nor to be trifled with. Karl Abbas came next. He belonged to the military wing and was normally quite formal and stiff around others. Having taken part in his fair share of campaigns over the years, he now tended to do politics, dabbling in the CoCee appropriations along the way. He was known to split most of his time between Belshore and Kalany, though he had other estates elsewhere. Marina believed he was at one of his smaller estates now in one of the system backwaters. Rumour had it that he liked to go fishing, but looking at him now, you would never tell. There seemed to be not a relaxed bone in his body. The very last to join was Ananda Luck, a wealthy industrialist, and a firm believer in The Benevolent's principles. He, among their group had brought himself from nothing, from one of the poorer mining worlds that struggled to eke out an existence within the system's economy. Little by little he had, over the years, by sheer cunning and hard work built himself a vast empire of manufacturing, distribution, and warehousing. If there was a product to be found, rumour had it that it would be located somewhere within Luck's extensive network; you just had to tap the right people to get to it. Looking at him, sitting there in his casual street clothes, no ostentation whatsoever, you might be surprised at the level of wealth he commanded. And despite his name, there was very little fortunate about how he had come by it. Each of the newcomers took their turns greeting the room's other virtual attendees.

"I still don't see…."

Marina held up a hand.

"I, for one, would like some sort of report," said Kraus. "I believe we are owed at least that much." She looked around the other faces for support, receiving affirming nods from a couple of them.

"Good," said Marina. She slid her hand across a control on the arm of her chair and tapped it a couple of times. Moments later, a new presence took shape in the room's centre. "Let's hear it from the source," she said, lifting her chin to indicate the new arrival. This was no projection. The alien figure, the Sirona, for that was what it was, had simply appeared in the middle of the space. It stood there for a moment or two, then turned slowly, its head tilted a little to one side, taking in those that it was facing.

"What would—you know?" it asked.

"Tell us what happened. Let's start with that," said Marina.

"We—were there. The place we deci—ded. And then—the Sleeth."

"Who or what are the Sleeth?" asked Abbas.

"They. One that we—told you about. One—of others."

"So this is another alien race," said Abbas.

"One," said the Sirona in response.

"Okay and…."

"The Siro—na must leave."

"Why would that be?" said Garin.

"Sirona could not—remain. Too much—danger."

"So I am assuming that the Sirona and these Sleeth do not

get on." That was Kraus. She peered intently at the Sirona, but the short alien said nothing. Kraus sat back in her chair with a huff and looked away.

"Alta walks among us unseen," said Fren. "Alta gives and Alta takes away, steering us ever on to the path of betterment."

Abbas gave a barely concealed snort at that, glancing at Fren. Despite his reaction, it was clear to Marina that the philosophy of the Altans was very strongly aligned with that of The Benevolent themselves. Fren simply ignored him. Larit Fren had very little sympathy with the military path and Abbas's frequent argument for it as a solution to nearly every problem. In this case, with the goal of the Sirona's involvement, it had happened to be the right one. Fren had seen that and reluctantly agreed. Despite their large numbers, to convert many more of the population to the Altan way of thinking would take years.

The Sirona was standing quite still, seemingly waiting for further questions, but it appeared that Abbas was off on his own path now.

"Whatever these Sleeth are," he said, "what they did was a clear act of aggression. I say we retaliate, and we do it hard and fast. The time is now. We should not let the opportunity slip past."

"I don't think that's necessarily the wisest course of action," said Kraus.

"And why is that?" said Abbas.

"It is not—as you say—wise," said the Sirona, slowly and carefully.

Abbas turned and faced the Sirona, frowning.

"They have great—" It seemed to stop and search for the word. "Power."

"The reports we had from the fleet should tell you that," said Marina. "You of all people Karl, should be up to date with the little we learned from that initial encounter."

"What, I am supposed to ignore the fact that they

destroyed four of our ships, and their crews with them? We just sit idly by and take that? If that's not aggression, what is? That's an act of war, right there."

"I agree, it's not what you'd call a peaceful act. But, if what we learned is true, then they had the power just to take out the entire fleet without even thinking about it. That they didn't do," said Marina.

"On the one hand Alta takes away something and grants us knowledge in return." Fren again.

Abbas hissed and glanced sidelong with a little shake of his head.

"How can we know the extent of their power. Did the fleet stay around to test it? Not as far as the reports tell me. So who says they have that level of power?"

"They have great power," said the Sirona, this time without any hesitation at all. "Great pow-er. To think otherwise is foo-lish."

Garin was frowning too. Taking one last sip from his small cup, he placed it down somewhere out of sight and leaned forward.

"Regardless, and even if what Karl is suggesting is right, we are left with a problem, don't you think?"

"And what's that?" said Eleni Kraus, also leaning forward.

"Well, we had a nice little plan, didn't we?" he said. "Present the worlds with a single common enemy, one that would drive them to pool their resources and pursue a joint goal. It was just what we needed to draw focus away from inter-world squabbles and dissipation of energies. Give them a single challenge that presents several seemingly insurmountable problems, allowing us to steer things ever in the right direction. Give them a challenge that we can control and manage the expectations and the outcomes. Wasn't that the plan?"

"But I don't see…," started Kraus, but Abbas held up a

hand to still her.

"These Sleeth, or whatever they are, aren't something we can control. Unless we deal with them, then things start to unravel. All the forces, the combined fleets with a single goal. We had the CoCee unified, knowing what they were doing. Yes, the challenge was huge, perhaps beyond them, but that was ideal too."

"Yes," said Garin. "Exactly. Unless we control the source of the problem, then we lose our ability to control the wellspring of solutions. Karl is right."

Just then, Ananda luck who seemed to have been listening with half an ear while studying the tops of his fingers spoke up. His voice, quiet and flowing with the music of his lilting accent caused them to stop.

"Actually, you know," he said, folding his hands in his lap. "I don't think Karl is right at all."

This brought a splutter from the statement's recipient.

"No, listen to me," said luck. "Yes, we had a plan. It was a good plan. But, fate, or…" He lifted a hand of acknowledgment in Fren's direction. "Or Alta…." A slight inclination of Fren's head recognised the consideration. "Or whatever cast the fates in this direction, has dealt us an opportunity. We portrayed the Sirona as far much more than they were. Now, we don't really have to. The threat, or the perceived threat, whether it turns out to be one or not, just got even more substantial. We, humanity, now have more than one thing to worry about. I am sure that this will result in a bit more focus. Perhaps, for now, a scattering of the energies, but it sets the stage for us to provide more paths and solutions that might have otherwise become a little harder to portray as acceptable. So, that climate, that environment, isn't that what we are striving for after all?"

He looked around each of the room's participants, a faint smile upon his lips.

"But what about the Sirona?" said Kraus.

"I'm not sure I…."

"Well, what are they going to do now? Hasn't their home system been invaded now from two angles, once with our fleet and now the Sleeth, or whatever they are called?"

Luck closed his eyes and nodded.

"I think you'll find…," Marina started, but the Sirona who had been watching the back and forth with apparent interest, spoke up and interrupted before she could finish the sentence.

"This is not—Sirona—home," it said.

That clearly startled Kraus and brought a look of query from Garin.

"Does it matter," said Marina. "We kept that knowledge quiet in case of any leakage. And before you protest, there is always leakage. It was important for the CoCee to believe that they had discovered the Sirona home system, if not a home world per se. It also allowed the Sirona to act without fear of real reprisals."

"Ah, clever," said Kraus, nodding her understanding.

"We thought so. Our navigation capability is so limited that there was little chance of stumbling upon the real Sirona homeworld. So, we created an enemy and we built their source with enough evidence to support that belief, even though there was no evidence of an orbiting planet to be found. Not even debris. The focus upon Sirona as enemy was great enough that it allowed us to gloss some of the flimsy assumptions necessitated about the Sirona themselves. It also allowed them to remain all the more inscrutable."

Marina had been aware of the existence of the Sirona homeworld for some time. Further discussions had revealed that it was quite resource poor in certain areas. That went a long way to explain what motivated some of the demands they levied in exchange for their services. Despite that though, there were still some things that remained inexplicable.

"So what now?" asked Garin.

Benevolent

"Well," said Marina. "The ILGC work with Carr has been proceeding well. We are ready to embark upon the next stage. I have set that in motion. All it takes is final agreement from us here. And unless there are any objections, I will let that proceed." She looked around the other faces. There were brief nods of consent. "Good. I believe some of the associated work in Ananda's domain goes quite well also." Luck inclined his head. "I believe the facilities are almost ready to commence production. And I'm sure he will be reporting as soon as there's significant news."

"And what about the CoCee?" asked Garin. "Do we need to do anything there?"

"I don't think so for now," said Marina. "Karl?"

"No. If we are clear that we don't want to put together some sort of strike force."

"No, I don't think so," said Kraus. "As our friend here says," she said waving in the Sirona's direction. "That is probably not a good idea."

"Speaking of our friend. I believe I call you Tarn," said Marina, addressing the last to the creature itself.

"You can call—Tarn," it said. "Names un—important."

"I think, for the moment, it's simply a holding action until we work out what we're going to do. I have no doubt that we will be in need of your services soon, but not just yet. I think that's all for now."

"That is accep-table busi-ness," it said. "Not control."

Marina frowned at that, narrowed her eyes at the Sirona.

"What do you mean?" she said.

The Sirona met her gaze and then bowed its head and an instant later, simply popped out of existence without answering. It never ceased to unsettle her the way they came and went. One day, they might learn how they did that as well, but so far it was something that the Sirona had failed to share. She wasn't sure that they ever would. In the end, she was also quite at ease not having to attempt that particular mode of transportation. The last words it had said lingered with her though, and it too slightly unsettled her.

She thought for a moment before looking around the room, seeing if there was anything or anyone she'd forgotten. "So, with that, unless there's anything else….," she said, pausing, waiting for any interjections "Then we'll see how things with the CoCee, with the Sirona strike force develop. To be honest, this blindsided us a little bit, but as Ananda said, in the end, it could work to our advantage.

Garin nodded and winked out of existence. A moment later, both Fren and Kraus did the same. Abbas appeared to be waiting for something, and Luck was simply sitting there staring down at his fingers clasped together in his lap. It was not unusual for Abbas to hang around. They had so many dealing with the CoCee business together that they often strategized on their own. Under the current circumstances, it was probably to be expected. She turned her attention to Luck.

"Is there something else, Ananda?" she said.

He looked up slowly and met her gaze.

"Perhaps," he said. "Perhaps there is."

That was uncommon in itself. Wondering what it was, she leaned forward, waiting for him to reveal what might be on his mind.

Chapter Nine

Belshore

As she clambered down from the pod, Mahra was still searching for some sort of answer to the fact that she'd had no possibility to determine where the vast alien ship had gone. It was as if she had her eyes opened and in the next instant been blinded, taking away her capacity to use her newfound skills. That was only one of the frustrations though. The rest of the journey back, she'd been dwelling on what Timon had said, about not having a choice. For the last few weeks, she had not really been comfortable with where she was and how things had ended up. There was the whole Jacinda incident, of course, but that was not it, or at least not all of it. Before the whole CoCee thing, before she'd worked out how Timon and Jayeer fit into the bigger picture, Mahra Kaitan had been beholden to nobody except her current boss and she'd made sure of that. There were sections of her past where she had had no choices at all, and she didn't want to go back there, ever. In some ways, the current circumstance reminded her of those times, not having the freedom to choose, circumstance or other people dictating every step she took. As she reached the deck, she glanced up towards the bridge. Jayeer was already heading down towards her. She looked back up towards the pod, realising that there lay another source of her current discomfort. She wasn't happy with the new layout. It didn't feel right. She didn't think she'd get much of a say there, but she could be wrong.

"Where's Timon," she asked as Jayeer approached.

"He said he wanted to check a couple of things," he answered. "Though I have no idea what they might be."

"Should we wait?"

"No, no," he said, peering up at her through his lenses. "I think it would probably be better if we headed on in. He will catch us up."

She gave a quick nod of understanding and headed to the lock, Jayeer following quickly behind.

"Explain something to me, Jay," she said without turning round as they walked out from the ship.

"I will try."

"You look at Timon, you see his actions, you would never suspect he would be okay with this whole chain of command thing."

"I see," said Jayeer. That brought just a flicker of a frown to Mahra's brow.

"Well, it's a little complex. What you are suggesting is not always the case. You know that. But in the end, it's that chain of command that lets him be himself, lets Timon be Timon Pellis. He recognises that. It also keeps him in a place that lets him do what he wants. Ultimately, Timon is a pilot, and a very good one at that. It helps that he loves doing what he's doing. It's his vocation, you know. He understands, I think, that without that very chain of command, he wouldn't have access to the level and sorts of ships that he does. It's a trade-off."

She stopped and turned. "Is it?"

He bit his lip before answering. "I think it is." He gave a little nod and a shrug. "But that's just me. Really, in the end, I suppose I'm pretty much the same. Despite our differences, I'm like Timon. I would not be as happy somewhere else, if happy is the right word. Perhaps content is better…."

She looked back towards where the ship sat parked among the others, looking almost similar, but the differences were noticeable. There was a parallel there. As yet, there was no sign of Timon.

"But you...?" she said.

"Of course," said Jay, his expression open. "Look at the technologies at the equipment, the resources I have at my disposal. There's only two other possibilities where I might have that luxury." He lifted a hand and pulled at one finger. "One, if I were insanely wealthy, which sadly, I am not, though I am not sure that would make me happy either. And two...." He pulled on his middle finger. "...if I were a part of some big corporation, and that wouldn't suit me either. Here, at least, the chain of command is well defined. In the free market, well, you never know, do you?"

"Hmm," said Mahra. "I'd never considered that. Okay. We should probably get inside," she said and turned back towards the building and started walking.

"Don't worry. From time to time, I think Timon struggles with it too," said Jayeer from behind her.

She stopped at the hangar doors and turned to survey the ranks of ships, all neatly parked, most of them looking remarkably similar with very little to distinguish them one from the other. She saw that Timon had finally emerged from *The Nameless* and was heading their way. Ironic, she thought. Really, any of these production-line ships could bear the 'nameless' signifier. There was something else nagging at her as she surveyed the apron and she couldn't quite put her finger on it. And then she had it.

"Where is everyone?" she said.

Jayeer turned and also looked across the open space and then frowned.

"I don't know," he said. "Strange."

Any other time and there would be mechanics, others moving around and between the ships, servicing, loading supplies, performing other tasks, including cleaning. As far as she could see, there was not a soul in evidence.

"Yeah, weird," she said. "You would think…." But she let the thought trail off.

She turned back to the smaller door set into the larger hangar doors, opened it, and stepped inside, not waiting to see if Timon was following. This whole thing just didn't feel right. Once inside, she saw that the wide hollow hangar space was the same; no one to be seen.

"Huh," she said and listened as her voice echoed from the walls. "Is there something going on that we don't know about?"

"If there was an address, that would be here," said Timon from behind her, having finally caught up. He seemed to have caught up with their conversation too. "So it's not that. I spoke to Garavenah from the ship. She said that she wanted to talk to us. It sounded like it was something other than a normal debrief. Although, I have to say, I think we've got some things to report."

"I'd say you're right there, Timon," said Jayeer. "Shall we go and find out where she is?"

"Sounds like a reasonable idea."

Not waiting, Mahra strode off across the hangar floor sensing rather than seeing the others following her straight behind. As usual, the hangar smelled of fuel and lubricants, and the underlying scent of metals. She opened the double doors at the end and entered the wide hallway stretching off to office spaces and further down, quarters. She paused for a moment.

"Her offices?"

"Yes," said Timon. "She didn't say, but I presume so."

She gave a quick nod and headed down in that direction. Here, inside, everything seemed unnaturally quiet as well.

"What the hell's going on?" she muttered, quickening her pace.

"Yes, I'd like to know that too," said Timon.

When they finally reached the offices, the adjutant

Benevolent

ushered them in without delay. At least there was someone in place to do that outside Garavenah's door. As they stepped inside, Garavenah looked up from her display, a preoccupied look on her face, she frowned and then her expression relaxed a fraction.

"Welcome back," she said. "You may as well take a seat. So what happened out there?"

"Nothing," said Timon. "Not a damned thing. The system was empty," he said as he took the indicated chair across the table from her. Jayeer took another place, but Mahra stood where she was, slightly behind them. Garavenah waved at her to take a place as well, but Mahra shook her head. Garavenah pursed her lips slightly but didn't press the point.

"And clues? Traces?"

This time Mahra spoke. "Nothing. I couldn't even sense their presence, the Sleeth that is. There were fragments, the smallest traces of the Sirona ships, but they went everywhere, and I think really, they're next to useless."

Garavenah nodded thoughtfully. She still seemed a little distracted. "Well, that's disappointing," she said finally.

"So what's next?" said Timon.

"We wait," said Garavenah with a sigh.

"What?" Timon's expression was incredulous. The word exploding out of his mouth. It was enough to make Chutzpah start on Mahra's shoulder and dig his claws in, bristling. Mahra lifted a hand to forestall any action that might result in the inevitable consequences. She didn't really want that happening at the moment.

"Yes, I know," said Garavenah.

Timon got to his feet, strode across the room, stood staring out the window, his hands against the frame.

"How can they decide that? We've just been defeated on two fronts. Outsmarted and out…I don't know…out-weaponed, or something. We're just expected to sit on our hands?"

He turned then, crossed his arms, his jaw set. "Really, Gara? No. I am not going to do it."

"Yes, you are, Commander. Yes, you are."

He dropped his gaze then, but his jaw was still working. He turned again to look out the window. After a moment, his shoulders dropped.

"Think of it this way, Timon. It gives us a chance to explore the new ship's capabilities properly before we might have to use them in anger. I, for one, am eager to find out what she can do."

"Yes, of course you are, Jay," said Timon, more quietly, without turning around. In the next instant she could hear him muttering something under his breath.

"Where is everyone?" asked Mahra, finally.

"Minimal duties. Some have been urged to take leave."

"And how long is that supposed to last?" asked Jayeer.

"Until we are told otherwise," Garavenah answered, clearly not happy with her own response.

"Well then," said Timon, turning around again, "Let's all have a nice vacation, shall we? Twiddle our thumbs while the higher ups decide what they're going to do…."

Garavenah shook her head, her lips pressed together.

"It's not like that at all, Timon."

Although, by the look on her face, Mahra wasn't entirely sure that she believed her own words. Quite frankly Mahra was starting to side with Timon on this one. If this was the CoCee response, then she didn't think it was either logical or right.

"So where is this coming from?" she asked.

"I'm not at liberty to tell you that, Mahra."

Mahra caught her bottom lip between her teeth and nodded slowly, finally giving a heavy sigh. "And what am I supposed to do in the meantime?"

"I'm not sure I understand."

"Well, tell me what I'm supposed to do. If we're waiting

Benevolent

around for something to happen, I haven't got a lot to do, have I. The training program is over. We don't seem to be flying anywhere. What do you suggest *I* do in the meantime?"

Mahra's tack was clearly starting to annoy Garavenah. "I don't know Mahra. Whatever you want to do probably. I'm not in a position to order you to do anything. I guess maybe you could use a bit of a break too."

Mahra narrowed her eyes and gave a sniff.

"Yeah, maybe I do," she said. "If that's all?"

Garavenah didn't respond, merely returned the stare. And in that moment, Mahra decided. She pushed back her chair, got to her feet, and stepped across to the door. She hesitated for a moment, hand on the handle and then pulled the door open. She gave one last glance before stepping through. Jayeer was sitting where he was, staring after her open mouthed. Timon stood in his place by the window, arms still crossed, his eyes narrowed. Garavenah simply returned her look blankly, face completely expressionless. Mahra pressed her jaw shut, turned, and strode from the room, through the outer office and down the hallway.

Chapter Ten

Belshore

She didn't go straight back to her quarters. First, there was something she had to do. She remembered that her blade still sat stowed on *The Pilgrim* where she'd left it. It didn't take her long to find her way back to the spot where they'd last parked the ship. Thankfully, it had not moved, not been repurposed since they'd moved on to *The Nameless*. In the current circumstances, with the general stand-down, that was not altogether a surprise. She palmed the outer hatch, made her way in, and opened the locker where she had stored the blade, slipped into the straps that held the sheath angled across her shoulders and then turned, looking around. The ship was idle, but it still somehow, smelled like home, familiar, comforting. *The Nameless* had accrued no such scent; it just smelled new, industrial. Changing ships, in a way, was just like leaving home. She sighed. Things were transforming again in ways that were beyond her control. She gave her head a slight shake and then exited, making her way back across the stained apron to the building that held her assigned quarters within.

Back in her cramped space, Mahra looked around at the bare grey walls. The quarters were devoid of any decoration. There was the simple bunk, the lack of clutter, the absence of anything really that would identify the space as hers. Yes, there were a few clothes, but that was it. She opened the closet and stood staring at what lay within. Yes, a few more clothes, a bag of coz nuts for Chutz, his life box stashed below.

Benevolent

Shrugging out of the harness, she slipped her blade off and hung it there, not quite sure what she was doing yet. There it lay, slightly swinging still from the last movement, accusing her. That was another issue and she knew it. Over the past few weeks, she'd allowed herself to become slack. She'd been remiss about her daily rituals, lax in the required maintenance of her blade. Whatever happened to mind, body and blade sharp? Whatever happened to the routines that she'd developed and stuck to for years. The whole period with Jacinda had been partially to blame. She'd become indulgent, too content and with that came complacency. Thoughts of Jacinda brought a bitter taste to her mouth and she tried to shake the thought away.

"What am I doing, Chutz?" she said, stroking him gently. Strangely, he was purring contentedly at her shoulder, as if he was completely comfortable with where they had found themselves at the moment.

"So, you approve," she said. "Funny."

Though she shouldn't have been surprised. Chutzpah always seemed to have a way of knowing when she was in the right place, even if it was an unforeseen chain of events that happened to put them there. The thought was funny though, because it was her head that was in the right space, not her presence here in a generic set of quarters devoid of all personality.

With a sigh, she planted her fists on her hips and stood staring at the small room, at the absence of anything meaningful, wondering about her next step. Hopefully, the CoCee wouldn't throw her out of these quarters immediately if she followed through with what she was planning to do. She had nowhere else to go yet. Of course, there was always a hotel, and the steady stream of credits that the ongoing employment had provided had also allowed her to put a bit aside. There hadn't really been that much to spend it on, or the opportunity to do so. She'd had other funds put aside before joining up with Timon and Jayeer, but that wasn't the point. She just liked to have some sort of plan in place, even if it was only a sketchy one.

"What are you doing, Mahra?"

She turned to see Jayeer standing there. Of all of them, she supposed that she would expect him to be the one to come seek her out. Certainly not Timon at the moment, and definitely not Garavenah.

"To be honest, Jay, I'm not really sure," she said.

"Well, that was a bit dramatic, I think. That upstairs, I mean."

"Maybe so. But things aren't working. You can see that."

He inclined his head and closed his eyes in acknowledgement.

"Yes, they are not the best, that is true. Can I come in?"

"If you can find somewhere in this luxurious space, of course."

"So what are you thinking, Mahra," he said, perching himself on the edge of her bunk and peering up at her over his lenses.

She shook her head. "Not sure I know. I seem to have lost something. Really, I don't blame Timon and I certainly don't blame you, but if we're going to just be sitting on our hands, then I can't stay here. Maybe what I need to do right now is not going to end up with me finding what I'm looking for, but I'm starting to think it's what I've got to do."

"And what are you looking for?" Jayeer tilted his head a little to one side.

"Oh, the first part is really simple." She reached out and ran her fingers up the length of her blade, not meeting his gaze. "I want some sort of closure with the Sirona business. I need to see them getting some sort of retribution for their past acts."

"Hmmm. But as you say, Mahra. They are past acts. A long time ago."

She turned back to face him. "That doesn't make them

Benevolent

any less important."

He lifted his hand placatingly.

"No, no. I am not saying that. It's just that…." His voice trailed off as he saw the expression on her face. "No, I understand. It must be a great burden to carry around with you. But do you really think we have the power to do anything really? We only understand a mere fraction of what they might be capable of. And now, with what's happened…."

She sighed then and nodded. "No, of course, you're right. But we can't just do nothing. *I* just can't do nothing. And anyway," she started after a pause. "It's not only that. The whole relationship with Timon, the tension between us. It's just as much me as him. I know that. I think I need to take some time to figure out a few things on my own. Staying on here is not going to help that."

"So you are planning on leaving?

"Yes. I think I have to."

Jayeer nodded slowly, There wasn't any protest, but from Jayeer, she thought, she would have been surprised if there had been.

"So what are you going to do?"

"I have no idea. No idea at all. I might try to find a hauler, one with some resources. I mean I have some pretty marketable skills now. With the jump drive and everything. Perhaps they need a navigator. I do have some other skills as well."

"As I am aware," said Jayeer, again inclining his head in acknowledgement.

Despite his initial reticence—as she now knew, that was just Jay being Jay—she felt a bond with Jayeer Sind, and somehow, she thought, that feeling was reciprocated.

"Initially," he said. "I might have urged caution, but I have been hearing of some trials and work going on in the commercial arena, so I think that might be an actual possibility. A few of my contacts are playing in that area. You know, military technology remains military technology, but it has a way if creeping out to the civilian population. Not that I would ever suggest that a few credits help smooth that particular pathway. Anyway, there have always been strong links between industry and the military wing of the CoCee. Very much in bed together, you might say. I don't tend to get involved in those things, but there you have it."

"Well, that's some good news at least," she said. "At least they can't claim that what is inside my head is proprietary. Although, you know, it wouldn't surprise me if they tried."

He gave a short laugh. "True, true."

Mahra maneuvered her way past his knees and sat down on the bunk beside him, then placed a hand on his leg.

"You know, Jay, this has nothing to do with you."

He turned to meet her gaze; his eyes magnified through the lenses. "You know, I didn't think it did, Mahra, but it's nice to have the confirmation." He paused. "And you know, in the end, I don't think it really has anything to do with Timon."

She looked down then and sighed. "Maybe you're right. Anyway, I should probably start to get myself together," she said and stood. He also rose.

"Listen, Jay, what do you think? They're not going to toss me out straight away…. I mean there's not going to be any formalities involved. As far as the CoCee is concerned, I'm just a freelance consultant."

"No, they're probably not going to do that, and I'm not going to say anything. You're quite right about your status and that's likely to work to your advantage in that regard. After all, the CoCee is nothing more than another bureaucracy and it will probably take them a little while to catch up, or even realise. I'm not sure that Garavenah will have registered. She has a lot on her plate."

"Right."

"Are you planning to inform her?"

Mahra paused for a moment before answering. "Maybe

I'm being childish, but no, I don't think I'm going to. Let her work that out for herself."

"Mahra, I wish you lots of luck, really. I will be thinking of you. Of course, I am respecting your decision and I'm not going to argue with you or try to talk you out of it."

"I appreciate that," she said.

"And you know, Mahra, if there's anything I can do for you...."

She thought for a moment before deciding to ask him. "Listen, maybe you could put in a call to one of these contacts? Saves me having to randomly cast about trying to find out where I might be useful. And you know, if the jump drive is involved anywhere, that's got to work in my favour, right?"

"Of course, of course," he said. "I should have thought. Let me go and do that immediately. If you wait here, I will come back down and let you know if I come up with anything. It shouldn't take me too long. Not that I would like to be seen as aiding and abetting as it were. We will keep this between ourselves."

"Are you sure?" she said, placing a hand on his shoulder.

"Of course I'm sure," he said, giving her a little look of annoyance. "But I'm afraid you're going to have to move if I am to be able to leave."

She glanced at the small space and then laughed. "You're right."

She stood and stepped back, turning, and taking the couple of steps out to the hallway, giving Jay the room to exit.

"Thanks," she said to him as he walked up the hallway and out of sight.

He nodded his response without turning around.

Hartley James

Chapter Eleven

New Helvetica

Valdor Carr wasn't really much of one for scenery, but as their groundcar whipped along at a pace, he couldn't help but contrast the soaring cloud-wreathed crags, the verdant slopes, the couple of crystal-clear lakes, with the dark purples and so-different desiccated landscapes of Kalany. They were on their way out to one of the production plants now to assess the progress of the new installations. Beside him, Tsinda was also watching the landscape out the window, the few small villages they passed, the occasional herds of domesticated animals that roamed the steep slopes to either side of the straight smooth roadway. Despite the investment in chemicals and weapons tech, New Helvetica still had its proportion of farmers, harking back to its agricultural origins, grazing and meat and pelts. He didn't understand how anybody could spend their lives like that. He pitied them really. Perhaps it was the legacy of his own history, but in the end, he still maintained a deep contempt for the farming life.

 Tsinda hadn't said much since they'd set out. Despite his misgivings, she'd proved herself to be quite useful in an administrative sense, taking several of the more tedious tasks off his hands without hesitation, which in turn, had freed him up to think. As Marina had suggested, she seemed to be multi-talented. She still made him uncomfortable though, and he couldn't rid himself of the feeling that she was continually observing, taking notes, ready to report back. She probably

Benevolent

was. He could say one thing for her though, she seemed to be a good listener. A very good listener. Since Marina has foist her on him, she had asked him lots about himself and at least given the impression that she was genuinely interested in the things that he had to tell her. That was probably her real talent. At this point, she had probably been exposed to his entire life history, although he hesitated when she had started venturing into areas of his ideals and goals. Valdor let no one be a party to those. Once upon a time, Marina may have been a bit of a confidante, but certainly not anymore. He glanced back at Tsinda, but she seemed to be still occupied with what passed outside the window. He turned back to his side, although already he was bored with the passing scenery. Sometimes he wished that they didn't have to put these production plants so far out. Perhaps one day soon, they'd adapt the jump drive, put it into groundcars. Now, that was a thought….

"How long till we get there," he asked the driver.

"About thirty minutes yet, Mezzer Carr."

Valdor humphed and turned once more to look at the mountains, tracing the track of a ski-lift up one slope. He peered at the cluster of lodges further up. You'd never get him in one of those. In fact, you'd never get Valdor on a set of skis. He failed to see the fascination. Go up to the top and slide down again, then do it all over again a few times and pay a lot of credits to do so. And then do that over and over again. Pointless expense. He thought quite a lot of it was probably ostentation, doing it just so you could show that you had the means to do it. Certainly the outfit styles were garish enough to support that theory. No style at all. With a slight snort in support of his own wit, he turned back to face the road ahead.

Eventually, with enough of the picturesque scenery having passed them by, they pulled up to a narrow tree-lined drive that wound down to the building complex. There were no signs anywhere announcing what might go on in the plant, or who it belonged to. That was not so unusual for many of the ventures on New Helvetica. With so many of them involved in technologies with military endpoints, there were security considerations and other concerns, particularly if some of the work they were involved in may be a little clandestine or a little doubtful from the do-gooder point of view. Not that New Helvetica really suffered from protestors. That sort of thing was heavily frowned upon.

The buildings themselves, squat, grey, featureless, seemed to extend over a vast area. Again, there were no signs, no names, no windows. Valdor was sure there were defences, in fact he knew there were, but there was no visible indication that those existed either. He was fairly certain that their approach would have been monitored every step of the way as soon as they got within range.

"Well," he said. "Here we are."

He realised, of course, that the last was somewhat unnecessary. Tsinda didn't react, however, and she waited for the doors to open and then stepped outside. He followed suit and looked around at the trees and the buildings once he'd moved a little away from their vehicle. He didn't recall having visited this particular plant before, but then there were a number of his holdings that he'd never felt the need to grace with his presence. He wasn't actually sure that this *had* been one of his holdings. He had always had people to do that sort of thing for him and from time to time, it was better not to have public connections to some of his enterprises. He scratched the back of his neck and grimaced. He wasn't sure what he was doing here now, but the message had come through that he needed to show his face and there was little he could do in his current position except comply.

"Shall I wait?" the driver asked.

"Yes, wait," Valdor told him without looking at him.

The man could park wherever he wanted as far as Valdor was concerned. He didn't care, but he didn't want to be put in a position where he had to wait around for a ride back to the

Benevolent

city once he was done here. If there was a problem with that, then let the people inside sort it out. On the face of it, at least now, he actually owned everything that stood in front of him, so he could do what he wanted. On the face of it….

"Do you see a door anywhere?" he asked Tsinda.

"Um, no. Haven't you been here before?"

"Not to this one, no."

"We could always wave."

He pursed his lips and then decided to respond anyway. "I'm not going to stand around like an idiot waving at a wall."

"Well, no."

"They were supposed to know we were coming, weren't they?"

"Yes, of course."

"And who are we supposed to be meeting?"

"Hendriksen."

"Mezzer, Mez?"

"I'm actually not sure. First name Orlan. I am not familiar with it, so I suppose it could be either."

"Or neither."

"Um, true," she said.

Valdor grimaced again. "Well if this Hendriksen doesn't show soon, we're leaving. I have better things to do."

"Do you think that's—"

Valdor narrowed his eyes at her, cutting her off mid-sentence.

"Right," she said and looked off to the side, first at the trees surrounding the grounds and then up at the sky. He half expected her to start whistling.

Suddenly, a section of the blank wall in front of them and off to the right opened, revealing light beyond and some shapes that he couldn't make out from this distance. A figure emerged, definitely male, and he strode towards them quickly. He wore a long coat, pale blue, the protective sort you saw in labs and medical facilities. There was some sort of detector badge affixed to the front where a breast pocket would be. Valdor wondered briefly what it was for. Radiation? Contaminants? Either way, if he needed to know, he was sure he would be informed. Or perhaps not.

"Hendriksen, said the man. Orlan." He thrust out a hand, and Valdor touched fingers.

"You are Mezzer Carr," he said.

"That's right. And this is—"

"—Mez Bos," Hendriksen finished for him. No finger contact there. Apparently Tsinda was a known quantity.

"Please, please, follow me." He spun on his heel and walked quickly towards the open space in the wall. Valdor had to hurry to catch up. Funny, he hadn't even known the Bos part.

"Is there anything I can get you before we begin?" said Hendriksen. "It's a bit of a haul out here from the city. Perhaps I can offer you some refreshments. Kahveh? Something else?"

Valdor could sorely have done with a brandy, but he doubted that would be on offer at the moment. Maybe later.

"No that's all right," he said, looking around the space that they'd just entered. The walls that weren't glass were some kind of bilious yellow, with the hard, shiny floor a washed-out green that did nothing to enhance the impression. Already he felt as if he might be contaminated, if only by the décor. There was a single security desk and a row of hard chairs lined along one wall. The desk stood empty. Hendriksen clearly noticed Valdor's focus because he immediately piped up with an explanation.

"There's not much call to have someone here. Our systems cover most of the requirements. This here is for check-in of casual labour."

"I don't understand," said Valdor. "Why would you need casual labour."

"Well, sometimes there might be a number of things that need carrying from one place to another. Sometimes they need

Benevolent

a human touch, and well, we wouldn't expect our researchers or top engineers or scientists to do the carrying. Some of it we just can't trust to machines."

"I see," said Valdor, tucking the information away for later. "And where do you get them, these casual labourers?"

"Oh, there are places in the city. Sometimes they are itinerants, just looking for something to tide them over. Sometimes they've wound up here, come in on a hauler with a short contract and are looking for something to carry them over to the next one. They're plentiful if you know where to look."

"And doesn't that present a security risk?"

"Oh, no, no…. not at all. All of our casual labourers are vetted thoroughly."

"But what if they saw something, took the knowledge away?"

Hendriksen laughed at that, as if he found the prospect ludicrous. When he next spoke, he did so with a little smirk. "I can assure you, the types we are talking about, that wouldn't be an issue."

Valdor glanced at Tsinda, but she was betraying nothing. She certainly played things close, this one.

"Okay then," said Valdor. "In that case, we had better get on with why we are here. Lead on Mezzer Hendriksen."

"It's Doctor, actually."

Ah, thought Valdor, one of *those*.

"All right then. Lead on, *Doctor* Hendriksen."

As he led the way, apparently unperturbed by Valdor's pointed sarcasm, Hendriksen chattered on to Tsinda, allowing Valdor further space to observe. He led them past a couple of storage areas, and then what appeared to be offices. Everywhere was the same dreadful combination of nauseous yellow and putrescent green. At least they were consistent. When they reached the end of the corridor, Hendriksen paused and turned to Valdor.

"What we will be seeing is in the next building. It's connected by a long corridor. We prefer not to have to go outside when moving from one to the other. It is better if everything is contained."

"I see," said Valdor. "One question I do have…if you have to ship in labour, then what about your full-time employees? I didn't see any settlement that close by. We passed a couple of villages on the way, but they didn't look like the sort of places that might accommodate the plant's population."

"No, you are right," Hendriksen answered. "Well spotted Mezzer Carr. Though a couple of them have chosen to make homes in those places you've mentioned, most of the staff prefer to use the accommodations provided onsite. They are free to use for our employees."

"And how does that work?"

"Well, generally, we get longer workdays, there's a community here, we would no doubt be required to reimburse any travel costs. Of course we have the best medical facilities here. Far better than anyone would find in the city generally and naturally, fairly immediate in their accessibility. I think it's an equitable arrangement all round."

"I see," said Valdor. There was perhaps some logic to it, but he didn't agree with it completely. Not so important, but it might turn out to be something else to investigate. "So one of these buildings is devoted to staff quarters?"

"And a cafeteria, a retail outlet."

"Hmm, a regular home away from home."

"We'd rather like to think of it as a regular home at home."

"And you, *Doctor* Hendriksen, do you also make your home here."

"Oh, fire no. I have a house in a nearby village. Kinsderf."

"I see," said Valdor nodding slowly. The man's ebullient

Benevolent

arrogance was starting to grate, but he doubted that he could do much about it. Hendriksen seemed to be oblivious to the normal cues. He could sense Tsinda watching him and he looked at her with a slight tilt of his head. She shook hers in response. She certainly had no problem reading his cues.

"So, let's go," he said.

"Yes, yes, of course," said Hendriksen and led them round the corner and into the promised long corridor.

It turned out to be little more than a featureless tube. Yellow walls. Pale green floor. There was no way of telling whether it was above ground or below it. Hendriksen hadn't led them down any stairs, so Valdor made the safe assumption that it was the former. As they walked its length, Valdor tuned out Hendriksen's voice and let Tsinda absorb the wash of his words. He may as well make use of her presence after all. Finally, they reached the corridor's end and they stepped out into a more brightly lit area. A walkway encircled a vast sunken square space with staircases leading down at every side. Perhaps it was below them and out of sight, but with his initial scan, he couldn't see any way that they might get things in or out of the place. But get things in they must, because evenly spaced, one from the other, were rows and rows of the containment cylinders that he had first seen back at the ILGC building labs. From what he could tell from up where he stood, as yet they appeared to be empty. He started counting, then gave up. Instead, he counted the rows and the number of cylinders in one of them and did the sum in his head and stopped.

"How many," he said.

"Here, in this building, two hundred and twenty-four."

"In this building?"

"Yes, we have two more like this."

This time Valdor did do the sum in his head. Six hundred and seventy-two in total. He said the number out loud. "And how did we come up with that?" he asked.

Hendriksen shrugged. "It is what fit," he said.

"Can we go down and look at them more closely?" asked Tsinda.

"Of course, of course. Follow me."

As they moved on, Valdor was speculating. Six hundred and seventy-two in this facilities. At least a couple more plants like this one. Whatever was back at ILGC. He wasn't aware yet of more distributed facilities, but they were bound to exist or were in the process of being established. The numbers grew in his head, and he pursed his lips.

Hendriksen led them along one of the gantries and down a set of metal stairs to the floor of what had once been either a production room or a warehouse, Valdor was not really sure which. There was nothing on the floor or anywhere else that gave a clue. In the end, it was just a vast empty space that was now full of rows of large capsules, slightly tilted backwards and bearing tubes and cables all flowing down to disappear beneath the floor. Valdor pointed to them.

"Where do those end up?" he asked.

Hendriksen nodded. "You can't see from here, but there's a sub level below us, absolutely packed full of equipment designed to keep these beauties running. Over the other side there—he indicated the upper level—are monitoring facilities. You can't see them now, obviously, because the walls are opaqued, but I'll take you up there after."

Tsinda, in the meantime had wandered over to one of the cylinders. She stretched up on her toes to try to peer through the front piece. It only emphasised how slight she was.

"These are empty, right?"

"For now, yes. But we hope to commence production very shortly."

Production. He was thinking of this like a factory, clearly unfazed by the implications. Valdor looked away from the man and stared at the rows and rows of chambers thoughtfully. There was something going on here, but it eluded him. He

Benevolent

knew he should be making the connection, but there was definitely something he wasn't quite putting his finger on.
    It didn't matter now. It would keep for later.

Chapter Twelve

Belshore

Having taken stock of her meagre possessions, Mahra was at somewhat of a loose end. She had to wait until Jayeer came up with something. Or not. And then she would work out what she was going to do. She could, of course, just head out and find what she might find. She was no stranger to that particular strategy, but something was telling her to sit tight for the moment.

Just to pass the time, as well as perhaps doing something to assuage her own guilt, she hefted her blade and then looked around the small cramped space. There was no way she could really run through anything that even resembled her patterns here. She dropped the blade on the bunk. Instead, with a grimace, she rummaged around in her locker until she located the whetstone, pulled it out of the pack and then stood, staring down at it. Back on The Cradle, there'd been a special stone, dug from a specific volcanic area, blue on one side, yellow on the other, swirled with patterns. The stone had been unique for its sharpening properties effective on the metallic mineral blades produced back then, each side having a different coarseness to work through the sharpening process. This stone now, like her blade on the bed were fine examples, but in her mind, they would never equal the Old One's blade that had passed down to her, or the Lantanan whetstone that she had learned to use properly and effectively back then. Still, it would do, as would the blade, that had certainly proven itself

Benevolent

up to the task on more than one occasion. She crossed to the sink and moistened the stone slightly. Were she to use one of the artificially produced synthetic stones, of course, it would instead remain dry, but Mahra preferred the natural stone, the cool dampness, the feel of it in her hand. Despite the assurances that the synthetics did a better job, Mahra knew what she liked and what felt right for her. She didn't remember which world this stone came from, but that was okay. It was the feel of it that mattered, not where it came from. Somehow, she though that might be a completely different matter if she managed to somehow acquire one of the Lantanan sharpening stones, not that there was any chance of that now.

She had a quick thought, stepped back to the locker, and then tossed a couple of coz nuts off to one end of the bunk.

"There you go, Chutz," she said, gave her shoulder a quick flex, but he needed no prompting. He quickly leaped off and onto the bunk, chittering happily to himself as he grabbed one of the nuts within both clawed paws. Nodding to herself, she sat on the bunk's edge, reached for the blade, and laying it flat against her thighs, started to draw the stone along its length. Pretty soon, she was into the rhythm of it and all thoughts started to flow away.

"Ah," Jayeer said from the doorway.

Mahra ceased the motion, placed the blade back down beside her on the bed. She'd been right to wait.

"So, how did it go," she asked as she placed the blade down again, reached for the cloth and rewrapped the whetstone.

"Well, you were right, certainly, as I thought you might be. There is definite interest."

"Okay, that's good," she said.

"Mmm-hmm," said Jayeer. "But…."

"Don't tell me; there are some complications."

"Well…" He moved his head from side to side. He gave the barest grimace. "Not exactly complications. It's just not, perhaps, as quick as you might like."

"How do you mean?"

"Well, clearly, they are not quite as advanced as we are with the technology. Not surprising. Things might take a little bit of time before they are ready to make use of your talents."

"In other words, I should have held back from having my little explosion for a little while longer."

Jayeer scratched at the side of his face and grimaced again, looking down at the floor. "But, all the same," he said, lifting his gaze, "they would very much like to talk to you."

"Any idea how long?" she asked.

Jayeer shook his head. "Not really. Sorry. You will need to ask them that question."

Mahra sighed and looked up at the ceiling. "Well, it's not all bad. Looks like we need to find something to occupy ourselves, Chutz," she said.

"Thanks, Jay, anyway. Give me the details if you're all right with that, and I'll get in touch."

"Of course."

"After I talk to them, I can work out how much time I am going to spend in random bars getting into trouble."

"Well, yes," said Jayeer. "You do seem to have a talent for that."

"Mmmm," she said. "That I do."

He said nothing, merely blinked at her through the thick lenses that magnified his eyes.

oOo

Mahra stood outside on the street looking up at the building. It was just like any corporate office complex on Belshore, all faux stone and glass and crawling holos. She had her blade snugly in place in its sheath between her shoulder blades and Chutzpah at her shoulder. She wanted there to be no misapprehensions as to what they were getting when Mahra

Benevolent

Kaitan came on board, if she came on board. When she'd spoken to this Mezzer Dubois over the com, he'd seemed eager enough though. It wasn't as if they were likely to get anyone else with the same capabilities as Mahra Kaitan, so they were probably more than likely to take her as she came. After all, she reminded herself, she was the *original* navigator. Somehow, she felt that Jayeer had already made that plain to them. Still, if there were any qualms, she could deal with them if and when they arose, and she was prepared for that.

She looked up at the name above the door. Bathyscaphe. Strange name for a company in the hauling business, or that's what she presumed they did. Their interest in her was a fairly big clue. Perhaps they'd had some sort of marine origins in their past. Of course they could be some sort of marine mercenary contractor, but looking at the building, at its location, she doubted that would be the case. Taking a deep breath, she stepped through the front doors and walked over to the reception. A young man in crisp whites sat behind the desk. She knew that she'd been scanned as soon as she walked in the door. She was interested to see how they were going to react to her blade.

"Mahra Kaitan, here to see a Mezzer Dubois."

"Yes, of course, Mez Kaitan. You are expected. Please take the elevator to the twentieth. You will be met up there."

She nodded her response. Not a flicker about either her blade or Chutzpah. She had been prepared to put up a fight, but it seemed like that would be unnecessary. She crossed to the indicated elevator and stepped in. The door closed automatically as soon as she entered, and it smoothly whirred into operation. There was nothing to press, nothing to say. She raised her eyebrows at that and spent the ascent scanning the headlines scrolling across the news feed beside the door. That was another thing she'd fallen out of practice with. Before the whole CoCee period, she'd made it a habit of keeping an eye on the newsfeeds. Sometimes it had been the source of work or pointed her to things or events that might result in a short-term contract. Not anymore. She'd become complacent, uninformed, and that was always a dangerous state to be in. The elevator glided to a stop. A big '20' flashed on and off beside the door in red, and the doors slid open, soundlessly. She stepped out into an empty space, all glass, glass walls, glass doors. Had it been more reflective, it would have been like a mirror maze. She wondered briefly if they could be turned reflective. She could imagine that they could be opaqued. She could see people at desks, one after the other, and she could look right through to the sky and clouds beyond. She found it a bit unsettling. A holo appeared in front of her.

Mez Kaitan.
Please follow the indicated signs.

It faded and was replaced by a small scrolling group of circles floating just below ceiling level, pointing her off to the left. Doing as she was instructed, she followed the glowing shapes down the glass corridor, around a corner to the right, and along until finally they reached another see-through door within another glass wall, leading to yet another glass office. Behind a desk in a high-backed white chair sat a harassed looking man. As she reached the door and the lights above her faded, she heard a chime from the door beyond. The man, dressed in crisp white, but with a straight cut grey jacket looked up, saw her there and stood, quickly crossing to the door, and opening it. His neatly cropped hair matched the grey and white of his outfit. By the look of his face, and she quickly checked his hands, even though he was a corporate office type, it looked like he might do his fair share of outdoor activities.

"Mez, Kaitan," he said. "A pleasure to see you. I am Roland Dubois. Please, please, come in," he said, bowing slightly as he stepped back and held out one hand, to indicate a small table and two chairs in one corner of the office. "Please, take a seat."

She nodded and stepped past him, noting the way his gaze

Benevolent

flitted first to the zimonette at her shoulder and then to her blade, before he closed the door and turned to join her at the table. While he was crossing, Mahra did a quick assessment of the room. Neat, orderly. On a shelf to one side sat a model of a yacht. There were a couple of pictures also showing Dubois and someone else…partner? friend?...looking windswept and slightly damp. So it looked like sailing was the thing. As he joined her, he noticed the direction of her gaze, gave the slightest lift of his chin, but made no acknowledgement.

"Well, Mez Kaitan," he said as he pulled out a chair and sat. "My friend Jayeer speaks very highly of you."

Mahra inclined her head but refrained from commenting. The use of 'friend' was interesting.

"Right," said Dubois. "I don't mind saying, that if you are half as good as Jay seems to think, we want you. We would very much like to make use of your services if you are interested."

"Okay…," said Mahra.

"However," Dubois, elbows on table, steepled his fingers in front of his chin. "There's a slight problem."

"You're not ready," said Mahra.

"That's it exactly," said Dubois seemingly unflustered by her quick assessment of the situation. "But…there may be a compromise."

"What sort of compromise."

"Well, I suppose there's no harm. I am quite eager to secure your services. Perhaps we could come to an arrangement. Some sort of retainer. You could perhaps consult with the engineering team. I believe we are able to simulate the reality quite effectively now. It's in our interest to make sure you remain available."

As he talked, Mahra studied the man's face. He was quite thin, with a sculpted thin beard and moustache. Lines crossed his forehead and he had a slight squint. His face, however, was tanned and healthy. The lines could be there from exposure to the wind and weather rather than worry and stress.

"Um, I'm not sure that would work," she said. Mahra had no desire to get involved in endless simulations. "But a retainer sounds good," she added quickly.

"Good." Dubois gave a series of very short enthusiastic nods. "Yes, very good."

"Forgive me, Mezzer Dubois," said Mahra. "But I'm not quite sure how you fit into the picture here."

Dubois paused then. "Oh. I am sorry. Of course. I am COO of Bathyscaphe."

Mahra almost started at that. She barely managed to restrain the reaction. She looked around the office space, at the floor, at the similar layouts. She would have expected a grand office. Well, at least it was in the corner. Her quick looks around were clearly not lost on him.

"Yes, I know. We don't hold very much with titles and position here at Bathyscaphe. We are not a military operation after all." He gave a short laugh at that then shook his head. "I was just one of the technical guys, and here I am. We're sort of like that."

It could be just talk, but Mahra thought she liked the sound of that. Still, he seemed to have done all right out of it.

"I have to ask," she said. "The name…?"

"Oh, Bathyscaphe? Yes." Another series of quick nods. "Our original business was in the deep sea mine operations and transport here on Belshore. The company was very successful early on. We were the original discoverers of the undersea crystal caves. Of course from there, with the immediate commercial possibilities of that operation, we grew and expanded our horizons." He gave another short laugh. "And you know, space is sort of like an ocean. We still sail in ships. Space has its depths. It even has pirates." Another short laugh.

She smiled herself at that.

"So, yes, Bathyscaphe."

Really, if she'd thought, she could have looked all that up

Benevolent

before she'd landed on their doorstep. She simply hadn't considered doing so. Yet another example of how she had become lax over the last few weeks. Stupid, Mahra. Nonetheless, unless she was wrong, this Dubois had the authority to make the offer he was suggesting. They could work out the details of what she might be doing in the consulting role as they got into the swing of it, but for now, she was more interested in nailing down this retainer. That would, in turn, let her decide what she could afford and what sort of accommodation options she had and what she was going to do with any leisure time she might have in between. Hopefully it was going to be enough to keep her out of yet another seedy transit hotel, although it had been a while since she'd found herself in one of those, either from circumstance or expedience.

As those thoughts ran through her head, she flirted with the idea of picking up something else freelance in the meantime. A couple of shifts doing security, something like that. That too was always an option.

"So, what do you say?" said Dubois, his voice drawing her back to the moment.

"Yes, I think it sounds reasonably attractive," she said. "But I'd be interested in knowing what your plans are once you are ready. What's my role? What do you see me doing?"

"Well. Yes. According to Mezzer Sind, you have more than one skillset. I'll be honest; I've been doing a bit of digging, but I haven't been able to find out much of your history."

This was the part that Mahra wasn't exactly looking forward to.

"I understand that," she said noncommittally.

"But," he continued. "With the information that I have had from Jayeer, and the whole CoCee connection, I don't think we need to worry too much about that."

Mahra was both relieved and a little puzzled by that.

"And why is that?"

"Well, you see," he said slowly. "Bathyscaphe actually does quite a bit, um…." He pressed his lips together for a moment. "I suppose you could say…alongside…the CoCee. We have quite a few complementary undertakings. I don't think I really need to go into the details now. Suffice it to say, we have common interests. Of course, we are not the only ones playing with the drive at the moment. Inter-system, and even intra-system distances are a challenge for many of the players in the marketplace. I would say that our relationship with the CoCee is…special, however which does a lot to help us in that regard. With your knowledge of some of those operations and with your unique skillsets, I think we could really benefit each other."

"I see," said Mahra, trying not to narrow her eyes in response. More like Mahra could benefit them was the truth of it. Perhaps Jayeer Sind was not quite as altruistic as he might have seemed. Sometimes, she wondered what ran beneath that impassive surface, and here yet again was another example to give her pause for thought. Sometimes, Jayeer surprised her.

Benevolent

Chapter Thirteen

Belshore

"Fire, Jayeer, I do not know what we're supposed to be doing out here."

"We are where we are, Timon. Orders are orders."

As ever, Jayeer Sind was taking everything in his stride. Sometimes his passivity annoyed the hell out of Timon, but then Jay had other things going for him. Timon glanced over, narrowed his eyes briefly, and then shifted his gaze to the world that sat slowly turning below them. They'd been up here for a few hours now, 'monitoring for any unusual activity." As far as he was concerned, this was little more than something to occupy them while the entirety of the CoCee fleet seemed to be shut down. Yes, they'd been in this sort of position before, but if Garavenah was going to give them holding duties, the least she could do would be to provide some sort of covert courier mission or the like. Something with a little bit of substance.

"How are you doing up there?" he asked over the com.

"Yes, I'm fine, Commander Pellis," said their replacement navigator Kurasa in response. Timon hadn't even registered the man's rank. He was a navigator; that was enough.

"Good," he said. "No sign of anything?"

"No, Commander, not a flicker."

The use of the title was starting to grate, but to be honest, right now, Timon couldn't be bothered. Frankly, he was sort of missing Mahra, though he was a little loathe to admit it to himself. There had been something about their teaming, the three of them. There'd been a chemistry to it, had been since the very first time they'd met in that bar on New Helvetica. And now that she was gone….

He glanced at the displays. Still at least another hour to go before they were due to end this shift.

"Okay, Jay," he said after a sigh. "Let's swing round the other side and see if we can pick up anything there."

Jayeer simply nodded in response, punctuating it with a deep breath, indicating his own lack of enthusiasm, Timon, prodded *The Nameless* into life. Below them, the world transitioned to darkness as they cruised to the nightside. He eased her into a parking orbit, and once he'd let the ship take over maintaining their position, settled back and continued his musings.

The Nameless was still new enough that he hadn't yet got around to equipping anything that could be seen as personalisation. He hadn't yet bonded with the ship. Timon guessed that was the right way to look at it. As a pilot, he bonded. He gave himself a little nod. That was the right word. Still, this particular vessel was quite something. Everything about her was state of the art, and even though he felt a certain level of resentment, there was much to admire in it. She handled like a dream. Of course, he had yet to see how she might perform in a combat situation, not that his primary focus there would be on the weaponry except as secondary backup. His job was to keep them from being hit, and to put them in a position where they could do the hitting. Anyway, there were still things to explore.

"Have you worked out if there's any music?" he asked, reaching for the controls, and scanning through a series of options.

"No, I haven't seen anything."

Benevolent

Timon gave another frustrated sigh. "I'm boring my boots off here, Jayeer."

Jay just peered at him and said nothing.

Timon gave another sigh, shook his head, and went back to scanning the controls.

"Aha," he said after a couple of minutes.

"Did you find it?"

"No, not that." He manipulated the controls, setting the temperature down by a couple of degrees. Had he been looking for it, he would have really had to search.

"Damned ship is too warm," he said by way of explanation.

Jayeer nodded and went back to his own examination of the colourful displays arrayed around him.

"Commander Pellis." Kurasa's voice over the com.

"Yes, what is it?"

"I think I…there was something…oh, no. I'm sorry. It was nothing."

Timon drew air slowly through his nose, his lips pressed together. Of course, it was nothing. He tilted his head back and closed his eyes. Somehow, he thought, it was always going to be nothing. Despite the plentiful nothing, there was something going on here, and it was leaving an unpleasant taste in his mouth. He didn't like it one bit.

He opened his eyes to stare down at Belshore below them. What exactly was Garavenah up to? Or perhaps it wasn't Garavenah at all.

"Fine, Jayeer," he said after a couple of moments. "Let's call it done. I don't know about you, but I, for one, am badly in need of a drink."

Jay nodded,

"Good. That's that then," he said and spurred *The Nameless* into life.

Hartley James

Chapter Fourteen

Belshore

As usual, Mahra ended up in the same old quarters, in the same old stomping ground. One day she might actually spend the time to work out what attracted her to the seedier locales in cities like this. Perhaps it was simply the fact that these sorts of places attracted those without roots, the loners, those who had nowhere else to go. In that respect, there was a kind of kinship. She'd been here in the locale long enough now that it was more than just a haunt. Rather, it was starting to feel more like a base, something quite unusual for her. She was still stuck in a hotel though, one of those cheaper short-stay places, despite her initial thoughts after the retainer discussion with Dubois. The amount was certainly adequate, but in the end, she had decided that taking on another part-time contract would lose the opportunity that the current arrangement gave her. It had been a long time since she'd had anything that amounted to a quasi-vacation, which was exactly what she was having now. Mahra didn't need that much though. Shower, toilet facilities, the feeds, and a bed; that was about it. Anything else she might need, she could find in the neighbourhood without much trouble. The hardest thing was finding a decent source of Coz nuts for Chutzpah, but in the end, purely by accident she had stumbled across one of those little shops that seems to carry everything imaginable. She had no idea where the owner came from, but it certainly wasn't Belshore. The accent and the looks were nothing she recognised. She thought to ask, just out of simple curiosity, but in the end had decided against it. In

Benevolent

places like this, people tended not to appreciate random questions about their origins. That sort of behaviour was just as likely to get you into trouble or at least cause offence. She was good enough at that by herself without adding to it. Anyway, it was not something she was going to dwell on. As long as she had a good supply, enough to keep Chutz happy, that was all that mattered.

After one or two tries, she had fixed on a new watering hole as her regular. The old place, the one where she and Jacinda had spent most of their time was burdened with memories, and she no longer felt comfortable there, regardless of the fact that she liked the regular bar staff and the general ambience. The problem was that it simply reminded her too much of how blind she had been, how stupid. There wasn't anything else for it. For a time, she had tried convincing herself that something could have happened to Jacinda, that she hadn't been played, but deep down, she knew otherwise. She ran her fingers up and down the side of her glass, leaving trails in the beaded moisture, then lifted it and took a healthy swallow. Leisure or not, this waiting was starting to get to her.

Just as she was lifting her glass for another sip, giving the rest of the place a quick scan to see if anything interesting might have shown up yet, her palm comp chimed and vibrated on the bar. Timing.

"Huh, what do you think of that, Chutz?" she said as she reached to spin it around so she could see.

There was a message there from Bathyscaphe, almost as of she'd willed it into being. She wasn't going to kid herself though; she was under no illusion that her abilities extended that far. She peered down at it and nodded. They wanted her to come in. Looked like her little period of leisure was coming to an end. She'd go in in the morning. It was already early evening and she doubted that anything was going to happen in the next few hours.

"One more night, eh Chutz?" she said and lifted her glass

once more, tilting it in a slight salute to their reflection in the mirror behind the bar. She was about to see where this one was going to lead them.

Benevolent

Chapter Fifteen

Sapporan

As Mahra stepped out of the shuttle, the climate hit her across the face like a wet palm. It was hot, damned hot, and the air was thick with humidity and the smell of vegetation, both new, and old and fading away. She breathed a curse despite herself. Of course she'd researched the place before they'd arrived, but nothing could have prepared her for the change from the carefully curated ship environment and then that of the shuttle. It was more than the thick air though. Only worlds smelled like this. There was absolutely no doubt that there was life here. The place reeked of it, current and recently passed. Off to one side, a group of youths were playing hook hoops. She'd seen it once or twice back on Belshore, but not up close like this. Somehow, it was an unexpected outcome of the jump tech, but she had no idea how and what. The floating rings hovered stationary for a few moments and then darted to another position. The idea was to snag them with a long hook like device and lift yourself up, then, while floating, detach yourself and snag another before it whipped away and left you falling to the ground. She stood watching for a few moments. It seemed that a miss earned just as many hoots and cheers as a successful catch. In the end, she shook her head and turned away. The things people invented to fill their time.

"Seems a bit pointless, eh Chutz?" she said, but his attention seemed to be elsewhere for now anyway. She looked back over her shoulder, tracing his gaze. There stabbing up into the heavens was the elevator, almost directly behind them. She would have sorely liked to travel down on that, but Merritt, the captain, was having none of it. Too much expense, he'd said. Couldn't justify it. They were spending too much on the cargo as it was without adding to the overheads. Mahra had tried arguing the point, but Merritt had refused to budge. Apparently, as far as he was concerned, Mahra was overhead. Maybe another time, he'd said, just as much to shut her up, she thought. She doubted very much that another time was likely to come any time with this particular crew and their captain. Still, Lars Merritt *was* the captain, and his word would win out every time. She'd been in that position before. The way that Chutz appeared focussed on the elevator was almost enough to make her believe that he knew the source of her frustration. One day, she might get the chance to know for sure.

"You just know too much for your own good, don't you?" she told him and gave him a gentle scratch under his furry chin. "Let's go and see what we can see anyway," she said and started heading towards the gates. Sometimes there were real advantages to coming down at the docks rather than any of the passenger terminals. Here, it was just a quick scan, a couple of words, and she was through. No interminable queues and suspicious officials, always having to explain away the blade, and more often than not, the zimonette as well. Funnily enough, it was Chutzpah that prompted more comment than the blade did. Quite often though, she had to fall back on the religion argument to see her through. Essential to the observance of her faith. Over the years she'd constructed a fairly elaborate description of what the religion entailed, some of it based on the philosophies taught back on The Cradle. Sometimes they bought it, but not always. In the end though, it wasn't too far from the truth if she thought about it. Perhaps she'd be better off spending her time actually founding a religion.

By the time she passed through the personnel entry, Mahra was starting to drip with sweat, runnels of it running down between her shoulder blades and moistening her hairline, and already, the humidity was starting to drag her down. What she needed was a bar and some decent climate control. She had no doubt that both had to exist in a place with weather like this.

"Is it always like this?" she asked the man checking the arrivals.

"Mostly," he said. "Sometimes it storms."

"Does it cool down?"

"Not really. Not ever. Welcome to Sapporan," he said. "Well, welcome to Sinq City." He said the last with a shrug.

That had come as no surprise to her. Unlike many of the other worlds where the main city seemed to adopt the name of the world itself, Sapporan seemed to be different. Whether it was tradition or something peculiar in their history, she hadn't been able to work out in the brief time she'd had to research the place. Merritt had remained fairly tight-lipped about their destination until they were ready for the jump, and once her bit was over, while they moved into orbit and maneuvered into a position where the goods could be ferried across to the elevator she had just a short time to access the feeds and see if she could find anything useful.

Hartley James

They only had a few hours here, making sure the consignment was landed, shipped, and on its way to its eventual destination. Then it was back to Belshore, simple as that. In a way, she could be grateful that Merritt had insisted that she use the shuttle. It meant she was down a lot quicker than if she had actually managed to ride the elevator. She had every intention of using the time it afforded her before she needed to be back on board. It was only going to be a few hours.

Just outside of the port gates was the high-speed transit that would ferry her to the city's borders, and she wasted no time climbing aboard the one that conveniently waiting there at the station. There was no payment required, as the city's management offered it as a service. Something she supposed that they needed to do. Otherwise, the port would be full of pirate taxis ready to gouge the uninformed newcomer, but of that particular feature found in most port cities, there was no sign. She glanced back towards the elevator, casting a long shadow across the landscape as it soared up into the heavily overcast sky. It was almost as if it was propping up the clouds, or that the clouds were some strange dark and fluffy foliage sprouting from the elevator's trunk. She supposed it made sense to have the thing a way out from the city itself.

Thankfully, the transport itself had climate control, protecting her from the wet towel heat as they skimmed into the city. As they travelled, she kept half an eye on the displays and half on the passing wet lushness, full of deep greens and purples, or the occasional muddy patch of ground. There didn't seem to be much going on, but she learned that the transit itself ran about every fifteen minutes, even throughout the night. She tucked the information away for later. Before long, they reached the transit stop, and she climbed out, looking up and down the platform, but there was no one else. Not a soul. It appeared as if she'd been the only passenger.

The little research she'd had time for had given her a pretty good picture of Sinq City's layout. It was relatively small, clustered along the sides of a slow-moving muddy river with encroaching jungle all around. Despite the damp and the humidity, the locals seemed to do a pretty good job with their buildings, square, raised on stilts for the most part and painted in various pastel shades. She wondered about the stilts. Was it because of the river, or something else? She made a note to ask someone about it if she got the chance. It was these little oddities that helped make a place unique. She didn't know enough about the place to entrust herself to public transport though. That would take a good deal more research and she didn't really have the time for that, so she started walking in the direction that led down to the centre. Thankfully, the place was small enough to make that possible. It gave her the chance to see and absorb more of the exotic sights and smells that abounded, and of those, there were many, especially the smells.

As she moved passed buildings and streets, the number of people grew. There were individuals from multiple races, origins. She noted a couple in Belshorian outfits, and one or two looking like there origin was probably New Helvetian, but there were many more that she had no idea where they hailed from. Tall, short, stocky, thin, distinctive styles of clothes, different shapes, and colours, all were on display. There was one thing common to all of them though; they were all human. She had marvelled at the number and variety of ships parked in orbit when they'd first arrived.

They too had shown great diversity, speaking of a multiple of origins.

She passed a street full of traders, not shops, but stalls set up along the length of the street with various goods out on display, cluttered and clustered close together. For the most part, they seemed to be run by locals. The native Sapporans were fairly easy to identify; they tended to be shorter and darker than the most of their customers with broad round faces, but the stallholders were in no way restricted to Sapporans. Here, now, the smell and humidity had been joined by a multiple of voices, some speaking in common, some in various dialects or tongues that she'd never even heard before. As she got closer and closer in to Sinq City's centre, she started to realise how much there was here to see and experience, and in a way, she began to feel a little sorry that she didn't have longer to explore the place. Perhaps she'd have another opportunity to come back. She passed yet another roadside stall, this one selling fans, the owner waving at her, beckoning for her to approach and see, demonstrating, but she waved her off, as nice as the idea of having something to stir the sluggish air would be. Every few paces there were food stalls, or open servery windows, serving quick bites with doorways leading in to darker, cooler places where more substantial meals could be had. All of it was new, the smells, the sights, the noise. It was chaos, but at the same time, there was some sort of order about it as well.

The heat and air were starting to drag on her even more now. If she had more time, she might be able to acclimatise, but not with this short hop. She needed to find somewhere that was cooler, replenish the moisture that was leaving her body with every step that she took. An exceptionally

Benevolent

bearded local stepped almost directly in her path, waving what looked like on overly large crisped cockroach on a stick. Mahra quickly sidestepped, reaching up to contain Chutz at the same time. That sort of sudden action was usually not good for the health, but there was barely a bristle from him. She frowned pointedly at the local and waved him away, but he persisted. Mahra firmly shook her head at him, and then made a show of reaching up for her blade. It seemed that he suddenly registered, because his eyes went wide and he stepped back rapidly, holding his hand up placatingly. Mahra nodded and wandered on, turning away. She was fairly certain he wouldn't be following her.

As she wandered further, she started to become aware that despite the apparent chaos, the mix of inhabitants, that underneath it all, it was really quite neat and ordered. There was nothing lying around in gutters, no piles of refuse. Sure there was the underlying smell, drifting through the odours of cooking, food stalls, some of the more exotic fruit and vegetables, but that was something that came with the world itself, she had decided. Her attention started to move away from the cacophony, the bombardment of sights and differences and moved to identifying those things that were the same. A place like this, she would expect to see hustlers, either goods or services, but she could spot neither. Perhaps all that was confined to a certain section of the city. Even if she couldn't find that, she needed to find some sort of place to get out of the heat. There just didn't seem to be anyone she would readily ask. She pulled out her palm comp and started looking for ideas. Despite the variety of people, Mahra, zimonette and blade standing in the middle of the thoroughfare scanning through her comp didn't take long to attract attention.

"Perhaps I can provide some assistance, Mez."

Mahra looked up from the comp to see a short, uniformed individual looking up at her, inquisitive, round faced, looking helpful, not hostile. She took all that in, especially the uniform, and decided that this was an opportunity.

"Looking for somewhere to get a drink out of the heat."

He gave a quick nod.

"There are many small cafés along the way. They are not always so easy to spot." He waved his hands up and down the street, indicating.

"Yes, well. I was looking for something a bit stronger than a café. Perhaps the chance to try out some of the local product."

The official, for that's what she had decided he was, cleared his throat.

"Oh," he said.

"Oh?"

"Well, yes, um...you will probably want to head down that way for about five blocks and then take a right. Continue on. You will eventually come to it. You won't miss it."

"What am I looking for?" she said.

"The compound. You'll see it."

She thanked him, and he ducked his head, moving away from her. If anything, he looked slightly embarrassed. She shrugged and decided to follow his instructions anyway. The whole compound thing was a little strange. As she travelled further, the number of stalls dwindled, storefronts giving way to residences, their stilt-like foundations taking over once more from the ground-level enterprises. Still she walked, and still there was no sign of what she was looking

Benevolent

for, and even now the sweat trickled in little runnels down her back and pooled under her hairline. She stopped, debating about whether she should proceed any further. She realised then that without any knowledge of the local public transport, if there even was any, because she had not yet seen anything that even looked like a cab or a shuttle or anything like it, that if she gave up, she would simply have to walk all the way back, wait around at the docks until the shuttle was ready to take her back up. There was nothing for it. She started walking again. Sometimes, she wondered how it was that Chutzpah seemed totally impervious to changes in temperature. He might, from time to time, become a little sluggish, but that was about the extent of it. It wasn't long, however, before she saw exactly what the official had meant.

In front of her stood a large walled area punctuated by a pair of double gates with a security entrance in front of them. There seemed to be a pair of smaller doors cut into the gates themselves, clearly to allow access to people rather than larger vehicles, she presumed for the entry and exit of goods or construction vehicles and the like. An official in a similar uniform to the one who had spoken to her on the street, stepped out of the grey and opaqued glass booth and waited for her to approach, assessing her all the way. As she neared, she could hear a baseline issuing from somewhere beyond the tall pale walls.

"Good day, Mez," she said.

"Hello."

The scrutiny continued. "You are a visitor to Sinq City?"

"Yes, that's right."

"And you are not in any way a resident?"

"No." Mahra shook her head. "What is this about?"

"As you may know, residents are not permitted in this area."

"I don't…." said Mahra and shook her head.

"Can I see your identification?"

Mahra pulled out her palm comp and the official linked, looked at the results and nodded.

"Very well. You may proceed. Through those doors there. But be aware that you are not permitted to transport any intoxicants outside the area of the compound. If you do so, you are liable for heavy fines and may be subject to a period of confinement."

"Confinement?"

"Imprisonment."

"Oh," said Mahra. "Yes of course."

As she headed towards the door, her frown was deepening. How had she missed this?

Through the doors, there was a single street, the double row of buildings completely enclosed by the tall, shielding walls. She wasn't sure if this was a security measure or just a way of hiding what went on in here from the rest of the local population.

"Wow, this is weird," she said quietly, as much to herself as Chutzpah. She took a few steps further into the compound, for that's what it was she had decided, and then hesitated. This wasn't exactly what she had been looking for, but then she realised that there was unlikely to be any other real option in the vicinity, so she picked one of the colourful doorways at random and headed towards it drawn as much by the music issuing from that direction as anything else. So far, she hadn't seen any sign of other visitors, but it was still relatively early in the day. She could imagine that things picked up at night, or maybe she was wrong about that as

Benevolent

well. She was tempted to whip out the comp and do a bit of research, but it would keep until she was out of this direct heat.

Hartley James

Chapter Sixteen

Sapporan

Thankfully, her surmise about it being cooler inside was right on the mark. Although there was no evident sound of air conditioning—the music could have masked it, she supposed—the cool air washed over hair, chilling the moisture on her skin, and bringing an actual sigh of relief. She scanned the place quickly, but it was quiet, perhaps too early. A group of what looked like haulers sat at the back, subdued and by all appearances, they'd probably been there for a while. They seemed to be doing little else than staring down into the drinks that they were clearly nursing. Maybe all-nighters just killing time until their shuttles left. It was always like that the last few hours before shore-leave ended. You didn't want to be back on shift with too much of a hangover. She chewed at the inside of her cheek, grunted to herself and headed to the bar. The individual serving there didn't appear to be local either.

"Hello, Mez, can I get you something. Good to be out of the heat, eh?"

Kalany? Perhaps. He had one of those ag world twangs.

"Yes, it is. Um, I was hoping maybe to try something local, if I could."

That bought a quick laugh. "A lot of us would like that," he said. "Not to be, I'm sorry. That will be the day."

Benevolent

She shook her head to indicate her misunderstanding.

"Oh, sorry," said the barman. "Most people who end up here already know and come forewarned. Sinq City is a clean town. No intoxicants whatsoever. They even class kahveh as an intoxicant. A few herbal teas get buy, somehow, but nothing else. For the locals, there's not a drop. Random haulers who are here for a layover, that's permitted, grudgingly, but only inside this walled compound."

"You're joking."

"'Fraid not," he said.

"Fine. Just bring me whatever's good."

"Ale, something stronger, or perhaps something else….."

"No, no. Ale is fine."

Peculiar. So they banned everything outside and yet permitted the supply of what might be considered illegal on some other worlds, inside the compound. Again she shook her head. She turned, looked down at the group towards the end of the long room. No wonder they looked like they might be depressed. She maneuvered herself on to a stool and waited for her drink to come back.

"Tell me if you like this," he said as he placed a tall foaming glass full of dark brew in front of her. It's not to everyone's taste, but I have a particular fondness for it."

"And why would that be?" she asked as she reached and took a tentative sip from the heavy glass. He seemed to be a talker. Not surprising in a place like this, but then for now, she didn't mind that at all.

"Well, it comes from the same place I do," he told her.

"And…." She took another sip. It wasn't bad. It had a sort of nutty flavour to it.

"Oh, yes. Lumiere. Not sure that you will have heard of it. It's kind of a backwater, out of the way. Mainly agricultural."

She placed her glass down, looking at him again more closely. "Really? Lumiere? Backwoods world with a surviving nobility and indentured labour? Almost feudal? That Lumiere?"

He looked at her and grinned.

"Seems you know the place."

"Oh yes," she said and reached for the glass again. "I spent some time on Lumiere. It wasn't the best time, but in the end, I suppose it wasn't the worst time either. Still, better to be well away from that particular world than still be there. Not planning on going back there in a hurry either. Yep better away from Lumiere."

"That it is. My sentiments exactly."

"Huh. So how'd you end up here? And I have to ask….is it any better."

Again a brief laugh. It wasn't unattractive either, like some people can be when they laughed like that.

"No, you're right about that. But, well, I don't know. I took the first opportunity I could to get off Lumiere, as you can imagine. Just by luck I managed to sign on with a hauler. Got me offworld, which was the intention. So that worked. The hauler itself, well…." He grimaced and shrugged.

"Yeah, I know *that* story."

"So yes, that…and then another, and then another, but in the end, I simply got tired of it. There were no connections, nothing to hold on to. Weeks and weeks confined in a metal box breathing recycled air, smelling nothing but machinery and your fellow crew. Privacy isn't something you want to talk about. Some of the cheaper ones, well."

"I know that too," Mahra said and took a healthy sip this time. On some of the haulers you learned to keep to yourself as much out of necessity as anything else. You let people get on with their things, and they let you get on with yours. If it didn't work like that, she was pretty sure there'd be substantially more violent crime or 'accidents' between the stars.

"So, you still haven't told me why here."

"No, you're right. At first, it was probably that it was so different, such a mixture of races and cultures. That's kind of attractive in and of itself. Or at least it was to me." He shrugged. "You can get your hands on just about anything here, well, apart from the restrictions and there's enough of those. There's always some new sight, smell, display going on. If you look back on the life of a hauler, or even as far back as Lumiere, it was such a contrast. I jumped at it without really thinking about what it meant, working bar inside a compound. Then the problem was, I just couldn't face going back on to the freighters. I'd had enough of that, and so now I'm stuck here in away, toiling away and saving bit by bit."

Mahra nodded her understanding. "So is it always so quiet here."

"Oh no, not at all. It comes in waves. Mostly the long haulers want to let off a little steam, but it's not so easy here on Sapporan. They tend to coordinate among themselves and come in a group. You never know when the place is going to be full and pounding. Just deal with it when it happens. All the places back each other up, run shifts if we need to."

She wondered briefly how much of that was going to change as the jump drive started to spread and become cheaper.

"Why the restrictions?"

"Funny. There's a core religious thread running through Sapporan society. *Very* conservative at the root. Sapporan just tended to be a natural hub for a lot of the earlier distribution and supply operations. One of the major outfits set up a headquarters here, and then the numbers started growing. More ships, more haulers, more activity that came with getting off several weeks in space. With the haulers, there came pirates, and then navy operations. Same sort of deal. Shore leave. None of that sat very well with the local Sapporans, and they started to pass some laws. The few laws became many, and, well…" He shrugged. "…here we are. The elevator, when it came, though that was a little before my time, just expanded the operations. Most of the world is geared around moving things from one place to the other. It's always been a trade and commerce hub, and somehow, I suspect it always will be."

Mahra nodded. "Well, it must be kind of strange though, for you, I mean. What do you do for entertainment? It's not as if you are likely to wind up back here to be entertained. Or maybe you do. I don't know really."

Again, he gave a brief laugh. "No, you're right. This is really the last place I want to be on my time off. As a local resident, I get a few options, but really, I like to get out and away from the city. It's one of the things that reminds me of back home. One of the things I like to be reminded of, that is. You know, wide open spaces, nature, that sort of thing. I cycle."

Benevolent

Mahra thought about that for a moment, and then looked him over again. Actually, now that she thought about it he did have a certain look about him. Well, to each their own, she supposed. Chutz chose that moment to dig his claws into her shoulder, hard.

"Ow, Chutz, what the hell? What is it?"

He was sitting on her shoulder, staring towards the door, quivering. She turned to follow the direction of his gaze.

"You'll have to excuse me for a second...."

"Ray"

"Yeah, Ray, okay. Mahra. As I said, you'll have to excuse me. Seems something is demanding my attention."

She gave a narrow-eyed pointed grimace in Chutzpah's direction.

The barman gave a quick nod.

It was only a few steps to the door and Mahra stood there, appreciating the flow of cool air that balanced the wash of humidity as she approached the outside proper. Chutzpah seemed to be focussed on the middle distance, but there was nothing that she could see, apart from the heavily pregnant dark grey cloud cover. Even that seemed fairly set in place, immobile. No vast channels of roiling air anywhere to be seen. She reached up to stroke him, but his back was knotted, hard as a rock. There was a faint sound coming from deep in his throat now, something she didn't like at all.

"What is it, Chutz? Dammit. Sometimes I wish you could just talk to me."

That being said, part of his tension was starting to seep across to her, and the edginess grew inside here, little by little. Still she scanned the sky, the buildings, the clouds in the direction of his focus. Still there was nothing. She shook her head and started to turn back inside, when she felt it. She couldn't quite tell what it was, but there was something in the vicinity that didn't feel right. How far away it was, she couldn't tell, but it was just like that feeling she got when something was about to emerge from jump.

"Oh great," she said to herself. If she was going to start feeling every ship equipped with a jump drive, then life was going to start becoming a little uncomfortable. She paused, gave a sigh, and then turned back towards the outside, but then it struck her. Unless she had been misinformed, the number of ships actually fitted with the drive were few and far between and nearly all of them belonged to the CoCee fleet which was currently grounded back on and around Belshore as far as she knew. Then who the hell was jumping here. There was her own ship, but she didn't think it was going anywhere. A little concerned now, she looked back up to the sky. Anyone else…or come to that, any *thing* else that might be jumping in this system was not something she really wanted anything to do with. At all. She swallowed back the immediate rush of feeling and steadied herself with a hand on the door. She hoped that it was something else. Something else entirely.

Just then, Chutzpah stiffened. There was a stirring, a vast pushing movement in the air. Off in the distance, something broke through the clouds, something slick, and vast and cylindrical. It pushed the cloud mass to either side, moving in slow motion. It looked like no ship she knew, and it was hard to judge the size of it, it was so far away. And still it came lower and lower. Was it landing? It appeared to be metallic. Then, further off, another similar shape broke through, stirring the clouds once more. It looked to be a little smaller than the first one. Then, off to one side, came another, but this one came plummeting through narrow end down. She watched them impassively, unable quite to process what she was seeing.

The first concussion knocked her off her feet and threw her backwards onto the barroom floor. The sound of glasses falling, containers toppling and smashing behind her came. Then there was a vast, deep sound, a roaring and a tearing noise that sounded as if the very planet was being ripped apart. She closed her eyes and grimaced against the wave. She reached for Chutz, but he wasn't there. She opened her eyes again, casting around to see if she could see any sign of him, but he was nowhere within sight. It was then that the vast wind came, carrying dirt and leaves and bits of vegetation, howling across the buildings, battering against the walls. The smell of wet earth and plant life was all around, cloying. It was not dust. The particles were too large for dust. It was as is if a mud storm had suddenly engulfed them. Another massive concussive vibration rippled through the ground, and still the wind came. She was glad that she'd been thrown back inside, glad that she was still in one piece, but despite the cacophony, the shaking ground, the wind battering against the building, all she could think of was the she couldn't find Chutz. Where the hell was he?

"Chutz!" she called out.

There was a strange sort of spattering noise coming from outside. She didn't recognise it at all.

"Chutz!" she called out again.

Chapter Seventeen

Belshore

"What do you suppose she wants now?"

"I don't know, Timon. I have no better knowledge of what goes on in Garavenah's head than you do."

"Well, if it's another stupid assignment to sit around smelling each other's gasses, I'll have a good mind to…."

"No you won't, Timon," said Jayeer with a little shake of his head. "No you won't."

Timon sighed. "No you're right."

"Still, even I am becoming quite frustrated with this current routine."

"Ha!" said Timon. "That I would almost pay to see."

Jayeer shrugged. "I am only telling you."

They both lapsed into silence as they wandered across the apron towards the building where Garavenah's offices lay. Timon cast an eye skyward, but there were no solutions to be found up there. He grimaced and returned his gaze to their destination, clasping his hands behind his back.

"To be honest, Jay, I'm kind of missing Mahra."

"Me too."

"I mean despite…well, despite everything, at least she brought a bit of conflict to the shape of things. Right now, everything's just the same. Day after day. Get in the ship. Hang around up there. Look for stuff. And what are we supposed to do if we find it? Scurry away like scared

Benevolent

rodents. I can't imagine that we'd stand much of a chance against a cluster of those Sirona ships, let alone that other thing, no matter how good the new weaponry might be. It's not what we do, Jay. It's not what we do."

Jayeer merely nodded and sighed.

As they reached the hangar door, Timon paused. "Have you heard from her?"

Jay turned and peered up at him through the thick lenses, blinking. "And what makes you think I would hear from her?"

"Oh, I don't know," said Timon. "Let's just say it's a gut feeling."

Jay gave a little snort and looked away. "No, Timon, I have not heard from her. If I had, I might even tell you about it. On the other hand...."

"Right," said Timon without looking at him and stepped through the door.

Their footsteps echoed from the hangar walls, the space empty for the moment. Timon opened the side doors granting access to the corridor running the length of the hangar's side and back to the staircases at the rear. The rest of the way, both of them kept within their own thoughts. And really, though he was reluctant to admit it, what Jayeer had said had annoyed him. It was not good. Just all this bland routine was making him edgy. He started humming tunelessly as they walked. Jayeer cleared his throat, but that was it. Timon decided he was going to keep it up all the way to Garavenah's place. When they got there, the adjutant ushered them in without any delay. As soon as they were in and the door was closed firmly behind them, Timon launched in.

"What is it now, Gara? Perhaps it's some babysitting exercise. Is that it? Fire. The least you could do is give us something to get our teeth into."

Garavenah let his bluster wash over her, stepped back behind her desk and sat.

"Commander Pellis, I would thank you to listen and take a seat."

"But...."

"Do it, Timon."

He pressed his lips together but held his tongue. Garavenah's use of his title was probably telling.

"At the moment, this doesn't leave this room. You won't see anything on the feeds, at least not yet. There's a total news embargo. It won't be long before one of the services gets hold of it though. Then, we can expect it to be everywhere."

That got his interest immediately. He glanced at Jayeer, then turned his attention back to Garavenah.

"What is it?"

She chewed at her bottom lip, crossed her hands on the desk, then lifted her gaze to meet his.

"There's been an attack. Another one."

"What? Where?" said Timon, leaning forward.

"What information we have is what we can piece together. Sapporan. The main space elevator."

"What...?"

"Yes, I know."

Jayeer gave a little shake of his head. "But that could be...."

"We don't know," said Garavenah.

"Fire," said Timon under his breath and then louder, "Who? Not those...."

Benevolent

"It's not domestic. It looks like the Sirona again, but once more, that's only what we can piece together. We have no real idea of the extent of the damage yet, but as you can imagine, it's not small. Not to mention the long-term impact it's going to have. There were several vessels parked in orbit, some of them making use of the elevator itself, but we don't know how many, or if there were any casualties among their number. Some of them simply took off as soon as they witnessed what was happening. Sapporan doesn't have a martial force to speak of. There's never been a need, as it's been in everyone's interest to keep the place running without any interference. Now that might change. You're going to head out with the fleet, get there as soon as we get everyone prepped and loaded. Some of our people will be there to help with the ground efforts. Ostensibly, that's why we're there, but also, we are going to be taking on a policing action and looking for any opportunities that might present."

"But groundside?" said Timon. "That's going to require a massive relief effort. We don't have the people, or come to that, enough ships to get enough people there in a short enough timespan. Isn't Sapporan weeks away?"

"With conventional drives, yes," said Jayeer.

"Then, what…?"

"Here, we're going to be drafting in assistance from some of the major tech industrials to do some build and refit. It might take a couple of weeks, a few days at minimum if they can rush it, but it's better than the time it would take to get there via normal haulers. Once they are available, we can start shipping supplies, personnel, whatever is required, in short order."

"One minor problem," said Jayeer quietly. "What about navigators?"

Garavenah nodded. "Yes, we've thought of that. Really, most of those we have are just too green for training. And then there's the associated medical procedure and…." She grimaced as the words trailed off and then she sighed. "Yes it's a problem. We are going through the logistics even as we speak. There are other sources though…" she narrowed her eyes as she looked across at Jayeer. "As you well know, Mezzer Sind, unless I'm mistaken?"

Timon looked at Jay and frowned.

Jayeer nodded slowly and then looked down at his hands.

"What, Jay? What's she talking about?"

"There's a…" He moved his head from side to side as he slowly spoke the next two words. "…kind of…commercial venture that is also doing a little bit of work with the drive."

"Who?"

"Bathyscaphe."

"Never heard of them. What sort of name is that anyway?"

Garavenah lifted a hand to still him. "That's unimportant, Timon. It suffices to know they exist and that they are positioned to help us."

Timon gave a little shake of his head, pursed his lips, and looked away. "I still don't see how any of this solves the issue at hand. When are we going to be able to take a stand against them? When are we going to be able to step up?" He cupped his fist in his other hand, rubbing it.

"You'll get your chance, Timon, just not yet. We have other things to do." The next she addressed to Jayeer. "I've been in touch with Dubois, not only to assist with the efforts, but also to see if we might do something about bringing Mez Kaitan back into the fold."

Jayeer had trouble hiding his surprise.

"Yes, Jayeer. My network runs just as widely as your little collection of science boys. It shouldn't come as a surprise to you."

Again Jayeer looked away.

"Wait…why…?" And then it struck him. He turned and gave Jayeer a narrow-eyed look. Jay refused to meet the look. "Fine," he said. "And…?"

"Nothing good, I'm afraid. We don't know. They don't know."

"But surely they must have some idea," said Jayeer.

"We have other things to worry about right now. When I know more, you'll no more. Until then, I suggest you prep. Remember, it's a relief effort. It's the CoCee reaching out to provide assistance in a time of disaster. I don't want any discussion of Sirona or the other race or anything else. How's your navigator?"

"Kurasa? He'll do I suppose," said Timon. "He's not going to light any fires though."

"Good enough to get the job done?"

"Yes," said Timon grudgingly.

"Good. Now go and prepare. I want this thing moving as soon as we can. And remember, no discussion, but I'm sure it won't be too long before it hits the feeds, and then, who knows…."

Timon pushed back his chair and stood, sparing a moment to give Jayeer another accusatory glance. Jay also stood, noting the look from Timon, but seemingly chose to ignore it and turned back to address Garavenah.

"Is there anything else we can do?"

She shook her head. "For now, no. Let's see if we get any more news in the meantime. Now go."

Benevolent

Chapter Eighteen

Belshore

Valdor paused in mid scan, rolled back, found what it was that had snagged his attention. He peered at the report for a moment, then sat back, running his fingers through his hair. They couldn't have been that stupid, could they? He looked out through the open space of his office, seeking any sign of the girl. He couldn't think of her as anything else, really. Young woman, female, it didn't matter. The word 'girl' stuck in his head whenever he thought of his involuntary companion, Tsinda. She had been a constant presence ever since Marina and The Benevolent had assigned her to him. Oh, she appeared to be competent enough at certain things, but she was not only a distraction, but also, more than that, an overt spy, which he was starting to object to quite strongly. He sniffed at the thought and glanced around the quarters. There was no doubt in his mind that they had him under surveillance anyway, not that he'd have any real way of knowing. The scans were coming up empty, but he had decided that he couldn't really trust them either. He had little chance of knowing which of his security personnel were Benevolent either, and he was sure there had to be some. Valdor have his head a little shake again and cast his attention over to the decanter, but then decided against it. He wanted to be razor sharp for this next. Now where was that Tsinda?

Grumbling to himself, he stood, crossed to the other side of the room, and went looking for her. It didn't take long before he found her, preening in front of a mirror, one of his own. Something he might catch himself doing. He watched her for a moment before clearing his throat. She glanced up from her own reflection and focussed on his in the mirror in front of her. She gave a little half smile.

That wasn't going to work on him either. There had been subtle signals from the girl ever since she'd joined him. Subtle enough that they could be denied altogether if subject to question, but, as attractive as she might be, Valdor just wasn't interested. He much preferred any of his entanglements, not to be entangled at all. He was busy rebuilding things and he didn't need that sort of distraction, not that he ever had. Marina had been the closest he had ever come to that sort of complication and look how that had turned out. He gave himself a little snort of derision despite himself.

"What can I do for you, Valdor?"

He took a steady breath. "Did you know about this?"

She turned then. "I don't know what you mean. What 'this?'"

"This attack."

She shook her head and looked genuinely confused. The reaction looked authentic enough.

"Then perhaps you should join me then. I am about to try to talk to Marina."

Tsinda still appeared as if she had no idea what was going on. Perhaps she didn't.

"All right. Where are you taking it?" she said.

Benevolent

Valdor spun on his heel and headed back towards his work space to put in the call without answering. His actions should be indication enough. Once there, he sat at the desk and gestured for Tsinda, who had followed, to join him in one of the chairs opposite.

"Marina Samaris," he told the system and waited.

"Marina Samaris in unavailable."

"Try again."

After a few moments, there was the same result.

"That's why I wanted you here," he told Tsinda. "I thought this may happen."

"But I don't know what I'm supposed…"

Valdor sighed, cutting her off, closed his eyes for a moment and pressed his lips together before responding.

"Really…?" he said, with a tilt of his head.

It was Tsinda's turn to sigh. "All right," she said, dropping the look of innocence. "Give me a moment."

She stood, turned, and quickly strode from the office area. A moment later, Valdor could hear her voice, speaking in hushed tones. A couple of moment later and she returned, resumed her place opposite and met his eyes with a steady look.

"Give her a few minutes. She's busy. She'll call you."

Valdor nodded once and looked up at the ceiling. "I thought so," he said.

"So, can I….?"

"No, stay here," he said, dropping his gaze again. "I want you where I can see you."

"Listen, Mezzer Carr, I am only here to assist you."

"Of course you are," said Valdor. "And you can drop the Mezzer business as well. Valdor is just fine."

He turned his attention back to the feeds and started scanning for anything else that would give him a better idea of what had happened, but so far the reports were far too young and sketchy as a result. All it told him was that there had been some sort of incident, and attack, on Sapporan. Normally, that might have passed him by entirely, but now, knowing what he knew, and what he was involved in, it was a different matter entirely. He didn't know that much about Sapporan as a world to be honest as he'd never had any real reason to establish an operation there. Certainly, it was a trade world from what he knew, import/export, but it dealt in the sort of goods and commodities that were a little more basic than Valdor's normal enterprises. As he scanned, he occasionally glanced up at Tsinda through the feeds, but she sat calmly, unflustered, her gaze wandering around the room, now and again looking down to study her hands and her nails, or to let her focus linger on Valdor's face for a moment.

After a time, his system flashed, alerting him to an incoming call. Marina, bedecked in the classic white suit she was most likely to be seen in these days swam into view as he answered, her expression firm.

"And how can I help you, Valdor?" she said. "Is there something you need?"

"This thing on Sapporan…."

There was the slightest flicker of a frown from her. "What thing? I'm not sure I…"

"Oh come on, Marina. Forgive me, but it has all the earmarks of a Benevolent action."

The frown became full blown then. "Valdor. We should talk. Not here. Not this way. We can discuss this better in person."

Benevolent

"What?"

"I suggest you come in. Bring Tsinda with you. I assume she's there."

"Of course she's here," said Valdor and severed the connection.

Where Marina's image had been, there was nothing, just Tsinda sitting across the desk, watching him. He met her gaze, chewing at the inside of his cheek and then looked away.

"Well?" she said.

"Yes. All right. Let's go."

"Shall I call some transport?"

He looked at her for a moment, considering. "No. We'll walk," he said, reaching down into the desk and removing the sliver that sat nestled there. He ran one finger along the choices, and then settled on tranqs before slotting them into place and laying the weapon down on the desktop. Tsinda observed all this without reaction. He pushed the drawer shut, crossed to retrieve the long coat that hung nearby, shrugged it on and then reached for the weapon and slipped it into one of the pockets. He glanced at his reflection in the window and decided that it would do. There was no room for fashion statements at the moment. This one would do. He turned and palmed the control that would call his private elevator. Tsinda stood, walked around the desk, and joined him. Moments later, they were down on the street.

As they headed up the street, between the tall stone building with their sculptured facades, past the wrought iron lighting and the low stone walls, neatly tended gardens, Tsinda spoke up again.

"Why did you decide to walk?"

"It helps me focus," said Valdor. "I also like seeing what's happening in the city. Sometimes there are clues there, little prompts that I can pick up on. It helps in the decision-making process. Besides, it's not very far. By the time a groundcar arrives and we get all comfortable, we would be halfway there. I don't like waiting around on the street wasting time for no reason." He supposed there wasn't any actual harm in answering the question.

After making their way through the old town and then through the bar district, fairly sparsely populated at this time of day, they finally reached the ILGC building. As usual, Valdor took a moment or two to stand and look from the opposite side of the street, then clamped his teeth together and crossed to enter the building proper with Tsinda in tow. Once inside, the same routine with his weapon, reception, being ushered to an elevator and being whisked up inside the building, no longer the master of his own movements. The elevator deposited them in the secure room from before, the place where they'd had that initial meeting that had introduced him to Tsinda. Once more, he took in the low leather couches and chairs, the grey-flecked polymer floor, slick and shiny, the glass sculpture in the corner and couldn't help thinking once more that it looked more like a reception area than a meeting room. Marina was there to greet them.

"I'm glad you came in, lover," she said as they stepped out of the elevator. It had been a while since she'd referred to him like that.

"So why couldn't we talk there over the com?" he asked as she gestured them both to chairs and she took one herself, not opting for one of the couches on this occasion.

She seemed to consider for a moment before answering. "I'm not sure how much information is out yet, and how it's

Benevolent

being treated. I didn't want to discuss this where there was any chance that the discussion might be compromised."

Valdor scratched at his chin. "I'm not buying that, Marina. Are you behind this? Did you do it?"

She let out a long slow breath. "Not me directly, no. I'm afraid this was a little out of my hands."

"Then who?"

"Oh, do not worry. The Benevolent owns this, directly and completely, but I can assure you that collectively, we feel it was the right move."

He narrowed his eyes a little at that. Did he sense a trace of dissension there?

"So what happened. And why Sapporan? Was it out little friends? And what was the point?"
She lifted a hand to still him. "One thing at a time, Valdor." She looked down. "Yes, the action was undertaken by the Sirona. Specifically, the main space elevator was the target."

Valdor's mouth fell open despite himself. He wasn't sure he was fully coming to grips with the enormity of what he was hearing. It only took him a moment to pull himself together again.

"But the devastation. That's a disaster, Marina. To what end?"

"Believe me, lover, there is one principle behind this action, and we know it to be true. If you think about it, you will too."

"And what's that?"

"Adversity banishes complacency."

He shook his head. "I don't follow."

"Just wait and see," she said. "Let's see how humanity pulls itself together now."

He looked across at her. There was no light of fanaticism in her eyes. It was as if she was reeling out words that had been delivered to her as part of a screed. Did she believe them? It was hard to tell. It sounded very like some sort of slogan.

"All right then, what's this supposed to achieve?"

Marina stood, crossed to the glass sculpture in the corner, started running one hand over the top of it. "We imagine there will be a necessary relief effort. Disaster management. The CoCee will not be enough to cope. We need to see how widely it extends now and what the consequences are. Before long, the Sirona involvement will become apparent. If it does not become clear through normal channels, then we will give it a little push. Once more, humanity will have its common enemy, something…or rather *someone* to strive against. They will unite in the face of a common foe. Humankind always has done. Once that focus has become clear, the we will determine when the time is right to step in. It will arrive."

She turned to meet his gaze, one hand still resting atop the sculpture.

"You can rest assured, lover. We know what we're doing."

She sounded convinced of her own words, but Valdor wasn't so sure. The sheer arrogance was astounding, and he himself had often accused of being a little too arrogant. He broke his gaze and looked over at Tsinda, but her attention was firmly fixed on Marina, almost rapt, it would seem.

"And what I'm doing…?" said Valdor.

"Just keep doing it," she said. "No need for you to be concerned with anything else. We will look after that."

Benevolent

He didn't respond. He wondered if there was any real point in doing so.

Hartley James

Chapter Nineteen

Sapporan

Mahra slowly pushed herself upright, working her mouth, scanning the area immediately around her. The air was still full of the scent of earth and torn vegetation, but there was something else now, and then she realised what it was…alcohol. The smell of hard liquor and fruity concoctions mixed in with everything else. That's right; she'd heard breaking glass. She levered herself up, got into a crouch and then pushed herself to her feet unsteadily, throwing out a hand to steady herself against a random piece of furniture. Nothing seemed to be hurt as far as she could tell. The few other people in the bar were also slowly getting to their feet or pulling themselves up onto chairs. Whatever had happened, it was like nothing she'd ever experienced.

Chutz. Where was Chutz? She felt the panic start to well up inside here like a cold hard knot deep in her belly. As if he had sensed her, cued in to the growing sense of helplessness, he was there, leaping from somewhere unseen to her shoulder. She reached a hand up, feeling him, then turned her attention to outside. The air was still muddy, and what had previously been a grey day filled with an overcast sky, was darker. Was it an attack? Had those things been ships? They were gone now though, and she had no way of knowing. She flashed back to The Cradle, those scenes of

Benevolent

devastation that would always stay with her, but if those things had indeed been ships, there were not like anything she was familiar with. If they had been Sirona, she would have known in an instant. They were c

A noise of something crunching grabbed her attention, and she turned to see the bartender, Ray, pulling himself to his feet. There was a nasty cut on one side of his forehead and blood trickled down that side of his face. Shards and a sprinkle of broken glass lay in his hair and scattered over his shoulders and front. He must have borne the brunt of a number of the smashing bottles. Not one of the things you'd necessarily expect working behind a bar.

She tossed her chin and he nodded.

"You're okay."

He reached up to probe at the cut on his head and she waved his hand away. "Too much glass. Get that off you first," she said. "You'll just do more damage. Wait, I'll help you."

"What the hell was that?" he said, reluctantly drawing his hand away.

Mahra just shook her head and turned to look outside again. Movement from further back in the bar caught her attention and she turned to look back over her shoulder. A couple of the other patrons—they looked like haulers—stumbled out towards the door. Ray made as if to intercept them, but they waved him away, shaking their heads and clearly intent on getting somewhere else, anywhere else. Without even thinking about it, she lifted one hand to stroke her fingers through Chutzpah's fur. He was chattering quietly to himself, but the tensions seemed to have disappeared for now. Whatever had been affecting him was gone now, at least for now. It was pretty clear that the presence, whatever it was, was linked to what had just happened. Once again, Mahra felt the frustration of not being able to see inside his head. What was it that he had known, seen…she didn't know how to describe it…that she had not been aware of? Sometimes it just didn't make sense. She glanced around the bar. He had probably just leapt free when she had fallen and that's why she'd been unable to locate him.

Other noises were starting to drift in now, far off voices, the sound of sirens swelling in the distance, but under it all was a low continual rumble.

She turned away from it then. There was nothing she could do outside. At least she could lend a hand here. She could finally focus on rendering the promised assistance to the barkeeper.

"Ray," she said. "Stay there, I'm coming over. Let me help you get cleaned up," she said. "Where's the bathroom?"

He indicated the back of the bar with a tilt of his head and then grimaced, clearly regretting the gesture.

"Here," she said, reaching out a hand, guiding him carefully through the small scattered piles of broken glass and intact bottles littering the floor. "Don't try doing anything yourself yet. You've got pieces all over you, really fine stuff as well. Is there a shower back there?"

"Um yeah. That's the staff locker room, but we need a card. Wait…."

"No, you stay here," she told him. "Just point to where it is."

She picked her way through the mess, found the card, snagged it, held it up between her first two fingers and after he had nodded his confirmation, just as carefully made her way back and led him towards the back of the bar. She could not help but cough a couple of times on the way with all the muck in the air, and Ray did the same, uttering an involuntary grunt of protest as a result, his hand moving up to clutch at his side. Clearly, he'd damaged more than his head on the way down.

"Looks like you might have done something to a rib," she said. "Take it easy. I hope you've got some clothes back there."

He nodded.

"What the hell was that?"

"I don't know," she said. "I thought maybe you'd have some idea. Whatever it was is gone for now. We have time to worry about that later." She glanced up behind the bar and over towards the corner. "The feeds seem to be out. Maybe it's just something broken in the network. I don't know. Anyway, first we need to get you sorted out. That's the priority right now. We can worry about what's happening in the rest of the world later. For the moment, we need to take care of what's within out control."

As she steered him back to the staff locker room, negotiated the door and helped him to a spot propped up against the wall, the sounds of confusion, people in panic, and then more measured voices started drifting through from outside. At least someone out there was trying to instil some sort of order. Best to let things run their course for the moment. Whatever had happened was bigger than she or this lone barman could deal with. She closed the door behind them and started helping him struggle awkwardly out of his shirt. She examined a deep mark over his ribs on the left-hand side. A full bottle of liquid weighs quite a bit and it's hard. If something had fallen from an upper shelf, it could do some damage. She balled his shirt and tossed it into a corner, allowing him to lean back against the wall as she picked out some of the larger pieces from his hair, and then offered her shoulder as a prop as he struggled out of his shoes and pants. She turned him around, looking for any further damage, but he seemed okay apart from the ribs and the cut. She'd learned more than once in the past that if you didn't check for other damage, you might end up regretting it.

"Listen, trying to get at any of the stuff in your hair is likely to cause more damage than solve anything. Get under the water, wash it out with a hard stream, don't rub your hands through your hair like you would if you were soaping it. You'll only tear up your scalp."

She turned the water on full, adjusted the temperature and then let him climb in.

"We can worry about the cut and those ribs once we're sure that you've got rid of all of that glass."

As he let the water do its work, she leaned back observing, watching him with a half critical eye. A bit wirier than what she'd normally be drawn to, but there was a lean hardness about his body too. Anyway, she was not here for that and she steered her thoughts away.

"But what about out there?" he said after a couple of minutes. "What do you think happened?"

"I guess we'll found out soon enough," she said. "For now, really, let's get you fixed up and into some fresh clothes. Is there a med kit in here anywhere?" He waved over to one of the lockers. She would have been surprised if there was not. The thing she was worried about most was the cut on his head. Especially with the current atmosphere, she probably needed to get that covered.

He stepped out of the shower, dripping and she tossed him a towel that had been hanging nearby. He wrapped it around himself and stepped over to one of the lockers, opened it, pulled out some clothes.

"Wait," she told him. She stepped across, tilted his head back to get a better look in the light, then, stripping off the outer skin to activate it, carefully applied the organic sealer pad she'd found in the medkit.

"Good," she said. "Now get dressed."

He nodded, wincing as he pulled a simple shirt on over his head and then again as he stooped to pull on underwear and trousers. Biting his lip, he sat on the bench that ran along one wall and leaned back against the wall.

"Can you hand me my shoes?" he said.

"Of course," said Mahra. She reached down, carried them over to where he sat then went down on one knee and slipped each of them on his feet in turn. If the situation had been different, she might have found the scene a little comical.

"What do you think that was?"

"I don't know. Some sort of attack. There's been some of that stuff going on elsewhere."

"Who? Is someone at war?"

She looked at him blankly for a moment. Did he really not know?

"Not war, no. Well, not as such." She sighed. "The Sirona."

"Wait. What?"

"You haven't heard about it?"

"No, I'm sorry. Am I supposed to? I don't really pay much attention to the feeds. They're just background noise." He shrugged and then grimaced for his efforts. "We're pretty isolated in here, in the compound. I just come in, do my shift, pay attention to what I'm doing. When I get back home, I'm usually tired. I might read a bit then fall asleep. The rest of it, well, I already told you. I don't really pay attention to anything else."

Mahra pursed her lips and looked away. She barely restrained the little shake of her head.

They needed to get out of here and it was probably time for her to find out exactly what had happened. She and Chutz were effectively down here alone, no idea what had happened, no clue whether her ship was still okay, or anything else for that matter. Time to find out.

Benevolent

Chapter Twenty

Belshore Space

"Some information's just come through from Bathyscaphe." It was Garavenah over the com, and that was unusual in itself. "I thought you two ought to hear it first," she said.

"So, tell me," said Timon, giving Jayeer a querying look. Jay just shrugged.

"It appears that Mez Kaitan may have been in the vicinity of Sapporan when the attack happened."

"Fire, Gara! What do you mean. Is she all right?"

"I don't know any more than that. The information came straight to me as a courtesy from the Bathyscaphe head. He knew about the connection, obviously."

"Nothing?"

"No, I'm sorry, Timon."

"So, do we know what she was doing there?" asked Jay.

"No, Jayeer, nothing more than I've just told you."

"Okay, thanks."

Jay turned to look at him. "If anything has happened to her…."

"What?"

"It's my fault she was with them. If it hadn't been for me…."

"Then what, Jay? She'd be somewhere else, and something else would happen. Things are like that. They happen. No one is ever really to blame unless it's a deliberate act. But, if you are more comfortable chasing guilt…it's up to you. I think it's time we got moving, don't you?"

Jayeer took a deep breath, gave a quick nod, and turned back to the controls. Timon put a call out to the rest of the fleet, assessing readiness.

"Okay, two more minutes," he told Jay, and then as an afterthought, spoke over the internal com. If it had been Mahra in place, there wouldn't have been the need.

"Kurasa, are you ready?"

"Certainly, Commander. On your command."

Timon narrowed his eyes, pressed his lips together firmly and shook his head. He wasn't going to say anything. He just wasn't. He caught Jay looking at him out of the corner of his eye, but he pretended he didn't notice. Now the impatience was starting to rise within him, and he began drumming his fingers on the flight couch's arm.

"Come on, come on," he said quietly.

"Commander Pellis, all systems ready."

Finally.

He opened the com again and gave the command.

He watched as the ships arrayed before him swelled and then popped out of existence one by one.

The Nameless was the last to jump.

Chapter Twenty-One

Sapporan

She started helping Ray towards the front of the bar, but he moved away, becoming all business as he assessed what he could see of the damage and the empty shelves behind the bar. Clearly, now, what had appeared to be perhaps a friendly overture was just a barman being a barman. Actually, she didn't blame him. He was right; there were more important things to think about now, like finding out exactly what had happened, for one, and also determining if she still had a ship anywhere in the vicinity. She hoped the shuttle was still there, if not, she could always reluctantly drain her funds a little to ride the…

"Space elevator," she said.

"What?"

"It was the elevator. Somehow it collapsed."

He shook his head, the expression on his face showing that the whole idea was beyond his reach.

"But…but how could that happen?" He blinked a couple of times.

"I don't know," said Mahra. "But it's the only thing that makes sense."

"But what…?"

"I don't know. Really, I don't know. Listen, Ray, are you going to be all right."

"Yes, fine," he said a little vaguely.

It didn't matter now. She'd done what she could, and she wasn't going to stick around and play concerned citizen because that's all it would be. There were enough other people, probably more qualified to sort things out here.

"Come on, Chutz," she said. "Ray, see you."

"Yes. Sure," he said, looking around at the mess on the floor, barely even acknowledging her.

Once outside, the air was still thick. A few confused looking patrons were still finding their way towards the compound's entrance, whatever they'd been doing in the meantime completely forgotten. Mahra had already spent enough time to get Ray's wound dressed, have him shower and changed into new clothes. A couple of them were a little unsteady on their feet, and Mahra doubted whether it had anything to do with what had happened a scant half hour ago. There were officials, she guessed local law enforcement by the uniforms, waving people out through the gates. That was the way she was headed. If what she suspected was true, then she wasn't sure whether the transit would be running, or in fact capable of running. It would have to be sheer luck if falling debris hadn't taken the thing out. At the gate, one of the uniformed officials gave her a quick up and down, paused upon seeing Chutzpah on her shoulder, then simply moved past it. He barely bothered with the blade. He too had more important things on his mind.

"Mez, where are you headed," she said.

"I don't know," said Mahra. "The port? I don't know. What happened? Was it the elevator."

Benevolent

"We are not sure what happened yet, Mez. And yes, it's the elevator. You need to get somewhere secure. Are you based here on Sapporan?"

"No, sorry. Visiting. I need to get to my ship."

"Did you come down on the elevator?" she asked.

"No, shuttle." She reached up to stroke Chutzpah, making sure that he was all right. It wouldn't do, particularly in the current circumstance for him to perceive anything this official was doing as a threat.

"With luck, it might still be there. That's not guaranteed though, Mez. Have you any way of getting in touch with the ship."

"No. Haven't tried. But even if I did, I can imagine coms are pretty jammed up at the moment."

The officer looked at her with a new eye, almost what Mahra might have interpreted as a touch of respect.

"Yes, you are right. I suggest you try and make your way to the port by whatever means you can. You'll be able to check whether your shuttle is still available."

"I gather the transit is out."

"Yes it is. And everything's a little chaotic as you might imagine. So, by whatever means."

Mahra paused for a moment and thought about what the official was asking her to do. "Is it really a good idea to head for the port?" she said. "If it's the elevator. That's in the port area. Aren't you going to be keeping people away from there."

The woman shook her head. "No. Quite the opposite. Most of the impact is away from the port, and we are going to need the port facilities for any incoming relief. From what I understand, it's already on its way. We'd actually like to get most of the ships cleared out of the vicinity. Some of them may be reluctant to leave crew behind, especially the larger freighters. The only thing we can do is get those crew back to those ships as soon as possible. I'm afraid, Mez, that includes you. Unfortunately, there's not a lot else I can advise you to do, so it's probably best if you get moving."

"Thanks," said Mahra and stepped past her.

The officer nodded and turned to the next person.

Outside the compound walls, the scene was nothing more than chaotic. People running, wandering around blankly, officials trying to herd them to wherever they needed them. Up in the sky, deep grey clouds rolled, giving no clue about what might be happening above. Mahra looked around, trying to remember which way she had come. She wasn't giving it too much attention, but as far as she could see, there was only superficial damage in the immediate vicinity. Most had been from the concussion, more like an earthquake than anything else, with several aftershocks following. The damage she could see was to the population and not a lot of it was physical. She flexed her arms, her shoulders. She hadn't even thought to check herself. She'd been more concerned with the barman's wellbeing. Strange. It seemed that Jacinda might have had an impact on her after all. That little thought brought dark memories washing in, and she shook her head to banish them. There were other things to worry about. She spotted a sign for the transit stop and took that direction, sidestepping as a blank-faced local almost walked straight into her without even looking. Everywhere, she saw the same vacant expressions, the lack of engagement and understanding as if something that they simply could not comprehend had taken place in their lives. It was exactly that, she supposed, especially in a culture where some sort of order seemed to

Benevolent

reign. The symbol of what they were had been broken and they'd watched it tumble to the ground.

As she walked, still having to stay out of the way of random locals, she noticed other things. The buildings seemed to be spattered with mud, bits of green plastered to the walls along with it. It was everywhere. Her first impression of the city had been one of chaos, but relative cleanness. Then she saw that it was not just the buildings. This mud drops splattered on clothing, on vehicles, on the awnings above roadside stalls. It must have rained wet earth, pouring out of the sky. She cast a glance skyward. What if it was going to happen again. Well, if it did, she'd deal with it if and when it happened. Head down. Get to where they were going.

She remembered the place when they got there. This was where the transit had stopped. It was as she recalled, not that far from the city's centre. At least not from the compound. A few blocks at most, though it had seemed like ages on the way in because of the heat. The heat. It was still there. It was funny how selective your perception could be about what really mattered. She wiped some moisture from her forehead and looked around. There was no sign of anything resembling the transit itself, so that had been a vain hope, and in the end, the official had been right. However, just as she suspected might be the case, there were already a couple of vehicles sitting there, biding time. It didn't matter where you wound up, there was always someone ready and eager to profit from misfortune. That didn't exclude disaster, whether natural or invoked. She nodded and made her way to the first groundcar. It wasn't a taxi, that much was clear. The driver was sitting propped up on the front, chewing on a thick stalk of something. As she approached, he slid off the vehicle, looked her up and down.

"Need a ride?" he said, a half grin on his face. "Let me guess. Offworlder right? Cute—" She cut him off before he could finish.

"Not a pet," she said. "And yes. How much to get me to the port."

He was sizing her up again.

"120. Advance."

She laughed. "Perhaps I'll go talk to your friend over there."

It didn't look like that was the reaction he'd been expecting as the grin slipped off his face. He looked over to the other driver, who simply shrugged.

"Come on, boys," she said to them. "Let's see who can do the best deal." She looked around. "Doesn't seem as if there's anyone else here to take you up on your offer."

Chapter Twenty-Two

New Helvetica

A mere day had passed since the meeting with Marina, a day in which Valdor had been chewing over the implications of everything that had been going on. Meanwhile, things were supposed to be business as usual for him and Tsinda. They were on their way now to another inspection of the plants and he glanced over at her, wondering briefly if there was such a thing as business as usual for the girl. It mattered not for now. He made no secret of the fact that Valdor Carr liked to be at the top of the food chain, but that was when things took place on a level battlefield. What the Benevolent were doing was making sure that the landscape was far from equal. There was an order and at the top of that pyramid sat no one else but them. He didn't like it at all. What it meant was that he was being held hostage to the whims of this group and as long as that was the case, he wasn't going to be in control of his own destiny. Well, he wasn't going to be a lacky to anyone, no matter how powerful they might be. He sniffed.

"Valdor?"

Tsinda reached out with one hand and placed it on his thigh. He looked over at her then pointedly looked down at the hand. After a moment, she withdrew it.

"And what do you think about all this, Tsinda?"

"Whatever happened, it was needful," she said and turned to look out at the passing landscape.

"In whose words? Marina?"

She sighed. "No Valdor. It goes beyond Marina. She and I are just tools for the cause."

"So it's a cause."

"Of course it's a cause," she said, turning back to look at him. "Don't you think that the advancement of humanity is worthy of being called a cause?"

"At what cost?" he said quietly.

"At any cost." Her expression was set and there was no wavering at all.

He was beginning to believe that the cost might be something he ought to consider. Maybe it was just a reaction to feeling constrained, under someone else's leash. He wondered if Marina felt the same thing or if, underneath, she too was a believer as Tsinda seemed to be. He didn't think so. He'd known her for a long time. Nevertheless, it remained unclear to him who the others might be. The Benevolent, as far as he knew, kept that information reasonably well guarded. He wondered how much the girl knew.

"Have you ever spoken to any of the others?" he asked her.

She turned to look at him again, clearly considering before answering. "Once or twice," she said finally.

"Was it for something special, or part of the normal course of operations?"

"I don't see why that's important."

He had to stop making the mistake of underestimating her. She looked harmless, maintained that demeanour, but there was obviously more going on under the surface with Tsinda.

"No, I suppose not," he said. "I am just becoming more interested in the people we are working for. That's all." He kept his gaze focussed on the road ahead.

"It's not people," said Tsinda. "Membership changes. People die. People move on. Accidents happen. The only constant is the organisation itself. We are just parts. Very small parts."

Valdor said nothing. This wasn't going in the direction he wanted. For now, it would keep. He lapsed into silence. There was still about half an hour before they reached their first destination. It was time enough to come up with a new strategy. He flicked on the in-vehicle feed and started scanning the business channels. Finance was taking a hit as news of the happenings on Sapporan started spreading. As a major trade hub, the disaster, for that's what it was being called now, was meaning that suppliers and producers would probably be taking a hit. In a couple of places more reliant on Sapporan as a hub, their economy charts were in steep decline. Well, there was no real surprise there. New Helvetica was relatively shielded from the impact, but it too was taking a minor hit, including his personal holdings. As with everything of that nature, this too would pass. It was nothing more than a minor distraction. He flicked the business channels away and moved to more mainstream news, seeing what else he could glean about Sapporan, spent a few moments filtering the most reliable streams and then comparing to try limiting the overall noise level and cut through the inevitable sensationalism that was the driving force behind their existence.

Hartley James

Initial reports had been correct; someone had taken out the main space elevator. At the moment, any discussion of Sirona involvement was just speculation, based upon one or two eyewitness reports who claimed to have recognised Sirona ships. Many of the vessels in the vicinity had already fled the area, so actual sources were fewer, and the news providers were having a bit of difficulty tracking them down. He glanced over at Tsinda, who was watching the feeds with interest. He looked back, flicked across to some of the more fringe feeds, to get some of the outlying opinion. It had been an act of domestic terrorism. Valdor dismissed that one without a second thought. Whoever was behind that particular feed clearly had an agenda. He found another. It was a covert operation sponsored by one of the industrial worlds to break Sapporan's monopoly on the trade routes. He tagged that one to his personal stream to look at further. Just as he was doing that, a breaking transition from the CoCee itself interrupted him. His hand hovered there in mid action for a moment and then he let it fall back to his lap.

A young dark-haired man, appeared in the image, one that Valdor did not recognise. The legend below said that he was Ari Martel, CoCee Representative. That surprised him. He would have expected someone more familiar, someone with a bit more kudos to be speaking for the CoCee. Someone with enough gravitas to instil calm. Perhaps this was merely an interim holding action. Where was the one called Aegis? As far as Valdor remembered, he had been the main public face. Valdor listened as the man ran through what was obviously a prepared script—no action at this time until they had established the facts. Relief efforts already in motion. Citizens to comply with directives. CoCee doing everything it could in this time of crisis. In the end, all they were doing were confirming their involvement. No real details of what they were going to do and how. In the end, they probably needed a bit more time to organise what they were doing and be confident enough with it to convey any more information.

"Hmmm," he said.

"What?"

"Well, they're not saying very much are they?"

"They never do," she said.

Valdor was almost tempted then to confront her, ask her what she was really doing here, but he held back. Besides, they were already pulling into the plant, and that too would probably keep.

As they both stepped out of the vehicle, the concealed door slid open, and, as usual *Doctor* Hendriksen was there to greet them, just like the time before and the time before that. This time, there was a sort of eagerness about him that Valdor hadn't seen before.

"Welcome, welcome," said the man as they approached. "We are so glad you are here. Timing could not be better."

"What is it, Doctor." Valdor was sure to emphasise the title, but he was sure the man was oblivious to the intended slight anyway.

"We are about to proceed to the next steps with our first ten subjects. They are ready to move out of incubation."

Valdor couldn't help twisting his lips with that choice of word. Didn't cultures, bacteria, diseases incubate? But then, so did eggs. He was reading too much into it.

"Good. And are we going to witness the procedure?" he asked.

"Well, yes. I was hoping you would want to," said Hendriksen. He was more animated than Valdor had ever seen him.

"Of course," said Valdor.

"Good. Very good. Follow me."

He led them through the biliously hued reception area and into the poisonous green corridors leading to the observation area. They followed in silence, as Valdor listened to the subtle noise of humming banks of machinery and took in the antiseptic flavour of the air. None of it was designed to increase his comfort level, that was for certain. It didn't take them long to reach the destination. Hendriksen gestured for them to take positions at the large observation windows and move to one side. Down below them, a bevy of white-coated technicians bustled around the relevant containment chambers, moving around individual gurneys set in place, one in front of each of the target subjects.

"How will you know if it's a success."

"Well, the first thing is if the subject survives exposure when we first detach the equipment, but we have every confidence that that will not be an issue. We learned quite a lot from our initial trials. From there, it will be a series of tests, first in isolation, then in groups. If those give us positive results, we will move the subjects into a training regime, and get ready for the next batch. But wait," he said, holding up a hand. "We are about to begin."

Valdor leaned forward. The activity around the first of the containers had heightened. Two of the technicians moved one to either side, simultaneously at some signal from one of the others cluster there, moved something and slowly, ponderously, the front of the container swung upward. There revealed, lying on the canted bottom, and

Benevolent

surrounded by tubes and leads lay a young woman, devoid of coverings and from what Valdor could see, in prime physical condition. One by one, the technicians leaned in and uncoupled tubing, thick leads, straps. Another one was running scans. One more was checking something on a control panel in front. It was a veritable flurry of activity down there. Whatever they had been checking, there seemed to be some sort of consensus, because the team activated another set of controls, and the large sarcophagus-like container started tilting back to a position horizontal with the floor. As soon as it had come to rest, four of the lab technicians moved, two on each side, took hold of some sort of handle and lifted the woman onto the gurney. Without any further ado, a pair of technicians wheeled her away, passing rapidly below the observation window where Valdor, Tsinda and Hendriksen stood watching. They didn't bother to cover her, and Valdor could plainly see the areas where tubes and other things had been attached all over the young woman's body. Again though, he noted; she was big and looked extremely well-muscled. It was not a body-builder's musculature though. This was something else.

"So far so good," said Hendriksen. Already the technicians were scurrying around the next…Valdor paused for a moment, thinking. No, it was right. It was nothing more than an incubation chamber. It was exactly that.

The lid slowly rose, this time revealing a young, dark man. Again there were the tubes and leads. Again the technicians fussed about on every side. Again he was fit, muscled, but differently muscled. He looked very strong.

"Are they all like this?" asked Valdor.

"Like what?" said Hendriksen.

"Their bodies."

"Oh, not only their bodies," said the Doctor. "Their minds as well, Mezzer Carr. Both are in peak condition, all of them. The final tests will tell, but I am confident. Especially now."

Valdor looked out of the room, over the row after row of similar containers. He knew how many there were in total. He knew how many similar rooms there were. It was part of his business to know. He thought about it then. And when this room was empty, would it fill up again? Would they have the subject to fill them? Would they need to?

He tried to do a quick projection in his head, ran through the amount of time he knew it had taken to bring them to this point.

Just for a moment, he felt a slight chill.

Benevolent

Chapter Twenty-Three

Sapporan

In the end, Mahra ended up with the first of the two drivers, who she managed to beat down to a price somewhere near a third of what he'd first requested. The other one had held firm at sixty and wouldn't budge. Though she didn't really approve of what the two of them were doing, she couldn't really begrudge them. It was a buy/sell economy on this world, and they had a product. Farin, the one who had won out had justified himself by telling her that he was merely providing a service to those who needed it most. Without him, the many offworlders who would be trying to get back to their ships would be stuck. Any official transport facilities and the local emergency services would be far too busy to lend aid to the hapless foreigner, unless, of course, they were physically injured and in need of medical attention. She had nodded her understanding, not buying into a single word of it, though she couldn't really argue with the logic. Anyway, he was there when she had needed him, so that would justify a lot of sins on its own. It was funny how things worked like that. She found it a little funny too that her capacity for wry cynicism still sat firmly in place amidst all this tragedy. Perhaps she was becoming inured to it. She wasn't sure she liked that possibility at all.

"How much longer?" she asked him.

"About forty minutes, give or take. It depends upon how many more diversions we have to make."

They'd already had to pass in a wide arc around one of the huge elevator sections that had smashed into the ground and torn up a good proportion of the surrounding landscape. Farin's groundcar had, however, proved to be fairly nimble and Farin himself reasonably adept at navigating the newly reshaped surface. As they drove, Mahra heard him tutting to himself once or twice, so despite her first impressions, the impact and destruction was not totally lost on him.

"And if my shuttle's not there? I'll have to try and call it down if that's the case. I won't even know if that's possible. Will you wait?"

"If you make it worth my while," he said. He turned to look at her and winked.

"If you think…"

"Joking, Mez. Joking. A few credits more will do the job."

She settled back in her seat and looked out the window. He may well have been joking but that didn't mean that she had to like it. She'd had too many experiences in the past to welcome any supposed levity in that particular direction. For now, she'd let it slide. She was dependent on him for the moment, but Farin had cooled her impression of him, when she had actually been warming a little up to that point. There were things she was still curious about, but now, she decided, she'd spend the rest of the ride in relative silence.

After another twenty minutes, another fallen piece of the structure loomed into view, rising like a sheer metallic wall through the continuing wet mist. First it was a blank bronze and then a pale sheen reflected light in places as they got closer. As they approached, it became clear that what had seemed like a vertical wall, was in fact curved, some of its bulk buried deep into the ground.

"Shit," said Farin.

"What?"

"It's right across the road." He craned his head in both directions, peering into the mist. "No idea how long it is. Nav systems aren't working. Haven't been since...well...so I'm going to have to just see what will work. It might be a bit bumpy. I can't tell the state of the ground. It might be too wet. Up to you. If you want to go back and wait until the situations clearer, we can do that too."

"What do you think?" she asked after a moment.

He shrugged turning to meet her gaze. "Seriously. It's your choice. You're the one paying. But if it takes too long, you're going to have to top it up a bit. I still need to get back too."

"Fine." She waved one hand, indicating that he should get going.

He nodded, turned back and seemingly at random, turned to the left the drive parallel to the vast metallic curved wall beside them.

"Why this way?"

"Just a feeling," he said.

There were some rough patches, where Mahra had to reach up to steady herself, Chutzpah digging his claws hard into her shoulder to maintain his balance as the groundcar shook and jolted.

"Give us some warning before the next one," she said after the first time. He nodded and proceeded on.

"Unusual times, you know. We can't expect usual conditions."

"Yes, yes," said Mahra. He was making light of it, but now his attitude was starting to grate.

Eventually, after a few more minutes of awkward progress, they reached the end of the toppled section and Farin negotiated the groundcar round the jutting edge and along the shorter hollowed end. It looked like the structure had been sheered right through, neatly on an angle.

"Yeah, that's not natural," said Mahra, more to Chutzpah.

Farin held his tongue this time.

She peered into the darkness contained within the tubular depths, the internal structures blurred by shadow. All they were, were shapes that meant very little to her in this unfamiliar context. Still, she ran her gaze over them as they slid past, looking for something, though she wasn't really sure what. And then they were round the end and heading back along the other side towards where she knew that the rest of the road lay.

"I think we're going to have to swing out a little bit across open ground to reach a spot where the road's not torn up," said her driver. "Thankfully…." He was peering into the distance, leaning forward in his seat. "It looks like there's not another one, at least for a while. If you're lucky, none of them came down on the port itself."

She hadn't thought about that. What was she going to do if that had happened? Perhaps there were no more shuttle, no port. She thought that the official at the compound would have heard something if that were the case.

"We'll see what we see when we get there," she said.

Farin shrugged and maneuvered the groundcar across the ground and towards the road, a little more smoothly than he had managed on the other side of the fallen structure.

Benevolent

Before long they were back on a road. To either side, smooth boled trees, trunks pale green and broken with rings, reminiscent of the structure of the fallen elevator draped with hanging vines and deep emerald leaves, now spattered with mahogany brown splashes, lined the avenue. Above the clouds swelled and swirled, just as they had before all this had happened. It was the same landscape she had watched out of the transit windows, absorbing the lushness and the steaminess of the atmosphere. Lower down, between the trunks, grew clumps of bright shiny leaves sprouting succulent flowers in deep pinks and carmine with the occasional splash of purple. Even despite the groundcar's air system, the smell of deep rich vegetation crept into the car along with the scent of damp earth. Compared to a ship's atmosphere, it was just so organic.

Mahra's thoughts turned to what had happened. She tuned out the landscape and conjured up the image of the severed elevator section. It was clear nothing natural had done that. It was a slice. There was only one thing she knew that could do that, and across such an area, and that thing would have to be carried by a ship, and not a small ship at that. This had been an attack, pure and simple. No matter how she wanted to, she was never going to leave it behind, and once again, her head was full of images of those large silvery ovoids hanging in the sky, the blue beams lancing across the domes and the buildings erupting. All that back on The Cradle so long ago, and here it was again, back to haunt her. She grimaced and shook her head. Chutz clearly picked up on her feelings as the cold hollow dropped inside her, and he nuzzled close in to her neck.

"Yeah, thanks, Chutz," she said. "I'll be okay."
"Huh?" said Farin.

"Nothing. Wasn't talking to you."

He grunted and turned back to the road.

The rest of the way to the port proved uneventful. As they approached, she could see that it had survived unscathed, but it was clear that they also weren't the first to head this way. A crowd of people stood clustered around the main entrance. As they drew up, she could see why. The main gate allowing access was firmly closed, with a pair of uniformed and armed officials standing guard behind.

Mahra opened the door and a clamour of confused voices washed over her along with the humid air.

"Right," she said. "Farin, you can go. Thanks. No point in you sticking around."

"No. Thank you," he said, waving his card. As soon as she shut the door, he was already heading out, likely off to see if he could score another fare back in this direction. She doubted he was going to get any going back the other way, but time would tell. Anyway, she suspected he'd be back, so if she had any problems here, which it looked like she might, she could worry about trying to negotiate a price back to Sinq City.

From here, she didn't have a clear view of what lay beyond the gates, so she moved closer. The huddle of various people, some with possessions dropped at their feet didn't help. She tried to work her way through to the front, but her attempts were quickly met with fairly solid resistance. A man in a hauler's uniform turned and shoved her back.

"Wait your turn," he said and then his eyes widened a little as he took in the blade, the zimonette on her shoulder and his hands rose in a pacifying gesture. "Sorry, I didn't mean…," he mumbled.

Benevolent

Mahra stood back, her hands on her hips, trying to decipher individual threads among the cacophony of voices.

"No." That was one of the uniforms behind the gate. "Until we can establish you are legitimate, we can't let you through."

"Listen, I'm from the hauler *Kayram.* Check me out. Here, here." He was waving a card in front of the officials face.

"Please step back. We'll deal with you in turn."

"Can I have your name? Excuse me?" A woman in a hat, with shadowed glasses. She obviously thought she had a better shot than others below her station. Well. Mahra had seen enough of that in other places. She was glad to see the woman ignored.

"Listen, all of you."

A pause.

"Listen!"

That brought a slight hush to the crowd. Behind her, another groundcar was pulling up.

"We are doing everything we can to verify. Those here with shuttles already on the ground will have first priority. Please form two lines. Have your identifications ready. We will check them, and if they match, we'll let you through. Others will just have to wait for due process. I'm sorry everyone, but that's the way it is."

She could sense a presence behind her left shoulder and a quiet voice spoke in her ear.

"Have you got credentials? I am willing to pay quite well."

She turned to look at a rather short man in a crumpled suit with a distinctly furtive air about him.

"I don't think it would do you much good, friend."

He looked her up and down and then sidled away towards the edge of the crowd, clearly to try his luck with someone else, but looking like that, she didn't think much of his chances. She turned her attention back to the crowd, and it appeared that the uniforms were starting to have an impact. All she could hope for now was that there was still a shuttle there waiting for her. She took a place in line behind a stocky woman in coveralls. She looked like a hauler. Maybe an engineer. As Mahra stepped up, the woman turned, scowling, and then grinned and gave her a nod. For some reason, Mahra seemed to have passed. It took several minutes, but one by one, the people were dealt with, either turned away, or the gate was opened just far enough to let them through. The woman in front made it past the gate, then it was her turn.

"Mahra Kaitan. Bathyscaphe. Here with *The Outrigger*." She passed her credentials through the gate and waited while the uniform disappeared, went through a brief consultation in an office off to one side, looked further into the dock area, shading his eyes for a moment, and then, seemingly satisfied, made his way back.

"Mez Kaitan, please step through. The shuttle is still here waiting. They are quite anxious for you to join them."

I bet they are, she thought to herself.

Benevolent

Chapter Twenty-Four

Sapporan

She recognised the crewmember standing in front of the shuttle door waving to her. It seemed they really were quite eager to have her back.

"Garrick, hi," she said as she walked up. The ever-present spatter was all over the shuttle too.

"Can't say I'm not glad to see you," he said. "You ready to make this place a memory?"

"Oh, it's going to be that regardless," she said. The other crewmember shoved her head out of the shuttle's rear doors.

"Welcome back." Her name was Nissa if the remembered correctly. "Can we get going."

Mahra nodded, clambered through the side door, moved through the now-empty transport bay, and took a place in one of the seats towards the front.

"Did you see anything?" she asked as the doors shut and the other two joined her up front.

"What, apart from chunks of stuff raining out of the sky? And then smaller stuff raining out of the sky after that?" said Nissa. "Usually, I'm okay with a bit of water. Maybe more than a bit. Occasionally ice. But that will do me."

"I know what you mean," said Mahra. "But, no I meant anything apart from that."

Nissa shook her head. Garrick followed suit. "Nah. The clouds. One minute we were unloading stuff, the next...boom," he pantomimed a splash with his hands. "And then...boom. And...well, so on. You were down here too. You see any of it?"

It was Mahra's turn to shake her head. "I was inside."

"Wish I had been," said Nissa.

"Come on, let's get off this world," said Garrick, giving each of them a quick check to confirm they were settled and strapped in.

"Fine with me," said Mahra, glancing back into the transport space. "Weren't we supposed to be waiting for something to go back?"

Nissa gave a short shake of her close-cropped head. "Captain Merritt wants us away from this place. Besides, you think anyone down here is going to be worried about a load at the moment?"

Mahra gave a small grunt of confirmation and felt an almost sense of relief, as at the same time, Garrick kicked the shuttle into operation, and they started to lift slowly from the parking apron. As the shuttle rose, she suddenly realised what it was that was out of place; there was no chatter, no traffic control.

"What's happened to traffic?" she said.

"Every one for themselves at the moment. Traffic, some of the other systems have been knocked out by the stuff coming down. Don't ask me how long that's going to take to get back under control. Anyway, you don't see a lot of other ships in the vicinity do you?"

Benevolent

He was right. There were only a few shuttles and smaller ships parked down there below them.

"Have they gone already?" She tried to remember how many there had been when they'd first come in.

"Oh," he said. "As soon as they could, if they could. We're only here because the Captain told us to wait for you. Nothing against you personally, Kaitan, but I'd have been gone if it weren't for the Captain. But hey, you know, orders are orders and here we are."

"Sure," she said. "No offence there. But you've got to see his point, right?"

"What?" Their pilot looked a little confused by that.

"Well, without me, you're back to standard drive, aren't you? How long would it take to get home?"

Enlightenment seemed to hit him then. "Ohhhhh."

"Yeah," said Mahra.

Nissa reached out a hand, briefly rested it on her shoulder and gave a nod.

As they reached the cloud layer, dim grey light shrouded them and Garrick waved the internal lighting up. Then they were through. A billowing cushion of clouds sat beneath them, darkness above. Up here, it was as if nothing had ever happened, except, of course, for the missing structure that had dominated the sky on their initial approach.

"So you've been talking to the Captain," said Mahra. *Obviously*, she thought to herself.

"Yes," answered Nissa.

"No problem with ship coms?"

"No, they were all right."

"Did he talk about what might have happened?"

"Not really. Called it an attack. Though he didn't seem to know who or why."

That much confirmed part of her suspicions. "No description of the ships? Nothing? I presume they were ships, plural?"

"I don't even know that much," said Nissa.

"Nah. Captain wasn't exactly in a chatty mood," said Garrick. "There we are," he said gesturing to a point above them with his chin. "Let's get you on board so that we can get the hell out of here…quickly," he said.

They'd be docked in a couple of minutes, but for now, Mahra wanted to try something. Already some time had passed between the events groundside and now, but there still might be traces. She reached up, felt for Chutz just to steady herself, and then closed her eyes. Carefully, she focussed, narrowing her concentration, stretching out with her senses, and probing nearby space. What she found brought a sudden gasp from her. There they were. Although she hadn't really wanted to find them, the familiar signatures were there, and she believed she recognised them. Four ships had jumped in concert, and not too long ago. Their identifiable traces marked those ships as Sirona, no one else. She let out her breath and opened her eyes again, her jaw set.

"What was that?" said Nissa.

Mahra shook her head. "No. It doesn't matter. Nothing. I guess the impact is just starting to hit me."

Nissa peered at her, then seemed to accept it, and turned her attention back to the approaching ship.

They docked without any fuss, and once the doors had closed, everything sealed, Merritt was there to meet them.

"Glad you could make it back," he told her, though the expression on his face said that it was something he saw as a

Benevolent

necessity rather than anything to be pleased about. His use of the word 'glad' she was going to take under advisement. In response, she merely nodded.

"We should get moving as soon as possible," he said, turning crisply away and heading towards the lock.

"Where to?" asked Mahra.

"Back to Belshore. Until we receive any further instructions."

He stepped through the lock then and apparently the conversation was over. She looked at the other two. Nissa gave her a sympathetic look, but Garrick was just grinning all over his tanned square face.

"What?" she said.

"Good with the whole feeling stuff, our Captain, eh?" he said. "Don't think I've ever seen him raise a smile. Think his head would shatter if he tried."

"Mmm-hmm. I'm starting to get that," said Mahra.

"Oh, don't take it personally," said Garrick. "It's not you; it's him."

For some reason, there was a tension starting to creep into her thoughts and across her shoulders. There was a dull, almost buzz just below her perceptions. She tried to shrug it off, probably a reaction to everything that had happened in the last couple of hours. Her suspicion of Sirona involvement certainly didn't help, but that too was out of her hands now. Let the CoCee deal with it, however they might. It wasn't her business anymore, though in a way, she thought, it always would remain so.

As she stepped through the lock and into the ship proper, heading for her station, the sensation grew and Chutz was becoming skittish, moving staccato on her shoulder.

Either he was picking up on what she was sensing too, or she was simply feeding him unwittingly.

"What is it Chutz?" she said quietly, reaching to soothe him, but he wasn't having any of it.

It would keep. She clambered up the staircase to her flight couch, strapped herself in, tuned into the preparatory chatter from the bridge.

"Set," she told them.

She closed her eyes, reached out with her senses, sought the pathways. There. There was Belshore. The jump point was about a minute, up and to the right. She fed that information to the pilot and the ship's drives hummed into life, a familiar vibration running through the ship and all of them. When she used to run the long hauls, that intermittent sound, the constant minor adjustments of the course necessitated by the influence of various passing gravity wells used to lull her to sleep. There was something familiar and comforting about it. One day, now, that too might become a thing of the past.

They were close now, and she fixed the point clearly in her mind.

But no, there was something else. She could feel other signatures nearing through the void. She didn't recognise the signatures. It wasn't one or two. There were many, and they were bearing down on their position. She wasn't going to wait around to find out.

"Jump. Now!" she said.

And then they were in void space, the traceries filling her mind.

Chapter Twenty-Five

Sapporan Space

"Have you ever been here before, Jay?"
"No. No reason to really. I've seen pictures of course."
"Yes, me too."

The Nameless was sitting in relatively high orbit, and below them sat Sapporan filling most of the viewscreen. It was a reasonably large world, shrouded in an almost perpetual layer of cloud. Now and again, it broke, but not for very long. With the cloud cover, there was no real way of telling how significant the damage was below. That was, of course, if you discounted the missing space elevator jutting up through the cloud layer that was an ever-present feature of the widely available images.

"So, what's wrong with this picture?" said Timon.

"Well, I have to say, apart from the missing elevator, Timon, the fact that most of the nearby space is occupied primarily by the CoCee fleet...."

"Yes, that.".

"I don't understand," said Kurasa from the pod.

"Simple. This is a trade hub. The whole economy survives on import/export. The sky should be full of freighters, long-haulers, ever short-hop carriers. There's virtually nothing here."

"Oh, I see."

"Are you getting anything?" Timon asked him.

"Uh...anything? Commander Pellis I..."

"Fire, man! What use are you? Any sign of Sirona ships. Any traces of anything."

"Wait um...hold on a moment. Let me see."

There were a few moments of silence in which Timon ground his teeth, waiting, staring out at the rest of the CoCee ships.

"Uh, no. I can't pick up anything. Only the marks of our own ships, as far as I can tell."

"Not sure you could tell anyway," he said quietly, lifting his eyebrows in Jay's direction. He really was starting to miss Mahra now. Why was it that they had been stuck with this green recruit. Though to be fair, in comparison to Mahra, they were all little more than green recruits these CoCee navigators.

"Well, keep looking, Navigator."

"Yes, Commander. Of course."

"Let me know the minute you sense anything." He turned his attention to Jayeer. "Meanwhile, we ought to find out what we can about these rumours of Mahra's location," he said.

Jayeer nodded. "I'll send a message out to the crews going groundside and see if they can pick anything up. From what I'm hearing here, the communications network has suffered some heavy damage. Comms are patchy all over."

"Do we know what ship she was on?"

"Something called *The Outrigger*. No sign anywhere in local space. Any calls are coming up empty. There's far too much chaos down there to get any sensible record checks either, though they would have had to log if they were docking."

Benevolent

"We can presume that it was fitted with the drive if Mahra was with them. That means it could be anywhere by now."

"Or nowhere."

"Well, that's not a possibility we want to consider right now."

Jay nodded. "True. So let's see what any of our people pick up down there. We'll ask around. It's not as if she blends into the landscape. Lone woman carrying a blade and a zimonette. It is not exactly your normal visitor and I doubt very much that she has changed that much. Although…we have no idea of knowing if she was alone."

"True."

"There's been some reports of casualties, but relatively few…. It seems the main impact has been to infrastructure. And…." Jayeer cocked his head, listening. "…to breathability, apparently."

"Huh?"

"Yes, I don't know. Your guess is as good as mine."

"Still nothing, Commander." Kurasa's voice broke in between them.

"That's all right," said Timon. "I don't want you to give me reports when there's nothing to report. Only tell me if something actually happens." He scowled at Jayeer and shook his head again.

Timon called up the planetary scan. It wasn't as good as direct visual, but with the cloud layer, it was the next best option and he looked as the graphic display delineated the primary areas of impact. There was damage, all right, but as far as he could see, it was restricted to outlying structures rather than Sinq City itself. To be honest, he was itching to get down there and have a look for himself, but orders were orders.

"Blast Garavenah," he said.

Jay gave him a quizzical look.

"Oh, you know. Hanging around up here doing nothing, listening to reports of nothing, watching nothing. Except preparations to go where we're not supposed to go, that is."

"It's all right. We will start to get feeds from our crews pretty soon. We will be able to see what's going on down there and where we might be able to direct our efforts. As Garavenah says, Timon, we need to be ready. We need to make sure that we're prepared and ready if they decide to come back."

"Yes, you're right," he said. "I just can't help feeling frustrated. Fire, Jay. I want to be doing something."

"Mmmm," said Jayeer and went back to listening to the come.

Timon was left to watch as one by one the other ships broke off and started drifting down towards the thick, dark, cloud layer below.

Benevolent

Chapter Twenty-Six

New Helvetica

He supposed it was his own arrogance as much as anything else. He didn't have a lot of time for people generally, and that was as much because he thought he was smarter than the vast majority, that he had a better mind. Their stupidity annoyed him, and when it didn't do that, it just meant that he became rapidly bored. Spending time with the machinations of his own schemes was a good antidote to that, or at least had proved to be so in the past. Now, though, he had a real problem, and that was that the machinations were no longer truly his own, so it was, in a way, as if he was merely playing at being Valdor Carr. Going through the motions. And he was beginning to like it less and less. He drummed his fingers on the desk, pushed back the tall wing-backed chair, and stood. It didn't matter what time of day it was; right now, he just wanted a brandy. He crossed to the shelf, poured himself a healthy measure, swirled it a couple of times before breathing in the aroma. At least that he could appreciate. He took a small sip and followed it immediately with a larger one which he swirled around in his mouth before swallowing, letting the warm burn give him focus. He turned to the window, looked out over the building old and new, not really seeing them, not even feeling like they were part of his domain anymore. He focussed on the reflection of the room behind him. Thankfully, for the moment, the girl was nowhere to be seen. She was probably off somewhere poking through his things. Well, let her. As long as he didn't have to put up with her increasingly annoying presence for the moment.

"Come on, Valdor, think," he said to himself. If they were listening, let them. He glanced around the shelves and the walls.

Everything he'd had was gone now. There wasn't even anyone left that he could truly trust. Even Milnus, the man he would have trusted his life with had turned out to be working for someone else. How had he not seen it? How could he have been so blind? Once more, it was probably nothing more than his own arrogance that had led him into that trap. Partly it was also the aura of blankness that Milnus maintained around himself, the typical New Helvetian, grey on grey, and really, one of the reasons that Valdor had trusted him in the first place was that he was damned good at what he did, which had generally been whatever Valdor asked of him. Marina, no. She was well and truly Benevolent and what a surprise she'd turned out to be. And then there was the CoCee. He could never really trust anyone in the CoCee. Normally Valdor trod a fine path between acceptability and legality, quite content to hover in the grey areas that had more than once had the CoCee looking his way with suspicion. Mostly, with them, he'd weathered the little storms that had arisen, relying as much upon his own network as his own wits. And that there, was another thing. The network. A series of business relationships, careful alliances, contacts that he'd spent time and energy cultivating over the years, and now, he had very little confidence in any of them. He called a couple to mind, but

Benevolent

no. There was no way to tell whether they might be Benevolent, might even be CoCee. He grimaced, shook his head, and took another healthy sip.

"Mezzer Carr?"

The girl was back. He took another swallow, peering at her over the top of his glass.

"Is there anything you want me to do?"

He paused before answering, biting back his response. Yes there was, but he wasn't about to tell her what it was. If it had been Milnus, Valdor would have delegated some of the business and finance monitoring, but that was also when Milnus had been someone that he could trust. Besides, right at the moment, he didn't want this Tsinda anywhere near his business transactions, eager to flag anything he might be off doing on his own well and truly away from The Benevolent's direct gaze. Nevertheless, he had a thought. With a barely perceptible nod to himself, he crossed back to the chair and sat, places his glass down on the desk and gestured with one hand for Tsinda to sit opposite him. As she joined him at the desk, took one of the chairs, he studied her.

She had a roundish, slightly oval face. The eyes were large, dark. Maybe a little too large. It reminded him a little of some of the animation feeds. The straight bobbed blonde hair added to the image. Full mouth, narrow chin, and a short nose. He'd not really paid that much attention to her before this. He wondered briefly if any of it was tailored. As far as he could see, there was no skin art in evidence, either implants or colour enhancement. Who knew what lay below the clothes though? He had no plans to explore that thought any further. She was clearly aware of his scrutiny and just sat there impassively, neither accepting or rejecting his gaze. Normally, anyone sitting across his desk being subjected to that level of drawn out and deliberate scrutiny would begin to show signs of discomfort, but not this one.

"I never asked you, Tsinda," he said finally. "How is it that you come to know Marina?"

She gave a little smile. "I don't know her, exactly," she said. "I work for her."

"And how did that come to be?"

She shrugged then. "The organisation puts people where they need to be. It happened to need me reporting to Mez Samaris."

"And you're fine with that?"

"Why would I not be?"

He nodded. She returned his gaze impassively.

When Valdor didn't say anything, she spoke. "Are you sure there is not something I can do for you now, Mezzer Carr?"

If there was an implication in the question, it was very, very, subtle. Valdor decided then that he had to stop thinking of her as a girl. She was, he thought, dangerous. Dangerous in the same way that Milnus was dangerous, but in a different way. The most perilous relationships were the ones where you underestimated the other person.

"No, but that's okay," said Valdor. "I do have some things I want to discuss though. Perhaps you can give me answers. Marina seems to be a bit busy these days and just a little short on information. Seeing as you report to her, perhaps you have some insight I can use to help me assist the program."

Tsinda tilted her head a little. "I will do what I can," she said. "Though I really wish you would think about making a bit more use of my presence. I can be useful," she said. "I really can."

"Oh, I don't doubt that," said Valdor. "Let me think on it. So…," he continued. "Stop me if I get anything wrong. Bear with me, because some of this is guesswork on my part, though it may be glaringly obvious."

She crossed her hands in her lap, leaning forward just a little, waiting.

"The facilities, the subjects, they're being readied to take over something. I hope or believe that they are not some sort of revolutionary force or something similar. Not some private army?"

"Not as such. No."

"Good. And…let's see if I have this right. After the latest thing on Sapporan, the CoCee will rush to their aid, but, they will prove ineffective against the mighty Sirona. Confidence in their capability will dwindle."

"Yes, and no," said Tsinda.

"How so?"

"Well, because of the relief effort, there's going to have to be massive upgrades to ships system wide. Whole fleets of ships. Installation of the jump drive. Training of navigators. All of it will be the CoCee's idea, of course, but it was always something that was necessary."

Valdor looked off into the middle distance as he absorbed that. The Benevolent were being quite clever in that regard. He didn't know why he would have expected otherwise. It wasn't the overt outcome that was the main aim. What they had been trying to achieve by the action was a side-effect. One that would not be immediately obvious as the desired result.

"Huh," he said to himself. "Nice."

She looked at him expectantly, but he took a moment more to process that, took a healthy sip from his glass and framed his next question.

"And the Sirona?"

"I don't know," she said with a shrug.

"And how exactly are these new elite supposed to step in to save the day?"

She lowered her gaze a little. "I don't know that either."

Either she didn't, or she was pretending that she didn't. Either way she was not to be trusted. He needed to think.

"Actually, I have something for you," he said. "If you can put together for me a complete projection of readiness, give me the timeline. We need to think about accommodating the subjects, equipping them. We need transport capabilities. Are we going to have uniforms or generic outfits? We have access to weaponry, but which weaponry? I don't think some of this has been thought through. Details. We need details. Can you start putting that together for me? Then I can make sure that what is necessary will happen. I am guessing that your contact with Marina will help you get the answers to some of the questions. Sometimes those with the grand ideas don't necessarily delve into the necessary detail required to support them."

As he'd expected, the sudden flurry had caught her a little off guard. It would certainly give her something to do and, for the moment at least, keep her out of his way while he made plans of his own.

"Is that all?"

"That's enough for now," he said, waving her away, sealing the statement by picking up his drink and swinging the chair to face the window. As he watched her retreating form in

Benevolent

the reflection, there was the vaguest hint of a smile etched upon his lips.

oOo

Just sometimes, when he was unable to resolve a problem, Valdor wandered the streets. There was something about the mist-borne glow of street lamps in the early evening and the history of the old town that set his mind at rest. Of course, if his wanderings took him into the entertainment district, there were risks to be had. The same with the commuter hubs like Central Station. For some reason, they seemed to attract the lesser end of the demographic, those with less to their name, and even less morality. Valdor didn't care whether it had been fate or something else that had driven them to their state, it just was, and he liked to be prepared for eventualities. He guessed that those coming and going from major ports were sometimes less aware, more concerned about working out where they were going than what might be occurring in their immediate surrounds. Most certainly that was true of the resort set the frequented New Helvetica. And Valdor, because he prided himself on his appearance, the impression he left on people, the state of his clothing, was sometimes confused with a potential mark. If that happened, whoever it was soon learned the error of their ways, because Valdor Carr was generally not to be trifled with and his handy little weapon tended to back that up. He supposed he could have had security, a bodyguard, someone to watch his back, but that would mean having to put up with another person in his orbit. No, he was fine looking after himself. This evening, however, he was confining his wandering to the old town, the quiet streets, the stately buildings, the streetlamps lending a slight yellow glow to the facades. He could taste the river in the mist, there despite the chill, always there.

As he walked he was considering the possible outcomes The Benevolent might have. Tsinda had given him something, but not quite enough. Yes, their stated aim was one of the betterment of the race, but as he slotted the little puzzle pieces into place, it was becoming clearer to Valdor that what might be their stated aim was nothing more than propaganda. In the end, what they were aiming for amounted to little more than a 'benevolent' dictatorship, serving no one really but themselves. Despite everything that had happened, he still couldn't help retaining a fondness for Marina. They'd worked together a long time and though she'd turned out to be someone completely other than what he believed, he wasn't sure that she was the sort that would aspire to true believer status. No, Marina was, in the end, out for Marina. He could appreciate that. She had always been one to dissemble when necessary and she was very good at it. As long as it achieved the required aim, then that was all right. So, if she was just working for someone, for whom was she working? That was the question. Valdor needed to know more about The Benevolent, understand where they were coming from. Who were the individuals behind the name? There had to be weaknesses there somewhere. Knowledge was a good bargaining chip. The problem was how.

He stopped and stood staring up at the front of a large building, statues propping up balconies on their backs, carved faces of old gods staring down at the street below with horrified expressions on their faces. That façade, that structure, reeked of belief. A belief in their own superiority. What had happened to them, to the builders, to the wealthy who wanted to construct something so grand? They were gone, all of them.

Benevolent

Valdor drew a deep breath through his nose and turned away. It could be him too. It could be all of them. Arrogance, Valdor. Arrogance and hubris. It appeared he was not alone in that. It still didn't solve his problem, although he was starting to have a germ of an idea about what he might do.

Chapter Twenty-Seven

Belshore

A welcoming committee was there waiting for them as soon as they landed. Dubois in the centre of a concerned-faced group of company functionaries and technical folk. So much for the supposed casual nature of Bathyscaphe.

"How was the drive?" was the first thing he asked.

"Optimal," said Mahra wryly.

"Hum, I see. So I hope you avoided most of what happened out there," he said.

"Yes, well, large chunks of infrastructure falling around our ears and then a rain of mud and who knows what else. Don't think it's actually avoidance."

Dubois looked away and cleared his throat. He looked to Merritt then.

"We're shutting down operations for the time being."

"Of course. I understand," said Merritt and immediately started walking towards the main building, a couple of his crew in tow.

"Seriously?" said Mahra, watching their retreating backs and then turning back to Dubois. "Why? If it hadn't been for the drive, we might still be back there, waiting for something, anything to happen. None of it good. Shouldn't

Benevolent

we be doing just the opposite? Pushing this forward? Trying to get it out there as soon as possible. From what I saw, the little I heard from the Captain, what I *felt* out there, it had to be the Sirona."

Dubois blinked, clearly a little taken aback by her barrage.

"I appreciate your eagerness, Mez Kaitan, however…there's just too much investment involved. I am not prepared to risk it at this stage. Do you know how much it costs to outfit a ship like that, make the modifications that are required? We are gearing up for production with others, but at the moment, this is our prototype. I would have liked to see a few more trials before we took the next step, but in this scenario, that will have to wait. So far, I am satisfied that the drive works and that the ship held together."

"Well, it might not have done, considering," she said.

"Exactly."

"But…."

"No, the decision has been made. We will just have to wait and see how this all plays out."

"But the Sirona. We have to do something."

"That doesn't matter to us, Mez Kaitan. Risk is risk, wherever it may come from. I don't care if it's the Sirona or some rogue pirate."

Mahra didn't quite know what to say. Reflexively she reached for Chutz.

"And what am I supposed to do?"

Dubois pressed his lips together. "Well…," he said. "That's a question isn't it? For the moment, I have nothing for you. I suggest you find an alternative in the meantime. Once we're ready to start up again, we'll get in touch, see if you're available."

She opened her mouth, but there were no words. He was serious, she could see that.

"So you're just going to leave me hanging."

"Well, I thought you had a pretty good run of it while Bathyscaphe had you on retainer, Mez Kaitan. Wouldn't you say? So far, that's paid off for us, but in light of the current events, I'm not sure that's really the case anymore. We'll just have to wait and see."

He turned then, and Mahra was left once more staring after a retreating back. A moment later, Nissa walked past her, briefly resting a hand on Mahra's shoulder as she passed before also heading towards the main building complex. Garrick was long gone, having headed off in that initial group with Merritt. The last thing she saw of any of them, was Nissa's upraised hand as she entered the building and disappeared from view.

"So what now, Chutz?" she said. "We're back where we started."

She looked back at *The Outrigger* and was relieved to see the rear bay doors open. She still had a couple of things inside and she wandered back to retrieve them, shove them into her carryall and head back out. But to where? That was the question. Her certainty about the Sirona was chewing her up inside, but she wasn't going to find a sympathetic ear in Bathyscaphe it seemed. And add to that the whole thing was all pretty short lived. She still had some funds put aside, but they'd only last so long with rental chewing up a piece of it. She'd have to find something. Maybe another short hop. Or even, now that she'd made the split from the CoCee, a longer haul job. It just seemed a pity to waste all the work they'd put in and the knowledge that they'd gained. She was still thinking as she grabbed the last of her gear, wandered

Benevolent

out the back of the ship and towards the main gates of their landing field. She was still a little ill-at-ease though, so perhaps she should just go and drop off her stuff and then find a bar, spend the rest of the evening trying to wind down.

"Dammit, though," she said with a shake of her head. "I can't escape them can I?"

Perhaps she needed to see Jayeer, tell him what she'd seen, what she'd felt. She still wasn't comfortable with approaching Timon. Maybe one day, but not yet. No, Jayeer Sind felt like a good option. She looked at her feed, checked the time. It was sometimes hard to keep track bouncing between worlds and systems. It turned out that it was earlier in the day than she'd thought. She could find a place to check in, drop her stuff, head over and see if she could find Jay. She needed to talk to someone.

The transit into the city hummed along, relatively empty out here in what amounted to the suburbs. Bathyscaphe was hardly likely to have a landing field in the middle of the city, so it was a good twenty minutes and then a change of line before she got within walking distance of the place she had been staying at. The whole way, those images, those vase shapes pushing the clouds apart, the slamming concussion, the sound of breaking glass, ran over and over in her head. She leaned back, resting the back of her skull against the window, trying to let the vibrations soothe the feelings, lull her into some sort of state where she was no longer thinking about it. They pulled into stop, the doors slid open and someone got in. He gave her a glance, looked away and then did a double take, and then quickly tried to hide it. She didn't even acknowledge it; she was so used to it now.

Finally back at the low-end hotel, she got through check in formalities, dumped the gear, took a few moments to give the sparse environment a quick scan, realising how little she had with her, how little she always had with her. The brief time with Jacinda had been a welcome change in that regard, but here, it was just Mahra, her blade and Chutzpah and a few bare necessities to keep them going from day to day. The rest of it was foraging. The way things looked now, it was just as well, because once more, the Sirona seemed to have stuck a hefty branch into the stream that was her life. For some reason, she was always fated to run in with the alien creatures, although on almost every occasion, it had not been the Sirona themselves, but rather, their ships. She let out a deep sigh. And once more, Mahra Kaitan would be scanning the feeds and cruising port bars on the chance that she might pick up some work. Of course, now, with her jump capabilities, she might be a little more marketable but somehow she thought she was probably a little early for that. Apart from Bathyscaphe, she doubted there was anyone out there yet with access to the drive. Anyway, first call was Jay.

Her hotel wasn't that far from the CoCee compound, so it took her about twenty-five minutes walking through the less reputable areas of the city and into the more ordered. When she got to the gate, she was about to blithely walk through when a uniformed guard stepped out in front of her, holding up a hand.

"And where do you think you're going, Mez?"

"Um, inside. I'm here to see Commander Sind."

"And your name?"

"Mahra Kaitan. He gave her the once over and then stepped back."

Benevolent

"You're not CoCee. I don't see a uniform. Identification?"

"Listen, I used to be. I only stopped a short while ago. Commander Sind and I happen to be friends, crewmates."

She passed him her device and then waited while he scanned it.

"I understand that, Mez," he said as he reviewed the details that came up, gave her a slightly suspicious glance, which she confronted, and then shut down the reader and handed her device back to her.

"I'm sorry, but you are not authorised to enter the facility."

She hadn't even considered that might be a possibility. But of course they were going to close down her access eventually.

"Listen," she said. "Would you be so kind as to contact Commander Sind. I'm sure he has the authority to allow me access."

"Please wait here."

He stepped out of view for a moment, before returning. "I'm afraid the Commander is not on base at the moment."

"Um. All right." And as much as she was reluctant to pull that card: "What about Commander Pellis."

"No need to check that, Mez. I know for a fact that he is not on base."

"Maybe…." No, there was nothing for it. "Can I leave a message for Jayeer…um, Commander Sind for when he gets back? Or maybe it could get to him wherever he might be."

"We might be able to arrange that, Mez," said the guard. "Seeing as you were with us for a time." There was a hint of reluctance in his tone. Of course the guard had no way of knowing under what circumstances she and the CoCee had parted ways.

"Thanks. I appreciate it," she said, keeping her tone as pleasant as possible. There was no point in trying to bully her way through. That certainly wouldn't work. She nodded and turned around again.

"Thanks again," she said as she wandered away down the street, fighting yet another sigh of frustration.

"Well, seems we've been told what we need to do," she said to Chutzpah. "I think we need to find a bar. Maybe something will come up, but until it does….."

And in the meantime, she needed to think about her circumstance. She couldn't afford to stay in hotels forever without some other income source, and if she was going to pick up a short-hop or longer, there'd be no point renting something that might be more within her budget. She'd be going back to being without any fixed base. She wasn't too sure whether she wanted that any more.

Benevolent

Chapter Twenty-Eight

New Helvetica

Valdor Carr had spent time carefully constructing a network of contacts, useful individuals, those with particular skills for a reason. As the public face of a series of corporate entities, he had sometimes been limited in the actions that he could be seen to be doing. Sometimes, however, those limitations were just that…limitations and he had to have ways of getting past them. That's where the network came in. If he needed to get into a particular secure system, then he had someone for that. If he needed to gain access to a building or a facility, then he had people for that, or rather people who could do the accessing for him. If, on the rare occasion, he needed someone taken out of the picture, he had also had people for that. It all depended on what the most urgent needs were at the time. Sometimes, he couldn't afford to wait around for due process to take its course. It was far too *limiting.*

And now was just such a circumstance.

He'd spent some time working through what he'd need for this to work effectively. The problem was, he was bound to be under scrutiny, and that was from more than the girl, the true believer. She was there not only to report back to Marina, but also to distract him. He was awake to that. The problem The Benevolent had was that once Valdor got something in his sights, he would not be distracted. He thought they'd also miscalculated putting her in place, which surprised him a little, considering how long he and Marina had known each other. Perhaps she had simply been under instructions. If Tsinda was to serve as a distraction, it could just as well have been to divert his attention from anything they'd put in place, whether it be here or elsewhere. It didn't make any difference though; the intent was clear. It was a pity that he no longer had in-house people who'd be able to root out any surveillance equipment, something that he'd had done regularly in his former tenure here. Just in case though, he had decided that any transactions, any conversations, any meetings related to the current project were going to take place outside of his offices and well away from the buildings. They were also going to take place in person. The Benevolent could have people following him, but that too shouldn't present too much of a problem. If they were skilled enough to have the job, he'd probably never spot them, but at the same time, the things he would be doing, the locales that he would be visiting, none of them presented a great variation from what he normally did or where he usually went, so they shouldn't raise any particular flags.

Before the whole takedown of Carr Holdings, he had, he thought, also become a little too complacent, relying too much on his own people instead of the extended network. A mistake he was not going to make again. Most of the broader contacts could be trusted because that trust was part of a business relationship. That form of relationship sometimes consisted partly of credits, partly of other give and take. It worked. He was pacing as he ran all this through in his head.

Benevolent

His feeds were off, the space was quiet. Tsinda was nowhere to be seen. Around and around the desk he walked, head down, hands clasped in front of him. The more he thought about it, the more he knew what he had to do. As long as he continued working with…or rather for…The Benevolent, nothing was going to get any better, and he would remain someone's vassal rather than the master of his own fate. He stopped mid-step, turned, walked over to the window. What he was about to do would put him in a role he never imagined he would be playing. He chewed over the thought for a moment or two. In the end, he thought, he was probably okay with that. The Benevolent and their Sirona friends had taken too much away from him. It was time to start taking some of it back.

Valdor glanced across at the shelf, at the crystal decanter, at the cut glass tumbler, both symbols of status and his own indulgence. He thought about pouring a drink to seal the commitment, but then decided he didn't need it. He had people to see. He crossed back to his desk, retrieved the weapon, shoved it into his pocket then turned to the elevator. His mind was made up.

It was relatively early in the day for Valdor to be conducting any sort of business. He hoped he'd be able to see who he needed to. At least one or two of them should be available, that is if they were still alive and in business. It had been that long that he really didn't know. What he did know was that he had to do this in person, of that there was no doubt. Doing any of this from his offices would be too much of a risk. As his elevator door slid open, and he stepped out into the street, he tilted his head back and took a deep breath of the cool mid-morning Helvetian air. He could smell the mountains, the freshness in it, perhaps a hint of the river. It was clean. A lot cleaner than most of the enterprises that did their business here. And that being considered, in the end, it was not that surprising that The Benevolent might have a significant presence here.

He wandered out of the old town, through the streets, still running things through his head, formulating his plan of action. When there were so few that he could have faith in, and even fewer that he could trust, things were going to be a little difficult. He barely registered the other people he passed, some workers, some resorters, some just simple tourists. A city maintenance vehicle hummed past, cleaning, it's program keeping it where it needed to be. Not that different from most of the population, he thought wryly to himself. What more were they other than programmed automata?

His first stop was a disappointment. The man he wanted to see was either not there, or Valdor really was simply too early. He shrugged, looked up and down the street at the glass fronted establishments, simple holos crawling above and beside the displays, some messages scrolling through the glass itself. This was a low-end commercial district. His next stop was right at the border of where the enterprises started to become a little grander, targeting those shoppers or potential walk-ins with a bit more resources. A few minutes later and he was standing in front of a modest shopfront with the name SEED in simple letters above the window. All sorts of small gadgets lay on a clutter of display shelves inside. Under the shop's name, ran a small set of words. 'From the smallest seed....' Indeed, he thought to himself as he pulled open the door and stepped inside. There was no one inside, just shelves and shelves of gadgetry, most of which Valdor would have no chance of defining the purpose.

Benevolent

He crossed to one of the shelves, lifted up a device, turned it over and over.

"Unless you are going to pay for that...."

Valdor placed it down and turned slowly. "Nathan Seed. It has been some time," he said.

"Well, well, Valdor Carr decides to perform an act of benevolence and join those less fortunate than himself."

Valdor winced at the choice of words, despite himself. The man in front of him was tall, wiry, with a shock of curly red hair. His thin freckled face held a grin, but there was a look of calculation in his eyes. The clothes were basic streetwear. No style there, but really, thought Valdor, there was no need for there to be. Nathan Seed was very good at what he did. The shop itself was more of a side-line.

"I need some help, Nathan. There's a situation and I need some tracking and identification."

Seed pursed his lips and nodded. "All right. You'd better come in to my office." He stepped aside and gestured with one arm towards a door at the rear, standing there and allowing Valdor to pass first.

"My, my, Valdor, but you've aged so much. That corporate existence doesn't treat you at all well," he said as Valdor passed.

"Yes, yes. Thank you very much," he said in response.

Seed's office was a tiny long room, more like a galley than an office, Shelves and boxes cluttered the walls. A couple of swivel chair sat next to a workbench that bore a pair of mismatched lamps, a magnifier, assorted tools, and a scattering of various parts.

"Pull up a seat," Seed told him. He waited for Valdor to get comfortable then sat in the other chair, leaned down to a small refrigerator below the bench and handed him a bottle.

Local ale. Valdor cracked it and took a sip. There was a ritual here and he needed to follow it.

"So, what can I do for the mighty Valdor Carr?" he said after taking a healthy swallow from his own bottle and smacking his lips appreciatively.

"Well, I've got a slight problem," Valdor started.

"More than one," said Seed with a tilt of the bottle in Valdor's direction.

Valdor rolled his eyes. "Thanks, Nathan, but this is a little serious."

"Go on."

"I came to you specifically for a reason."

"And that is?"

"Well, you helped with the outfitting of the ILGC building. You probably know more about the inbuilt surveillance measures than anyone else."

Seed nodded.

"The problem is that I don't really own the building any more, but, I want access to some of the feeds inside."

"Huh. You can fill me in on what happened later, but for now, let me understand what you want to see or listen to."

Valdor nodded. "I believe there may be a series of meetings taking place inside that building. I need to know firstly who is involved and as a secondary, what they might be discussing."

"And why do you need me?"

"A couple of reasons. Most of these meetings are probably distance casts. I don't think they'd be meeting in person. That's just supposition, but I think it's a reasonable bet."

"And who are they?"

Benevolent

"Hmmm. That's a little more complicated." Valdor bit his lip and thought for a moment. He wasn't ready to reveal too much yet. "Let's say they're a group who are involved in planning a hostile takeover. One that I'm not too eager for it to take place. I need to know who they are and the factions they represent. Once I know that, I should be better equipped to go after them, find out their weaknesses, look at what leverage I might have." He took another sip from his bottle. Ale really wasn't his thing, but he had to be seen to enjoy it. Seed was a huge fan of the local product. It was almost like a religion with him.

"All right," said Seed. "I think we can do that. Depends on whether there's been modifications since last I was there."

"I think there may have been," said Valdor.

"Let me have a look."

Seed waved his displays into life, conjured a few routines, and peered at some images that scrolled past.

"From what I'm seeing," he said finally, "there have been. There's a space there that I can't get into from here."

Valdor had always suspected that Seed maintained his own backdoor access to anything he set up. If it were Valdor, he'd do the same. It was a good thing that Seed was one of the few people he still trusted.

"Let me think about this. In the meantime, you can fill me in on what happened, why you suddenly disappeared from the landscape a while ago. Oh, and just so you know, the fact that you haven't been in touch up until now wounds me deeply. I expect you to show the appropriate level of contrition."

Valdor snorted at that, turned to look at the displays. He delivered a highly edited version of the happenings of the last several months.

"Huh. CoCee," said Seed as Valdor ran out of words. "That can't have been fun. And then that whole stuff on Kalany." Seed shook his head. "I'm starting to wonder if I should be associating with you at all." He reached down, pulled out two more bottle from beneath the workbench and handed one to Valdor.

"Okay, so," he said. "For this to be able to work, I need access to that room. Can you get in there? Because if you can, we might have an option. There are other ways, but this would be the easiest."

Valdor nodded, watching him over the top of the bottle as he lifted it to his lips and took a polite swallow.

Seed rummaged around on the table surface, found what he was looking for, lifted it in one hand above his head, peering up at it.

"There you are," he said.

Valdor narrowed his eyes. All he could see was a small box.

"Oh, well you might look sceptical, Mezzer Carr, but in here, is my little miracle. It's a little paste keyed to certain channels. It's almost invisible once applied. All I need you to do is to, I don't know, have it on one of your hands, spread it on the back of a chair, on the underside of a table, a desk. Do that and we're inside. Okay, there's a possibility that it could get cleaned off, but normally, it stays around for a while. All you need to do is to get it in there. Up to you where. And that is all. Well, not quite all. You need to activate it before you put it in place."

"And how would I do that?"

Benevolent

"You will probably need to time it in case there are other security checks." He reached for something else, held it up. It was a small card. "This sends an activation signal. All you need to do is swipe it over the top of the tin, then take some of the contents and put them in a place where they are unlikely to be noticed. How you do that is up to you."

Valdor thought that he'd probably have to do all of that before he got anywhere near the inside of the building. Perhaps if he wore gloves…. But no, he could plan the details later.

"Good," he said. "Are you sure this stuff will work?"

"Oh, I would stake my reputation on it."

"Such as it is," said Valdor, tilting his bottle towards him.

"Ha ha. Yes, thanks," said Seed with a half grin.

"I'm going to leave this stuff here for now," Valdor told him. "Too dangerous to carry it around at the moment and I don't want to leave it anywhere back at my place considering the current circumstances. I'll come back closer to the time, once I've been able to organise the appropriate access."

"As you like," said Seed.

"Anyway, I need to get going," said Valdor. "I have another couple of calls to make. And I thank you for your hospitality."

Seed gave a dismissive snort. "Yes, sure."

Valdor placed his half-empty bottle down on the workbench, sidled past Seed's lanky frame with barely enough space to do it, and then passed outside into the cluttered shop. He did have another call to make. This one with a slightly different purpose. But as he stepped out onto the street, he was feeling a slight sense of accomplishment.

The first small piece had been enacted. Now he needed to put some other things in place.

Benevolent

Chapter Twenty-Nine

Belshore

Over the next couple of days, Mahra spent her time either scanning the feeds or finding a place with deep thumping music and sketchy population to while away her time. More than once, she went back to the CoCee, but each time her efforts met with the same result. There was no access and no response from inside. Wherever Timon and Jay were, they weren't immediately reachable, or they had more important things on their minds. It would have been deeply ironic, she thought, if it turned out to have something to do with Sapporan. Of course, her personal feed and those constantly playing in the bars were full of speculation, reports on the clean-up and relief efforts. Apparently the CoCee had dispatched a fleet, so it was highly likely that *The Nameless* and its crew were a part of the whole thing. It had not been one hundred percent confirmed, but the belief was that this had been some sort of inexplicable action by the Sirona. Something to damage the system's trade capability? It didn't make sense though, because this, the actions on Kalany, all of it was nothing less than war, and many of the commentators were calling it just that. Some of the feeds were becoming increasingly outraged and militant in their commentary. War or not, Sirona or not, Mahra still had to find something that was going to provide her with a source of credits. She hunkered down over the feeds and started skimming the notices. Sapporan didn't help matters at all. There seemed to be a creeping reluctance to get involved with long-haul trade at the moment. Apparently many of the haulers were being refitted to help the efforts on Sapporan, but that was going to take some time. There might be an opportunity there. They were going to need navigators with the new drive, but perhaps there was already some sort of deal in place with the CoCee. Not having access to any information from inside the CoCee didn't help her at all.

Just then, something came in on her personal feed, something addressed specifically to her. The whole thing had been encrypted. She frowned, not recognising the name. Perhaps it was something from Bathyscaphe. Thinking that, she opened it without hesitation, but then as she read through it, her hand hovered, and then withdrew. It was nothing to do with Bathyscaphe. It was nothing to do with the CoCee either. The message was from a Lars Rimmel, a name she didn't recognise. There was no company associated with it, nor any ship call sign. It hadn't originated on Belshore either.

Mahra Kaitan. We have an assignment which may interest you. It's a specific courier job. You may find the work familiar. It involves a very small and special package, not unlike one you carried before. Slightly unusual.

Please respond if interested and we will communicate further.

Lars Rimmel

Mahra sat back, staring at the display. What the hell?

She certainly didn't recognise the name, but a courier assignment and one she'd done before. There was only one thing that came to mind and it was that whole business with Valdor Carr. The little side mission that had started this whole chain of events. She looked back at the display and read through the message again. There was nothing else that it could be. But it was a little strange. She'd lost track of what had happened to Carr. Why would he be contacting her this way, or, rather, why would he be using someone to act on his behalf? She bit off that thought. It would not be unusual for Carr to have someone else working for him, but the whole vague and mysterious nature of the communication was strange to say the least. There was something else going on here. She peered at the tags. The source of the message seemed to be New Helvetica, so that would fit with Carr. Visions of that sterile, frigid world swam into being in her head and she grimaced. Not somewhere she particularly wanted to be again in a hurry. Snowsports were not exactly her thing.

"Remember New Helvetica, Chutz?" she said, scratching under his chin. "Remember Valdor Carr?"

She shrugged. At this point, there was nothing to lose. She thought for a moment, constructing the words.

Mezzer Rimmel
Possible interest. More details needed.
Mahra Kaitan,

There. That was vague enough but gave the message that she needed to send. Now to sit back and wait.

Chapter Thirty

New Helvetica

At his next port of call, Valdor had leveraged another of his old contacts. He'd instructed him to have secured communications sent to a couple of places. One, he thought might be a bit of a longshot, but the other, well he'd have to wait and see. The problem was that right at the moment, he had no confidence that the CoCee was free of Benevolent operatives, and that meant that he couldn't trust anyone there. He had to come at them from another angle. The other issue with that was that in the end, he thought they'd probably need the CoCee's resources to accomplish what he needed, but he needed to be sure of them in the meantime.

First, however, he needed to get into the ILGC building, and more specifically into that particular room and then let's Seed's toys do their job. He called Tsinda and asked her to join him in their offices.

"Mezzer Carr?" she said as she arrived.

"Have you got those reports for me?" he asked. "And you know, it's been long enough; let's not keep up the charade. I've said it before, Valdor is fine."

Tsinda gave a nod of acknowledgment and took a seat. "They're nearly complete. There's a lot of stuff to go through."

Benevolent

"I'm going to need what you have by the end of the morning. Then I'd like to meet with Marina, confirm the direction, some of the talking points. We can fill in the rest of the details later. I also need a status update on production readiness and how far along we are with the program."

"Um, yes, of course, Mezzer...um Valdor."

"Good. Well, you'd better get to it," he said, waving her away.

She pushed back her chair looking a little unsettled. Well, she should get used to it now. This was Valdor Carr in full flow. He watched her retreating back as she scurried off to do his bidding. That was a bit better, and rather more in keeping with the way he liked things to be. Nonetheless, he wasn't going to fool himself about the situation that he found himself in. And, really, he missed Milnus, not that he'd gone anywhere particularly, just somewhat in the background with the stigma of his Benevolent association hanging above him every time Valdor saw him. Milnus would have scurried too, but somehow, he believed, perhaps with a bit more dignity about it. Anyway, if he could keep the girl busy, immersed in things that needed doing, he might also keep her off her toes, more likely to miss something when he needed her to do just that. Speaking of which, he had a couple of hours now. Time enough to check on progress. Again, something he needed to do in person. Maybe, a little later, he might talk to Nathan Seed about his offices and living quarters and what to do about them. Of course, and this was the thing, if there was surveillance there, shutting it down was going the alert The Benevolent immediately. He needed them comfortable at the moment if he was going to be able to do what he needed to. Perhaps all he needed was a more secure channel. That thought would keep for now.

He stood, grabbed his coat, and made for the elevator. As he stepped inside and waited for the doors to close, he sniffed at himself. He really needed to shower when he got back. When he was in full stream, he sometimes forgot about it, getting so caught up in the little manoeuvrings that the mundane just slipped right by his attention. That was a little dangerous in itself. He needed to be more on top of things, on top of everything.

Out on the street, he glanced up at the sky, threatening dark clouds stirring above him. He sighed thinking about going back up and grabbing something, but it was too late now. If he got wet, he got wet. He'd just have to risk it. It was only a few minutes' walk and he might just be lucky. By the time he reached his destination, the first fat drops were slapping on the pavements and buildings. He pressed the entry and waited, hoping this time that Rimmel was in. A moment later and he was buzzed inside, just as the heavens opened.

"Lucky, Valdor," said Lars Rimmel from the top of a narrow staircase. "It's all in the timing right?"

"Including the fact that you're actually here," said Valdor.

Rimmel, dark, squat, a belly extending over casual trousers too small for him waved Valdor up into the gloom.

"Yes, well," said Rimmel, here I am.

At the top of the stairs lay a landing which accounted for the gloom as it was barely lit. Doors on either side sat closed, concealing whatever lay behind. Rimmel turned and opened one of the doors, which immediately flooded the space with light.

Benevolent

"Come on," he said. "Something to drink? Kahveh?"

More out of politeness than any desire, Valdor accepted the offer.

"There, find yourself a place. Be back in a moment."

Valdor stepped into the room proper. Wide, brightly lit with an array of feeds on every wall. A few chairs sat around, and every bit of desk space had cups, drinks, disposable wrappings, evidence of takeaways. Rimmel came back, cleared a space on one of the desks using the side of his arm, and placed two mugs down.

"Just natural, if I'm right," said Rimmel, gesturing towards one of the mugs.

"Yes, thank you," said Valdor, reaching for the indicated kahveh. He held it in both hands, feeling the warmth through the sides of the mug, breathing in the rich smell. It wasn't Kalanian premium, but it would do.

"So, how did we go?" said Valdor.

Rimmel plumped himself into a chair and nodded, reaching for his own mug, dragging it across the desk towards him, and then turning to rummage around in a corner behind, finally coming up with a bottle, pouring a jolt in his own mug and then tilting the bottle in Valdor's direction. Valdor shook his head.

"Well, yes," said Rimmel. "One I'm waiting on. The other. The one on Belshore, she came back."

"Good," said Valdor. "Good. I'm going to need a secure channel somehow. We need to distance cast, but without any possibility of leakage. I can't have the discussion heard by anyone else. No one at all. Can that happen?"

"Yes, we should be able to manage that. I have some people on Belshore. They will have to line up a facility, put the safeguards in place. Might take a day or so."

Rimmel peered at him over the top of his mug, waiting for a response.

"That should be fine. I need to put some other things of my own in place anyway in the meantime. And where will we do it? Here?"

Rimmel shook his head. "No, not here. Somewhere else. I'll let you know when the time comes. It's not quite as easy as it sounds, Valdor."

Valdor gave a short laugh. "I thought everything was easy for Lars Rimmel."

That brought a shrug. "Well…. This one better be worth it. I am going to have to call in a couple of favours."

"I understand," said Valdor. "Don't worry. I'll be sure that you'll be taken care of."

"Can I ask…?"

"No. Sorry."

"Fair enough." Rimmel gave another slight shrug. "I guess I don't need to know."

"Better if you don't," said Valdor. "Believe me."

Valdor placed his mug down on the bench—it wasn't that good in the end, anyway—and stood.

"I'll be back tomorrow afternoon to see where we are. Unfortunately I can't do any of this from my place for now. Maybe soon, but not at the moment. You of all people can appreciate that I am sure."

Rimmel lifted his eyebrows in assent and took another sip. "I'll try to be here," he said.

Valdor nodded, turned, and left him sitting there. Rimmel seemed in no hurry to get on with it, but then Valdor supposed that he might just be a little reluctant to talk with some of his people with Valdor still present. He would do exactly the same thing.

Benevolent

As he walked down the stairs, he felt a little touch of satisfaction. There was much more to do yet, but for now, that was yet another small step. He opened the door and looked out onto the street, the smell of wet stone and clouds pervading the air. At least the rain had stopped for now. He thought about checking on his other contact but decided it would keep. More important was getting the whole ILGC feed thing in place. He had to make sure that the girl didn't surmise what he was up to. If he made some excuse like needing to use the bathroom on the way in, it was bound to arouse suspicion, so he needed to activate the stuff, have it in place and probably keep the treated hand safely tucked away in his pocket. With this weather, and with his penchant for long flowing coats, that shouldn't be too much of a problem for Valdor. He usually kept one hand in his pocket as he walked the streets, keeping his little friend in quick and handy reach. He hadn't thought about the rain though. Was the stuff proof against weather? He glanced up at the cloud-filled sky again and grimaced. He'd just have to take his chances with that. There was too much that he was leaving in the hand of simple fate and it didn't make him comfortable at all. All of it detail, all of it. First a brief stop at Seed's to pick up the tool and then back to his place.

oOo

All the way back to his accommodations, the weather held. There were more people out on the street now. He glanced at a couple of them as he passed, but there was nothing to arouse his suspicion. Once or twice, he stopped in front of shop displays, seemingly to browse casually what was on offer, but also surreptitiously checking reflections.

He also glanced upward once or twice checking whether he had acquired an aerial companion, but it didn't look like it. That, of course, was harder to determine with any certainty. He made it back and into his offices without incident, fairly confident that his little excursion was not subject to any direct observation.

Once back inside, he triggered his secure desk drawer, allowing it to slide out, and digging into his pocket, ostensibly to replace the small weapon he kept there, but also revealing the little present that Nathan Seed had left with him. He crossed to the shelves, poured himself a brandy, as much to get rid of the taste left by Rimmel's dreadful kahveh, then pulled out his chair and sat. He placed his weapon on the desktop, as if it was an oversight and he'd simply forgotten to put it back, then he thumbed on his display and called Tsinda.

"Hello. What progress?"

"Almost there," she said. "I need perhaps about fifteen minutes more, then we'll be ready. As much as we can be, anyway."

"Good. Once you're done, we can review it here. My office."

"Right."

"And Marina?"

"Yes, yes. It's all set up. She's expecting us in a couple of hours."

Valdor grimaced at that. He needed to perform a bit of a juggling act.

"I'll tell you what. Come to my office about half an hour before we need to leave. I want to review some market stuff in the meantime. Just let me know when you're on your way."

Benevolent

If she was suspicious, there was not a trace of it in her response. And why should she be anyway? Now he was getting paranoid. He glanced down at Seed's container lying there accusingly in his drawer. He glanced at the weapon, and then decided he'd leave it there, glanced up at the time display and nodded. For just a moment, he considered applying the paste and then pulling on some gloves, but he had no idea what impact that might have, so decided against it. No best to be simple. The more complicated a plan was, the more potential failure points existed. He kicked some of his algorithms into life on his display, watching some of the curated feeds scrolling through news items, market responses, prices. Of course Sapporan was still all over the feeds, but that was to be expected. He cupped his hands around his glass and scanned the displays with bare attention. To any casual observer, he'd be going through his usual routine. Instead, as he slipped slowly at the glass, he was running the plans through his head, poking at them from different angles and searching for weaknesses. The biggest one that he could see was that so much of what he planned now was reliant upon simple chance. Valdor didn't like that. He far preferred that he was the one well and truly in control.

Chapter Thirty-One

Belshore

"Mahra Kaitan, thank you for agreeing to this."

"Valdor Carr," she said.

"Ah, you have your little friend with you," he said.

"Always, Mezzer Carr, always."

"What's his name again?"

"Chutzpah. No reason why you'd remember."

"Right," he said. "Right."

She couldn't tell very much about where he was from the cast. There was some sort of generic blue-white lighting in the background and that was it. There was the chair he sat in and Carr himself, looking perhaps a little more worn than last time she'd seen him. She supposed that the view she presented was pretty much the same on her end, because this location, some building that looked like nothing from the outside, was also free of identifying features. She'd followed the instructions, turned up, been ushered inside by faceless individuals in non-descript gear with few words, just those necessary to get her seated and the whole thing rolling.

"I have to say, the nature of your message is interesting," said Mahra. "Why the intrigue?"

"I thought it might get your attention. These are secure channels, and what I have to tell you is one of the reasons for the secrecy."

"All right. But why me, Mezzer Carr?"

"You can call me Valdor. Where we are has taken us well beyond formality."

"Fine, but again, why me?"

"I'll get to that, but first I need to fill you in on a couple of details, and please, hear me out, because some of it's going to sound a little bit like a grand conspiracy theory, but you'll have to believe me when I tell you that it's more than a theory. And please, please, hear me out. We have a limited time on this channel, and I need to make the best of it. Next time we talk, it will be on a different carrier."

"If there is a next time...."

"Oh, I think you..." He lowered his gaze and lifted one hand. "All right. Yes."

At the moment, she was feeling nothing from Chutz, but then she'd never really been in a circumstance like this. She doubted whether his senses could extend that far across the reaches of space. Regardless, the fact that he seemed to be at ease, made her more ready to continue.

Carr lifted his gaze again and continued speaking.

"Let me start by telling you that on New Helvetica, there's a program of human enhancement going on in a number of clandestine facilities. I am involved in the program in an oversight role."

"You'll forgive me if I don't find that surprising," said Mahra. And in the end, it was just the sort of thing she'd expect from Valdor Carr. "And really, I am already wondering what that has to do with me, unless you are planning bringing me into the program, because for now, I think I have all the enhancements I need. Partially thanks to you, I might add."

"Yes, I acknowledge that, but please," he said. "The aim of this program is to replace the CoCee and act as a military enforcement arm of an organisation that intends to take over all of the civilised worlds that make up the membership of the Combined Council."

"And still…."

"I think the next thing that I'm going to tell you might change your mind."

"And what might that be. So far, Mezzer Carr, Valdor, I am beginning to lose interest. Unless this represents an opportunity for me, some sort of real contract, then I really do have better things to do."

She was already suspicious of the man, and nothing she'd seen of him in the past had given her any reason to trust him. Valdor Carr was generally out for the betterment of Valdor Carr, nothing else.

"Well," he said. "Let's say I told you that the Sirona are working for that organisation too."

He paused, waiting for the statement to sink in.

"What?"

"The Sirona are nothing more than a mercenary force working for that organisation. They probably do work for others too, but I know for a fact that the actions on Kalany, those on Sapporan, were undertaken at the behest of this group I'm talking about. I don't know what the recompense might have been or how that happened, but I do know that it was not their own initiative. The Sirona were merely weapons for hire pointed in the right direction."

"What? Who? I mean…."

Benevolent

Mahra's voice trailed off as she thought through the implications of that statement. If it was true, how long had that been going on? How about the devastation back on The Cradle? Were they working for someone else then too? Was it the same people. The questions kept popping into her head, one after the other. She tried to shake them away. Chutz was clearly picking up on her mental turmoil, because he started to become jittery as well.

"How do you know this, Valdor Carr? How do you know?"

"Oh, believe me, I know, first hand. I've dealt with them before, but I've seen…."

She was still processing.

"I can see that this means something to you, Mahra, as I thought. I remember your history. I don't know what I can say to convince you what I'm saying is true but believe me it is."

Finally, she found some words. "Okay, I can appreciate that, but again, why me? I'm nobody." She gave a short laugh. "Navigator and bodyguard for hire who sees things when she's on board a ship and sometimes off it. That's me. So, yes, tell me, why me?"

"I know you," he said slowly. "I have seen where you're loyalties lie. I think I can trust you. Forgive me for saying so, but I also think that what you do and what you want, what drives you is fairly uncomplicated. I don't think Mahra Kaitan has any hidden agendas."

She blinked at that, thought about it for a moment. Maybe he was right, but still…uncomplicated?

"So…?" she said finally.

"The organisation we're talking about runs deep, has been around for a long time, and I don't know how far their reach might extend or where they might have resources. I do not doubt that they have people within the CoCee, but, and this is the thing, if we are going to put a stop to their agenda, I think we are probably going to need the CoCee's help to achieve that, reluctant as I am to admit it. I cannot do it on my own. These people's resources and reach are too great."

Mahra held up a hand. "Stop."

"What?"

"How am I supposed to believe any of this? And I'm sorry to have to say this but coming from you as well. I've seen you in the past. I've seen what motivates you. Why get involved? Why this sudden turn of conscience? What's in it for Valdor Carr?"

He nodded then, apparently accepting what she was saying to him, about him.

"Yes, I know. You have no reason for believing any of this is true. You might understand this though. Valdor Carr has never been beholden to anyone but Valdor Carr. I have been my own master and everything I've built has been because of my choices. Everything I have lost along the way has been because of my choices. I have learned from those mistakes and I might have burned some others along the way, but that's all to me, for me. My choices. Now, the Sirona and their paymasters are taking that away from me. More than that, they are intending to take the capacity to choose away from all of humanity. Every one of us. I cannot allow that to happen. Not without a fight." The last few words he said with a set jaw. "If they do that, it all becomes meaningless. I have to be able to choose. I have to be able to act. We all do. They may spout worthiness and idealism, but the only people this group is serving is themselves. And at what cost?"

Benevolent

He was staring at her with a fixed intensity almost palpable over the distance of the feed.

"So yes. It may not be what you might expect, but it's something I need to do. I've never made any secret of the fact that most of what I do is far from selfless, but this is different. We need to find a solution before it's too late. Hopefully you also want to be part of a solution. It's up to you Mahra Kaitan. You have the choice."

For the moment, Valdor Carr seemed to have run out of words.

Mahra stared back at him. Words seemed to have deserted her as well.

"Think about it," he said after a lengthy silence, and he reached forward and cut the connection.

Chapter Thirty-Two

Sapporan Space

Despite the orders, Timon was just as tempted to land and have them go looking for Mahra themselves. There was nothing to be seen up here and nothing to see down below. Their navigator was proving to be next the useless and all of it was beginning to tighten the muscles in his shoulders and make him grind his teeth together.

"Fire, Jay, we should get down there, don't you think now? The crews are all too busy and there's nothing going on up here. It seems like there's a bit of property damage and clean-up. The coms systems are out but they'll come back eventually. We need to be doing something. Are we sure she was here?"

"Well, that's what Garavenah said wasn't it?"

"Yes, yes, I know. I just feel so…useless."

"Well, you've changed your tune, Commander Pellis," said Jayeer. "Unless you are simply using Mahra as an excuse to keep yourself from getting too bored, because I can see that as a possibility too."

Timon turned to look at him, narrowing his eyes. It seemed he was serious, although sometimes it was hard to tell with Jay.

Benevolent

"Gah," he said and turned to look out of the functionally limited viewports, having to stretch a little to see out properly. "It's been nearly three days that we've been stuck up here. Nothing. Simply nothing. How long before we are allowed to give it up and find something useful to do. We'll probably need to restock soon, no?"

Jay pursed his lips. "You know full well that we have enough provisions for at least three weeks, and now, with the jump drive, I would remind you that it is hardly necessary."

"Fine," said Timon. "Kurasa. Anything?"

"Nothing, Commander."

Timon gave a low growl. "Okay, enough. We are going down there."

"If you're sure…."

"Yes I'm bloody sure. Let's see for ourselves what those little buggers have wrought. I'm pretty sure it's them, and you should be too, Jayeer."

"You're right. I would find it hard to believe it was anyone else."

"Right then. It's settled."

Satisfied with at least that, Timon kicked *The Nameless* into life.

"Commander, forgive me for saying," said Kurasa over the com. "But should you—"

"You are not forgiven. And you are not saying any more," said Timon. "Just sit there, shut up and keep your eye out like you are supposed to be doing."

Any further words died in Kurasa's throat.

As they broke through the thick cloud cover, relying as much on their own instrumentation as anything else, the extent of the damage became clear. Large chunks of material lay scattered over the landscape. The sight of crews surrounding them, working to break them down, salvage what could be saved, was like a swarm of insects around fallen food. Jayeer pointed towards the port area, and Timon began to steer them in that direction. There were a few ships parked, but most of their own fleet were dispersed, landing instead in areas that gave the greatest access to places that needed their help. Timon tutted at what he saw.

"What would be the point of all that, Jay? I mean it seems somewhat vindictive," he said. "Do you think it's some form of retaliation for our little encounter before."

"It's hard to say," said Jayeer. "Who knows their motivation? Very little what they do has ever made sense to me. I thought they were supposed to be traders. I would think they are going to be doing very little trade from now on though."

Timon sighed. "Unfortunately, neither will Sapporan by the looks of things. Not for a long while. Not for a very long while."

As he set *The Nameless* down, started unstrapping himself, he was shaking his head.

"I don't know, Jay," he said. "There's something not quite right about all of this. Anyway, I'm going to start asking around. You might get to the control room, see if there's a record of that ship, if you can get any sense out of them."

"Commander," Kurasa called from up in the pod as Timon was off the com directly for the moment. "What shall I do?"

"I don't know," said Timon. "Wait there? Watch a feed. Sing a song. I don't know. I don't think we'll be that long. It's up to you."

There was only silence in response. Perhaps the young man was getting the impression that Timon was none too impressed with him.

"Do you think I hurt his feelings?" he said quietly to Jayeer, and then ducked out of the bridge and strode down towards the lock.

Chapter Thirty-Three

New Helvetica

Tsinda had finally sent him the requested report, and he scanned it superficially before taking a copy to a sliver and palming it, trying to be as surreptitious as possible. He had other plans for the information. Ostensibly, it was for the requested meeting with Marina, a review was how he was going to frame it, but the real destination was much further away. He crossed to the shelves, made a show of pouring himself a brandy and slipped the sliver into one of the books. He simply could not allow himself to transmit the report by any other means, just in case his systems were being monitored and if The Benevolent had access to the resources they hinted at, top class monitoring routines would be well within their capacity. Of course his naturally suspicious nature helped frame these decisions. Along with the report, and the digging expedition he was about to embark upon with Tsinda and Marina, it should give him enough he hoped. He had no doubt about Tsinda's smartness now, her capacity to read and ascertain what things, actions, turns of phrase might mean, but Valdor wasn't bad at that game either. Tsinda had made her allegiances quite clear. Nonetheless, in this particular case, he preferred getting closer to the source for this exercise. Satisfied that the sliver was properly stashed, he crossed back over to his desk carrying the glass. He arranged himself, pulling up a few of his monitoring routines, and then waited, glass in one hand, elbow on his desk propping up his chin as he scanned the displays. It wasn't too long before the girl arrived.

"Valdor?" she said. "We should leave."

"Right, right," he said, feigning distraction. "Sorry, I was just caught up in one of the companies I've been monitoring."

Tsinda glanced at the display and nodded.

"Good," said Valdor, hand hovering, making a show of looking at one last piece of data before shutting down the feeds.

He placed his glass down, crossed, pulled on his coat, and moved to the elevator.

"Aren't you forgetting something?" said Tsinda.

He turned to look at her. She was looking pointedly at the desk, particularly at the drawers and she inclined her head in that direction. All of a sudden his heart dropped. How could she know? He'd been very careful, even up to the preparation, all over the heel of his left hand where he had hoped it wouldn't be disturbed by a casual touch.

"What?" he said, almost catching his breath, but making sure to keep his outward demeanour calm.

"I've never seen you go out without a weapon, Valdor. Not once."

"I...of course, you're right," he said. "I suppose it's just how close we are. It's distracting me."

He crossed back to the desk, triggered the concealed drawer, and withdrew his small weapon and placed it in his pocket. The fist with the Seed's paste on it, he shoved deep into the same pocket. Of course he would be asked to surrender the weapon once they arrived at ILGC, but it all added to the picture of normalcy he was trying to convey. He was not at all surprised that Tsinda had noticed. It was those little things, those small, sharp observations, that gave the lie to what she was pretending to be, and over the last couple of days, though she had most certainly been observing him, he had been watching her in turn.

Once out on the street, he picked up his pace, striding purposefully, Tsinda in tow. Her diminutive frame, compared to Valdor meant that she had to hurry to keep up, forestalling any real attempt at conversation, which suited Valdor just fine. As they reached the offices, barely a word had passed between them. As he predicted, he was relieved of the weapon, they were directed to the appropriate elevator and it whisked them up to the floor with the shielded room. Of course they were expected, and no doubt Marina had requested that Tsinda be in attendance too. It actually suited Valdor's plans, because she could help explain what she'd put together, give a little more credence to Valdor's own stated concerns.

"Valdor, lover," said Marina as the doors slide open. "I understand from Tsinda that there may be some potential issues."

"Yes, that's right," he told her.

He moved into the room, trailing his hand along the underside of the curved upper back of one of the white couches. He made a show of removing the coat and she gestured towards a rack standing at one side of the room. He nodded, draping the coat over one arm, crossed to the indicated rack and placed the coat there, making sure to wipe his hand along the coat hook on one of the trees and also along the one that now held his coat. He turned, rubbing his

Benevolent

hands together. Marina indicated one of the couches, but instead, Valdor moved to one of the single chairs placed around the room, let his arms drape over the edges and slid his palms along both sides. Hopefully that would be enough, but now it was time to move onto the other business.

"You know how I am, Marina. I like to make sure things are in place, that the whole chain is thought through properly."

"I do, Valdor. I do. One of the reasons the group agreed to my choice for this particular task."

"Yes, well, understanding where we are, I need to be comfortable that there are other areas, not directly within my control, that are being taken care of. A proper outcome would demand that the right things are in place at the right time. You know that. Weakest link in the chain and all that. What is out of my control is…well…out of my control."

"All right," said Marina, leaning forward.

Valdor turned to Tsinda then, who had taken a seat on one of the couches opposite. "For the purposes of this discussion, I had asked Tsinda to prepare a status report, where we are, what our logistics needs are, if transport is not in place, the implications, etc., so that we have a full picture."

"So what is it you're missing, lover?" said Marina.

"If we look at the timeline projections, you can see that we're going to need transport, accommodation facilities, plus, if, as I believe, these enhanced resources are going to be used in various, policing or enforcement actions, then there's the whole question of appropriate ships, jump drives, all of that. I need to know what the plans are for the next wave and I am presuming a wave after that. I need to have the moving parts set in my head to be able to achieve optimal efficiency and cost effectiveness with what we're doing here."

Marina seemed to be accepting his concerns without any real difficulty. It was just the sort of thing that that Valdor would have been obsessing over in his past incarnation.

"All right, so show me, Tsinda."

Tsinda moved from her position on the couch sat next to Marina and then manipulated a small display unit. As she walked Marina through the projections, there were occasional nods, a pointed finger, a question. Marina had always had a good business sense, but she was nowhere in Valdor's league. He was quite sure that some of the implications were slipping past her. Hopefully, that would prompt a meeting of those involved, which was exactly the outcome he was aiming for.

"I see," said Marina finally. "But…no, wait. Let me paint a picture for you Valdor."

"Are you sure that—" said Tsinda, but Marina held up a hand to still her.

"While the relief efforts on Sapporan are underway, most of the CoCee forces will be occupied on the ground. Before the rest of the enhanced commercial fleet is ready to turn up and assist, there will be a second attack. Those available CoCee forces policing will be devastated. We have no doubt that our little friends will be quite capable of making that happen. Then they will concentrate on the ground forces. It will be a tragedy, but it will show how clearly the CoCee is toothless, unable to deal with the slightest alien threat, let alone a large one. When all is lost, our people will sweep in, dealing a vast blow to the alien forces, effortlessly driving them back and reasserting sovereignty. It will become clear that it is newly formed Union of Worlds that are the only choice for delivering humanity's salvation. Ta da!" she said holding her hands wide.

"The Union of Worlds?"

Marina shrugged. "Well, of course, lover. We have to have a badge, a flag, a rallying point. Of course it's us, but…."

Tsinda was watching her with slightly narrowed eyes and she glanced in Valdor's direction. Valdor made sure to keep his face as neutral as possible.

"I see," he said finally, then after a pause, "but you understand my concern."

"Of course, Valdor, of course. At the moment, ship production is underway, barracks are being constructed."

"Can I ask where?"

Tsinda's hand shot out then, touching Marina's forearm. Marina glanced at her.

"That's unimportant," she said. "Just be assured that it's happening. Every step has been thought through. We have some excellent minds taking care of what needs to be done. All we need from you is to make sure that some of these crucial steps happen and happen well. I have always been able to rely on you Valdor. Always there when I needed you. Nothing had changed."

"All right," he said after a pause. "I've done my part. You're aware of my concerns. Everything you've told me tells me that this needs to be a tightly coordinated plan. Unless all the parts work, none of it will."

Marina stared at him.

"Be assured…."

"Yes, yes, Marina. I know. My place is to make sure that my part works as it's meant to. Well, I can assure you that's happening, but a proportion of that part, my part, is ensuring the dependencies are catered for. If you are telling me that everything's in place, then I have to trust that. If it's not, there could be unintended consequences, including the failure of the entire enterprise. Just so you are aware."

He stood them having made his point. He crossed, retrieved his coat, pulled it on, still facing the wall, trying very hard to supress a slight smirk that threatened to play across his lips. He turned back to face them.

"I'm going back, Tsinda. Do you want to join?"

She chewed at her bottom lip for a moment. "No, that's all right. I'll stay for a little while, work through some more of the figures with Marina."

Her attention wasn't on Valdor as she said this. She still had her focus on the woman sitting beside her, the woman that Valdor had thought he had known once upon a time. How things changed. He turned and walked towards the elevator.

"Fine," he said, then after a moment. "Can you let me out, Marina?"

"Yes, of course. Sorry."

Moments later and the elevator doors opened. Valdor stepped inside without bothering to turn as the doors slid shut behind him. Down in the lobby, he crossed to the security station and retrieved his weapon.

"See you soon, Mezzer Carr," said the boy sitting at reception.

Valdor lifted a hand in response and stepped out onto the street. Once outside, he flexed his hand. Hopefully Seed's stuff would do its job and hopefully, Valdor himself

Benevolent

had done enough for that to happen. He looked down at his palm. Hopefully also the stuff wasn't going to have any lingering effects. With a grimace, he shoved the hand back into his pocket and headed away from ILGC. He had bigger things to think about.

Chapter Thirty-Four

New Helvetica

As Tsinda was now currently occupied, Valdor thought he could usefully make his way to Seed's place to check that what he'd done was sufficient. It didn't take him long to reach the shop and Seed was there, available and welcomed him in.

"Well, well," said Seed, beckoning Valdor to follow his lanky frame. "My little toys seem to have done the job, and timing could not be better. I don't know what you did, but already this some action underway."

"I hoped there would be," said Valdor. "I also hope that you're taking a record."

"Who do you think I am, Valdor Carr? Who do you think I am?"

"Yes, well, just checking."

Nathan Seed's technology had effectively managed to hijack the distance cast, feeding a collective viewpoint somehow stolen from each of the individual signals and melded together into one coherent whole. Valdor leaned forward eagerly, waving his hand at Seed.

"Sound," he said.

"Yes, of course, sorry."

Benevolent

The words became clearer.

"Do we need to worry about your little pet, Marina?"

Valdor grimaced at that but leaned in studying the speaker.

"Who is that?" he said.

Seed just shook his head and Valdor turned back to the feed.

Marina was in the process of assuring the others that her choice was sound. Valdor spent the time to study each of the participants in turn. A couple he recognised. There was that androgynous religious leader from the something-or-other Cluster. What was it they followed? Something called Alta, he thought. His/her name was Fern, or Fran or something like that. And the next one he recognised without hesitation, having had his own dealings with the man in the past, Ananda Luck. He was all over all sorts of industries, quite useful as a contact and a supplier both. It didn't surprise Valdor that Luck was also involved. His resources were enormous. And that was Eleni Kraus if he was not mistaken, the gold facial decorations served to identify her. She had deep roots in planetary aristocracy, again another that he was not too surprised to see. He was still struggling with that first speaker. Another member turned towards Fren…that was his/her name, Valdor was sure now.

"So, how are the quarters?" he asked Fren.

"They are virtually complete, well within one of the major Altan campuses. May the light of Alta illuminate their efforts." Fren steepled his/her fingers and bowed slightly.

The questioner turned back to Marina. "Karl is right, though Marina, I am becoming less comfortable with the Carr equation. We might have to do something about it. Surely we can find someone else to replace him."

"I don't think that would be wise, Dareth. He's very good at what he does, and he is ultimately beholden to us. It would not be in his best interests to do anything that doesn't support our goals. Valdor Carr has always been about the best interests of Valdor Carr."

"Yes, well, we'll see about that, Marina," said Valdor quietly to the feed, but now he had one more name, and with that small prompt, he recognised the man now. Dareth Garin. He'd been associated with ag world politics for some time.

"How's the ship production going, Luck?" That was from the one called Karl. "Are we ready."

"All production is at capacity. Final vessels should be rolling off the Ramada production facilities as we speak." Luck inclined his head in the questioner's direction. There was nothing about the man that was familiar to Valdor, but he had just gained another clue with the mention of Ramada. He knew of luck's Ramada facilities. Of course if it was production and manufacturing of any sort, Luck's empire had many arms. Thinking about it, he was pretty sure that ship production had been one of them. That would fit perfectly.

There was another voice then, one that didn't seem to be associated with any of the feeds that he could see.

"I do not need to remind any of you that we are mere days away from what we are about to deliver. It is nothing less than humanity's salvation. I do not need to tell any of you that, but you should not forget it."

Valdor glanced over at Seed, frowning.

"I don't know," said Seed. "If it's part of the cast, it should be there."

"Well who the hell is it?"

Benevolent

"Whoever it is has to be applying some pretty sophisticated masking technology. Whatever it is, is very, very good."

"Hmm," said Valdor. The unknown voice had gone quiet again.

"So, two unknown," he continued. "One of them masked. One we just don't know, but his name is Karl something. Luck we have for sure. Eleni Kraus. That Fren individual. And the Garin guy. Add in Marina and that makes seven. Not a bad number for a cabal."

"Should you be worried?" asked Seed.

"Probably, but I think I can keep it under control for now. One thing's for sure though now."

"And that is?"

"A lot is riding on my contacts at the other end. If we are likely to have any success here, it's going to depend on what they can do. And as uncomfortable as I am saying it, a lot is going to depend on the capabilities of the CoCee. I'm not sure I can comfortably say that I trust that at all."

Valdor turned back to the feed. He couldn't be sure if Tsinda was still there or not, whether she was allowed to be in the meeting. If she was, then it was clearly only as an observer. If not, then he probably needed to get back to his place fairly smartly. Everything was becoming a juggling act now and he couldn't afford to trip, or it was all going to come crashing down around his ears. He needed to get the report over to Rimmel and also whatever more could be gleaned from this cast. He needed to be able to send the cast recording through as well, as further backup to the report. First steps had been accomplished though, and he felt a sense of satisfaction in that much. The feeling was a little tarnished by the confirmation of how little Marina had really thought of him. Deep down, he had known it, had reached that conclusion for himself, but it didn't matter what came with such an awareness, having it confirmed to his face was something else entirely.

"Thanks for this, Nathan."

"Sure. As long as you're going to make it worth my while, of course."

"Do you doubt it?"

He laughed. "Oh, no. Not at all. Having a look at that stuff though, I am more than a little worried about you still being around to make good."

"Hmmm." He wasn't wrong. Valdor was now entering into an arena of significant risk. But that was okay. A bit of risk always sharpened the senses, kept him on his toes. "I think I'm okay for now," he said. "If I'm not, I'll let you know."

"And if you're not," said Seed. "I would instead ask you to keep yourself a significant distance from me and my operations." His face was deadly serious.

Valdor raised his hands in placation.

"Of course. No need to worry about that."

He just didn't need Seed off side for the moment. Well, he'd prefer not to have him off side at all, ever.

There was some unrelated conversation going on in the feed at the moment, but Valdor thought he had what he needed for now.

"Can you package this up for me some way? I will try to be back for it later if I can engineer it. May take a bit of manoeuvring, but I need to move quickly. As you heard, there's not a lot of time to have things in place."

"And how are you going to ensure that, Valdor?"

He fixed Seed with a steady eye.

Benevolent

"Sheer luck and good fortune mixed with a capacity for decent planning."

"Well, I hope that luck holds out," said Seed.

"So do I, Nathan," he said, standing. "So do I. See you soon, hopefully."

Chapter Thirty-Five

Belshore

Mahra had been waiting for a follow-up, but nothing had come through and she was starting to become a little frustrated with the whole thing. She went out for a walk, occasionally checking her feeds, but still nothing. Finally, in the end, she and Chutzpah ended up in their usual bar. She was already on her second drink when she received an alert.

"Now," she said. "It has to be now. I don't know, Chutz, these people have absolutely no consideration."

She put down the drink and read through the message. This Rimmel was requesting another call. It had to be Carr. The problem was, they wanted her to show up in the early hours of the morning. She'd had that before. It was often an issue when communication with other worlds. You never knew how to synchronise times. Yes, there were algorithms for doing that stuff, but in the end, most people just didn't bother. Everyone just ended up living with it, no matter what time of day arrived. She sighed and pushed the drink away from her, the glass still two-thirds full.

"As I said," she told Chutz. "No consideration. Not that I'd expect any."

Now she had more time to kill, and no idea what she was going to do to fill it. She supposed she could take

Benevolent

another run at the CoCee facility and see if their hardened stance had shifted any, but she doubted it. She also doubted whether Jayeer and Timon would be back, though she had a pretty good idea where they'd be. From the feeds, it looked like relief work would be ongoing for some time. She glanced up at the display above the bar. The whole Sapporan situation was still dominating, but it was already starting to fade as a priority story. The Kalany attack had only really lasted for about a week and then it had simply slipped away. People had no capacity for retention. Not Mahra Kaitan though. She was never going to forget. And if what Carr had said was true….

The Sirona had to pay. Whoever was behind them had to pay too. If she could do anything to make that happen, then she was going to be fine with that. Of course, there were still too many unanswered questions. Perhaps she'd never find answers for some of them.

After thinking about her options, staring at the untouched remainder of her drink, she simply wandered back to her hotel, grabbing a quick takeaway meal then slumped in front of a series of lifestyle and fashion feeds, flipping through them as there was nothing that sparked her interest. There was some sort of deep, moody criminal drama, but knowing what was to come, she just couldn't concentrate on the intricacies of the storyline, so she flipped back to random browsing, glancing at the time display far too often. Finally, the interminable wait ended, and she grabbed her blade and headed out into the early hours. It was mid-week and the streets were fairly empty. This time of morning there was always a risk, but with Chutz's senses and her own wariness, she wasn't likely to be caught off guard. Besides, anyone who thought about messing with

Mahra Kaitan ought to think again. She was in just enough of a mood to make that more than a simple threat.

When she arrived at the building hosting the distance casting facilities, it took a while to raise someone, but finally a scratchy voice came over the door system and she was granted access. There was no one to greet her, guide her to where she was supposed to be. She climbed the stairs in semi darkness, came to the floor and wandered down the corridor that she believed was the one she had been in before. It was hard to tell, but just as she was deciding to start knocking on doors, a head popped out further down the hallway and then an arm, beckoning her forward. She tossed her chin in acknowledgement and headed to the door.

As she remembered, the space behind the door was quite a bit larger than one might expect from the outside appearances. Various blocks of equipment sat around, arrayed in seemingly random spots, none of which meant very much to her. Her host, a stocky woman with shaved head gestured to a chair sitting in the middle of an open space at one end of the room. Bluish lights shone down illuminating what was a very basic piece of furniture in a slightly ethereal glue. The woman gestured again to the chair. Clearly this wasn't a time for conversation, or any words at all. Mahra raised her eyebrows and then turned to the chair and took up her place. She lifted a hand, checked Chutz, but he seemed to be fine. She relaxed a little. If Chutzpah was at ease, that was generally a good sign. The woman nodded to her and an image blossomed into a column of pastel light in front of her. It was Carr.

"Mez Kaitan," he said.

"Mezzer Carr."

"What time is it there?"

Benevolent

"Far too early, or far too late, depending on how you look at it."

"I'm sorry about that, but there have been some further developments since last we spoke. I have more idea about The Benevolent's plans and they involve a significant threat to the CoCee's fleet and operation. Just prior to this, I had a report put together showing production capability, facility locations and numbers of the enhanced forces. I have a good idea of some of the significant membership of The Benevolent, and also where their major fleet production is occurring."

He was all efficiency, rattling through the points one after the other, as if he was in a hurry to get through everything.

"You have been busy," she said.

He seemed to ignore the lightness of her statement. "This is quite urgent, and we need to be prepared for what's to come," he said.

"All right."

"The Benevolent are planning another attack using the Sirona as their strike force again. The intent is to damage the CoCee beyond recovery, humiliate them. They then plan to stage a sweeping victory with their own forces, showing to all that they are the superior force. The Sirona are mere hired actors in this charade."

"That sounds like quite a stretch, Valdor Carr," she said after a moment. "How is anyone supposed to believe all this? Even if I did, how am I supposed to convince anyone that this is going on? I can't even get access to the CoCee anymore. What am I supposed to do?"

Valdor shook his head. "No, Mahra, this is not going to be easy. That's why I sent you the material. When you see the feed, see who it involves and what they're discussing there will be no doubt. We have to be very careful. Very, very careful. The Benevolent have people in places you might not expect. Or maybe you would. I don't know."

Mahra did not know what to believe. "How am I supposed to...?"

"I don't know. That's up to you, Mahra. Do you want to strike a blow against the Sirona? Is that of any interest to you at all? Do you want to end up with freedom of choice or being subject to the rule and whims of people who think they know better than your what's good for you and for the rest of humanity?"

Again there was that fervour in his voice and in his expression. Somehow, she thought, she had underestimated Valdor Carr. She was a little taken aback by his passion, but he had chosen the words carefully, clearly designed to work against Mahra's specific trigger.

Again he pushed. "Do you want the Sirona to win...again?

She couldn't take any more of it.

"No," she yelled at him through closed teeth. "No...," and then "No!"

He sat back, apparently satisfied. "Well, you need to do something about it then," he said calmly.

"But I really still don't see...."

"You'll find a way. I'm sure you will. Watch the feeds. Look at the reports. Spend the next couple of hours working out what you've got to do, because seriously, I believe that's all you have. The CoCee needs to be warned, but at the same time, they need to be convinced. I don't know who you've been talking to there, but it needs to be someone who has enough influence, but at the same time, you feel you can trust."

She simply looked back at him. There weren't any words.

"Good," he said finally. "If you need to get through to me, you can do so via Lars Rimmel. Not direct. It's too risky."

He nodded and the cast was gone.

The bluish light illuminating her spot, winked out.

The woman who had set everything up had been lurking in background, and right then she emerged from the shadows.

"This way," she said. "Your choice. You can either look at the stuff here or take it away. Doesn't matter to me." She had an accent Mahra couldn't place, but now was neither the time or the place to try to find out. She was still a bit worked up after Valdor's assault on her sensibilities.

"Sooner the better," she said. "Lead the way."

"What do you want first?" asked the woman. "There's a couple of files or there's a recorded cast."

"Give me the cast."

The woman nodded and Mahra took the indicated seat. The recorded images blossomed into life in small form in front of her. It was a little hard to hear what was going on at first and she waved behind her, pointing at her ear, and lifting her hand up. Immediately the sound increased. As she watched, it was clear that Valdor had been telling the truth. She too recognised a couple of the faces. She was surprised to see Larit Fren among them. She'd come across the whole Altan philosophy, religion, whatever you wanted to call it on a couple of the worlds she'd visited. Fren was a familiar figure. Mahra would have thought that The Benevolent's plans would have been somewhat in contrast to the teachings of Alta. But then, how many times had it emerged that what was said in public and what went on behind the scenes were two completely different things? Betterment of humanity? Perhaps it fit in some strangely twisted way. She didn't want to think about the levels of self-justification it might take. Or maybe it was delusion. None of that mattered though. What mattered was that Fren's presence gave credence to Valdor's claims. She half recognised another of the faces, but she couldn't place it. Perhaps someone at the CoCee would be able to identify them.

She let the feed trail off and sat back. She could barely believe what she'd just witnessed and was almost tempted to watch the whole thing again. She sat back on the chair and tried to still the feeling of outrage that was growing inside her.

"Unbelievable," she said.

"That's some pretty nasty stuff," said the woman from the corner.

"You watched."

"Yeah. Hard to believe."

Mahra shook her head. "I'd better take a look at the files."

Her helper crossed, called them up and flipped them onto the display. Mahra skimmed through. There were all sorts of figures, numbers, graphs, risk assessments. Not a lot of it meant anything to her. She closed the first one, turned her attention to the second, but it was more of the same, this time with graphics.

"Yeah, no," she said. "I'm sorry, what's your name?" said Mahra.

"Liyanne." She shrugged. "Not important really."

Benevolent

"It should be," said Mahra. "Tell me, did you recognise anyone in the cast, Liyanne?"

"Yeah," she said. "There was that religious nutjob, but there was that other one. The politician, noble, whatever her name is. The one with all the gold. Her. Kraus I think, Always thought she was immensely entitled, full of herself. If there was a word, I would say it was 'privileged.'"

Mahra nodded. She glanced at the time display. There was still time.

"Can we watch it again?" she asked.

"Sure," said Liyanne. "I might be able to pin a name on another of them."

"Okay. Let's try."

Liyanne hunched down close and Mahra felt Chutz tense.

"It's all right," she told him. "She's with us."

Chapter Thirty-Six

Belshore

By the time she left Liyanne, day was already starting to break. Liyanne had provided her with a couple of slivers, one containing the reports and the other, the recording of the damning distant cast. She had only one option now and that was Garavenah. Mahra thought that if there was anyone she could trust, it was Garavenah. She'd known her long enough, seen the desire to do right under the chain of command thing. She doubted very much that Garavenah would be anyone's plant within the CoCee. A desire to stay away from official notice and simply come in the side door with the help of a friend had driven her last few attempts. All that was different now.

There were no strict hours at the CoCee compound, and she knew there'd always be someone at the gate. Not surprisingly a guard stepped out to stop her once again, but she'd been expecting it.

"Mahra Kaitan, here to see Brigadier Commander Garavenah Lish."

The name gave the guardsman immediate pause. He stepped inside and checked something, only to return a moment later shaking his head.

Benevolent

"There's no record of any appointment," he said.

"Oh, believe me, she's going to want to see me," Mahra told him, not breaking his gaze for an instant.

"Let me check, Mez. What was that name again?"

"Mahra Kaitan."

He nodded and stepped back inside. Mahra could hear one side of a conversation from inside and he was back again.

"Brigadier Lish wants to know what this is about."

"Look, just let me speak to her. Can you bring me the com."

The guardsman pursed his lips, processed for a moment, and then turned without saying anything. Again a brief conversation and he was back once more.

"Brigadier Commander Lish," he said handing her the device.

Mahra took it and turned slightly away, not that there was any chance she wouldn't be overheard. She doubted there was any risk from the guardsman, but she was reluctant to share too much over the com all the same.

"Garavenah, hi. I need to talk to you. It's quite urgent."

"Listen, Mahra. We're somewhat busy in case you hadn't worked that out. It's early. I've got quite a lot to do and agreeing to talk to you is just a courtesy."

"I understand that," said Mahra. "And I wouldn't expect anything else. You really do need to listen to me though." She kept her voice as low as she could. "There's probably another attack imminent. It's the Sirona certainly, but there's more than that, much more."

"You walked away, Mahra."

"Yes, I walked away. This is more important. You have to believe me. None of that matters. This is what matters. You have to listen to me."

"I don't *have* to do anything, Mahra." Mahra could feel she was on the verge of cutting the conversation.

"Please, Garavenah, please. Please give me a few moments. I have proof."

"Then tell me."

"I can't. You have to see it for yourself. Please."

Garavenah sighed. "All right. I can give you a few minutes, but no more. As I said, we're busy. Give me back to the guardsman. I presume you still know the way. It hasn't been that long."

"Yes," said Mahra, a sense of relief washing over her. The battle wasn't over yet though. She handed the com to the guardsman.

"Yes, Brigadier. Understood. He severed the connection and turned to Mahra. "I'll take the blade, and…."

Mahra screwed up her face and shook her head. "You can have the blade, but I think you'd regret trying to take anything else. We've both had a long night. We might be a little tired and on edge."

The guardsman looked from her face to Chutzpah already starting to bristle at her shoulder. He swallowed.

"Fine, the blade then."

Mahra nodded and handed it over. That she was prepared to allow at the moment.

The guardsman stepped back, allowed her to pass. Mahra walked into the facility, passing the first of the buildings, the landing apron virtually devoid of ships. She filled her senses with the familiar smells of the place, fuel, machinery, lubricant. She took a moment to orient herself

Benevolent

and then headed for the broad hangar building that granted access at the side to the complex of offices that lay on the upper levels. Without hesitation, she pushed the door open, entered the empty hangar, strode across the echoing space, and slipped into the corridors through the side doors. The tension, the lack of sleep was starting to wear, and she was starting to feel as if she was walking in a fog. Up the stairs, into the outer offices. There was no-one at the outer office desk. She crossed and knocked at Garavenah's door.

"Come in."

Garavenah looked up as Mahra entered. "This better be good, Mahra," she said.

"Nice to see you too, Garavenah."

"Look, I haven't got time for this game. You're the one who walked out. Tell me what you've come to say and be quick about it."

"Yes, yes. Of course you're right. Sorry." She pulled out the slivers. "Can you access these. Everything will be clear."

Garavenah waved with her fingers. "Give them here." She slotted both in, and called up the files, looking distracted. "You said something about the Sirona."

"Start with the recording first."

She did so. At first her eyes narrowed and then widened. "Fire, what is this?"

Mahra held up a hand. "Listen."

Garavenah leaned in to the display, a furrow creasing her forehead. As Mahra watched, her expression changed from disbelief to horror.

"This can't be real," she said.

"It's real," said Mahra.

"And where did you get it?"

"Before we go there, listen to the rest, get as much of the picture as you can, and then look at the other files."

Garavenah nodded and waved her to a seat.

"Wait, is that…. oh…." Garavenah stopped the feed. "I've seen enough for now. Tell me everything you know. Also where this came from and how you came to get it."

Mahra did exactly that. A couple of times Garavenah stopped her, asked for clarification. When Mahra mentioned Valdor Carr, her eyebrows rose.

"Carr," she said. "And you believe you can trust him?"

"This time I do. Everything he said made perfect sense. I don't doubt that dealing with what we're seeing is good for Valdor Carr, but as far as I'm concerned, it's also good for everyone."

"And why you?"

"For some reason, he seems to trust me, but his explanation also made sense, the Sirona connection, everything. Don't forget, he knows my history too."

Garavenah nodded, sat back thinking.

"So what now?" said Mahra.

"You were right to come to me," said Garavenah. "I need to tell…no…wait…that might be risky…."

"We need to be careful."

Garavenah nodded. "And why me?" she said in response to the last.

"The only way we are going to do this is with the CoCee. You I trust, Garavenah. I've seen enough of you to know that. My friend here also seems to have no problem with you either. That goes a long way."

Garavenah nodded. "I have to tell…," she started again and then trailed off. "I don't know."

Benevolent

"Exactly. Valdor says they have people everywhere. CoCee included."

It was clear then that Garavenah was torn. She was being pressured on the one hand by expediency and on the other by her own sense of duty. She gritted her teeth and looked away. Finally she turned back.

"We have to keep this off the sensors. I think the only way to get through this is to solve the first step, the attack. To do that, I will need you to get out to Sapporan and meet up with your old friends there. We can't be seen to be doing that." She paused for a moment and then clamped her teeth together again. "Argh, that won't work."

"What is it?"

"Well, the other thing is we're somewhat short of ships fitted with the drive here. Just about everything's already on Sapporan dealing with the crisis, and unless I'm going to flood the feeds with information that we don't particularly want out there at the moment, then we need to come at this a different way."

In the meantime, she had opened the pair of reports and was scanning through them, nodding as the figures and charts scrolled past.

"How many of those people did you recognise?" asked Mahra.

"Just about all of them," said Garavenah, focussing on her over he display. "Except of course, for the one we couldn't see. It's concerning enough who they are and the resources they have at their disposal but having an unknown as well…. It's never good."

She looked at the ceiling, again shaking her head.

"There is a way around this, I think," she said, dropping her gaze again to meet Mahra's own.

"And that is?"

"Can you get yourself to Bathyscaphe?"

"Yes, I think so."

"Well, it's ideal isn't it. If you link up with Bathyscaphe, no one should suspect anything. You are just continuing your contracted work."

"You know about that?"

"Of course I know about that, Mahra. What did you expect? Anyway, I think we know what we need to do. The rest of it we can solve as we go further. Anything more that happens on Sapporan will help make our case. As long as we are successful," she said. "As long as we are successful...."

"We haven't got a choice, do we?" said Mahra.

Benevolent

Chapter Thirty-Seven

Sapporan Space

It took only a couple of hours for everything to fall into place at the Belshore end. Mahra took the transit direct to Bathyscaphe's field, so she was spared the cool reception she had expected from Dubois. Regardless, she was already prepared for the stony-faced regard afforded her by Captain Merritt, but Nissa was there grinning and waving from the lock. Mahra nodded at the Captain and walked past him to greet Nissa. Garrick was nowhere to be seen. The Captain swivelled his head to follow Mahra, his eyes narrowed and his lips thin.

"So looks like we'll be going back," said Nissa as Mahra reached the lock. "Not sure whether I should be thanking you for that. If you leave us, we're not going to be able to get back in a hurry."

"Oh, I'm sure the CoCee will sort something out. They've got plenty of navigators out there."

Nissa shrugged. "Maybe. Maybe not. Anyway, let's get you to your station. We're leaving as soon as system checks are done." The next she said in a lower voice, her head closer to Mahra's "Don't think the Captain's too pleased about any of this."

"Is he ever pleased about anything?"

"Fair point. He's a good man underneath all that steely surface."

"I believe you. I've yet to see it though."

She didn't need the escort, but she still appreciated Nissa's accompaniment up to the pod.

"So what's this all about?" Nissa asked conspiratorially.

"I just need to be there with my old crew to check something out. That's all it is. *The Outrigger* is about the only ship equipped to get us there this month."

"Hmmm, you can't tell me more than that?"

Mahra shrugged. "Not that much more to tell."

"Fair enough."

Mahra climbed into the pod, nodded to Nissa, who then left her to perform her own preparations.

"Okay, Chutz, here we go," said Mahra as she reached for the controls.

A couple of hours later and they emerged back at Sapporan. As normal space coalesced around her, she scanned for any emergence signatures, but it seemed that for the moment, everything was clean. She turned her attention to the instrument displays. From what she could see there were only about a dozen ships in orbit. She focussed in on each of the callsigns. Half of those were freighters that had, for whatever reason chosen to hang around. Or who knew, perhaps they were new arrivals waiting around to see if there was any possibility of unloading their cargo. She could understand the sentiment having worked enough long-hauls. The last thing you wanted to do was arrive and then have to ferry your goods all the way back again. The whole point was to be able to take something else back. That's what made the enterprise worthwhile.

Benevolent

So, that meant only five CoCee ships. And there, of course was *The Nameless.* She opened the com.

"This is *The Outrigger.* Calling *The Nameless.* Requesting permission to join."

"Ha, Mahra Kaitan. What are you waiting for? Hop on over." She could picture Timon's half-grin as he said it.

"Be there in a few," she said

She wasted no time unstrapping and heading down to the bay. Garrick was already in place ready to pilot the shuttle across. There was no need for anyone else but Nissa was standing at the door as she passed, rested a hand briefly on her shoulder as she passed.

"Do good," she said.

Mahra stopped and turned to look at her. "How much do you know?" she said.

"Not much more than you told me. Captain briefed us though. Said it was something important for the CoCee and we needed to do it. Told you. He's a good man."

Mahra nodded.

"I'll try to do what I can," she said and headed over to the shuttle and climbed aboard. Garrick nodded at her, waited while she got settled and then hit the controls that closed the bay doors to the interior and cycled air. A couple of moments later and they were underway. Mahra looked out the viewport, down at the thick clouds roiling below them, not that she could see the movement from up here. It looked like some bumpily textured fabric. Something being *blanketed* in cloud certainly made sense to her. As she watched them thoughtfully, the images of the vast sections breaking through the layers took substance in her mind, and with them, the hint of an idea. For it to function, they'd have to be ready. She needed to talk to Timon and Jayeer though, see if it would actually work. Garrick maneuvered the shuttle into position and they bumped against the lock coupling once, twice, before they were married.

"Sorry," said Garrick. "Not too much call for ship to ship."

She waved his apology away. "Thanks. See you, I hope," she said.

He gave an uncertain smile in return. She stood, crossed, and opened the door. On the other side of the coupling stood an unfamiliar figure. He was decked out in CoCee Nav uniform, so she guessed he was the replacement.

"Hello," she said. "Mahra Kaitan."

"Kurasa," he said. Just that, and then sidled past her into the shuttle. Further back, behind him, partially shadowed, she recognised Jayeer's portly figure and she raised a hand. Sind beckoned her inside. She turned and watched Kurasa get settled. Good. That meant that *The Outrigger's* crew would be fine. They could get the hell away from whatever was about to erupt in Sapporan space. Unfortunately, she didn't think that the remaining freighters in orbit were going to be so lucky and that gave her a bit of an uncomfortable feeling. Perhaps they could stagger them leaving, but then telling them anything could be a risk.

"Come on, Mahra, what are you waiting for?" said Sind from inside. "Do we smell that bad?"

"Yes, sorry. I mean no, not about the smell. I just had a thought. We can talk about it in a while. I need to fill you both in before that."

"Hum, well let's get you inside."

Mahra stepped aboard *The Nameless* and the door slid shut behind her. She took the three paces between herself and Jayeer and threw her arms around him. Jayeer

Benevolent

immediately tensed, drew back, his attention completely on Chutz at her shoulder.

"Oh, come on, Jay. Still?"

He held up his hands. "Come on." He turned and headed up towards the bridge, Mahra following close behind.

Jayeer stepped in and moved aside to his place, allowing Mahra to enter. Timon turned, ran his finger and thumb spreading his moustache and grinned.

"Mahra Kaitan. So you've decided to grace us with your presence then."

"A necessary evil," she said.

"Hah. So take a place. I suppose we need to talk."

Mahra nodded and sat, took a breath, bit her lip, thinking for a moment and then started to fill them both in. It didn't take very long indeed for her to have both of their full attention.

"And you say it's Valdor Carr that set this off?" asked Timon.

Mahra nodded and Timon shook his head.

"But, anyway, we need to worry about what's coming. It depends how many ships there are on the surface."

"Most of the fleet are down there now, helping with the relief, you know," said Jay.

"That may work to our advantage, but….it has to do with Sapporan."

Timon frowned. "I'm not sure I see."

Mahra almost laughed at his choice of words. "From what Valdor said, what we saw on the recording, the plan is that the Sirona fleet comes in, quickly mops up those ships in orbit and then descends, catching those forces on the ground unawares and wiping them out. They then remain in place until the valiant Benevolent fleet of their enhanced troops arrives, dealing a crushing blow to the evil Sirona and sending them on their way. Or that's the way the story goes. We need to turn that around. We need to be prepared. We can use Sapporan to our advantage in that regard.

Benevolent

Chapter Thirty-Eight

Sapporan Space

All around her, there was blank space. They'd managed to convince a couple of the merchanters to leave, so, there were four of those left, and nothing but the half dozen CoCee ships, primed and ready, navigators on the alert. If Mahra's plan was to work, they needed to be quick on the response, very quick. She could feel Chutzpah's tension and it mirrored her own.

"Anything, Mahra?" Timon's voice over the com.

"No nothing." Her hands hovered over the weapons array. They were going to be here very soon. The Benevolent's plan relied just as much on timing as their own, and if they were to succeed, it had to happen now. Mahra reached out stretching her awareness as far as she could, alert for the slightest sign. At her shoulder, Chutzpah was doing something else. He was tense, trembling, but there was a low keening sound coming from his throat. She'd heard that before, but she couldn't afford the diversion at the moment. She couldn't remember. It had happened only once before. Whatever it was, it would keep. Her attention was elsewhere. Then there, the first tingling, the swelling in space.

"They're here," she said over the com. "Ready weapons."

"Fleet, on my signal."

It was on them now, *The Benevolent* and the other few ships that would need to weather the initial storm. After that, it would be up to all of them.

One after another, large silver ovoids popped into normal space, spread all over the field of stars. Right at that moment, Mahra hit her controls.

"Now!" she yelled.

Just to the right, she could see, actinic light pounding, concentrating fire on one of the CoCee ships. She stabbed at her controls, firing, on one, then another. The other CoCee ship was holding for the moment. It seemed the Sirona were still targeting. She had had the luxury of knowing exactly where the Sirona ships were going to be, so she was better prepared.

Then, below them—she could sense it as well as see it on the displays, all across the covering blanket of clouds, ships burst through from the positions they'd been holding within the concealing layer.

"Fire!" she yelled. "Take them out. Hit them."

There, lancing lights burst into being from all across the CoCee fleet, stabbing out, meeting silver ships. One of the incoming Sirona vessels succumbed, a moment later another.

"Fire," she yelled again. "Keep firing!"

She stabbed at her controls, willing the devastation upon them, her teeth clamped together.

It took the Sirona only moments to recover, and blue lights lanced out in return, stabbing into the CoCee fleet.

Benevolent

Two of their ships went in the next instant. There it was. The Sirona were coordinating their fire, concentrating on only a couple of ships at a time. One, then another of the CoCee ships blew apart, pieces of wreckage spiralling across the field of battle. Suddenly her displays were awash with bright blue light, her visual field disrupting into noise. She closed her eyes using her other senses and kept firing, sending beam after beam into the Sirona ships. She was too busy returning fire to be able to think, to worry about coordinating anything with the other CoCee ships.

"Damn you," she yelled at them. "Die!"

The sound in Chutzpah's throat had grown in intensity. His whole frame was quivering. His cry becoming louder and louder, hurting her ears now, but she couldn't afford to switch her attention to him, to work out what was happening.

And in the next instant, there was an all-encompassing emergence washing across her awareness.

"What the hell?" she cried.

Then there were no Sirona ships, just a field, bronze and green shapes blotting out everything, filling the viewport, alarms crying across the instruments. Once more it was there, that vast, impossible ship. The CoCee weapons washed across that surface and they were absorbed, sucked in and through, splashing against it ineffectively.

"Hold fire!" she screamed across the com. "Hold your fire!"

One by one, the CoCee weapons winked out. She could sense traces of the Sirona ships. She could tell they were still there, but everything was dominated by the vast presence in front of her. The shapes were in constant motion, forming and reforming across the entire surface, gold, bronze, green swimming like oil on water, drawing the eye to multiple places, but impossible at the same time. She was holding her breath. She had hoped she would never see that sight again, that otherness that defied her perceptions, and forced her to struggle with its reality.

"Don't whatever you do fire on it," she said over the com. "Wait. Nobody do anything."

They sat there for a few minutes, nothing happening. And then, she felt it. One by one, those traceries that were the Sirona presence winked out. She wasn't sure, but she thought that most of them had actually jumped. A few of them though, had not. They simply were not there anymore.

Mahra swallowed, her attention drawn to a revolving piece of debris moving slowly across the vast mobile surface before her.

"I think...," she said hesitantly. "I think the Sirona are gone."

"But what now?" said Timon. "What happens now?"

"I don't know," she said. "I don't know."

She couldn't see him, but she knew that he was staring out at that immense presence. All of them were.

Then she felt the first stirrings within her consciousness, a first gentle probe.

"Hello again, Mahra Kaitan."

The words formed within her mind, but they were not words, they were the concept of words, the essence of words, building little structures of knowledge in her awareness. A subtle pressure built and then faded within her head, like a pulse, a heartbeat, waves against a shore, sweeping in to overtake her mind, and then just as they felt too much, slipping away again.

Benevolent

"The Sirona are gone," said the Sleeth presence. "They will not be back."

The Sleeth presence swelled in her head, swelled, and faded, and then the words formed once more.

She narrowed her concentration. She didn't have any idea if they would be able to hear and understand her thought, her words.

"But how...why?" she sent.

She thought for a moment that she'd be left with nothing, that her thoughts were just echoing inside her own head, but then came a reply.

"Because it was asked," came the voice.

"I don't understand," Mahra thought.

"The zimonette."

"I don't understand," Mahra sent back.

"We have witnessed this before," came the words. "The zimonette, sometimes attach themselves to a species, ride along with them, adding their wisdom, their knowledge and their senses to the host. This time, they chose you. Without the zimonette, you would have been unable to do much of what you did, to sense much of what you sensed, to see what you have seen. Their wisdom is unknowable and boundless, though they do not think like many others. They work in synergy with the host species and bring them to their own version of the light. They are a very old species, an ancient race. Their intelligence is other, but it is great."

"Chutzpah?" she said. Turning to look at him. He was still. The keening had gone. He seemed at ease. She looked back to the great impossible ship before her.

"Mahra?" it was Timon's voice.

"Wait," she said. "Wait."

"They are an interesting species, the zimonette," came the multiple voices, swelling, dissipating, speaking as one, echoing inside her consciousness. "Once we were few," said the chorus. "Now we are many."

She thought they were about to slip away, and then they were back, filling her head with memory and knowledge.

"We have given him a choice."

"I don't know what..." she spoke to the empty air. Then she remembered the tricks that Aleyin had taught her what seemed like a lifetime ago. She focussed her will concentrating, seeking out the presence that lay all around her, honing in on it, not to let it slip away.

"His choice is made," they said.

As the next words expanded inside her mind, she reached up a hand to touch him, but there was nothing there. She felt, glanced around. She reached out for his presence, but she found nothing. He was nowhere. Where was he? A moment ago, he had been here. But where was he? Where had he gone? He wasn't on her shoulder anymore. She wasn't on the flight couch. Where was he?

And then she understood. Then she knew it. They had told her, Chutzpah had made a choice. That's why she couldn't find him. She understood.

She heard a voice inside her then, one that was achingly familiar and yet she'd never heard before, echoing with knowledge, and understanding, a tinge of sadness, but also a wave of inevitability. There was a finality in that voice that she could sense. It was unavoidable.

"Farewell, Mahra," he said. "I will be with you always as you will be with me. Our memory lives in fondness and it always will. We carry you with us. Be well, Mahra. Be

Benevolent

content. We will miss you, but now it is time. You are ready."

"Chutz," she said quietly as a tear welled in her eye and ran down one cheek. She reached out with her senses to find him, but he was truly gone, gone to be…what and where she didn't know. She somehow imagined that he was now a part of a larger whole, though she couldn't truly understand it. Already she could feel the ache of his absence.

More different words came then. "We gave to you, we showed you things, and we have taken. Now, as something in return, we will leave you with something else."

At first it was the slightest sensation inside her mind, like a flowing current, pushing at her rushing up and over her thoughts, her senses and filling with a cacophony of noise, pouring into her. She cried out, overwhelmed by the intensity as it rushed through and into her, filling her to bursting.

"Use it wisely, what we have given you, Mahra Kaitan," said the voice that was one and many and legion. "Perhaps one day, we shall meet again. We shall see. One day, you, all of you will be ready."

And then there was only silence.

She looked out of the viewport. The vastness, bronze green gold was separating into smaller components, large spheres and smaller ones scattering into a confusion of shapes, cluttering the space around them and then, all of a sudden, where there were many, there were none. She stared out into blank darkness, realising in that instant that she was on her hands and knees having fallen to the deck in the vastness of the assault to her mind. Slowly, gripping the edges of her flight couch, she dragged herself to her feet, still staring out at the blankness. She closed her eyes, reached out to the darkness, to the voidspace, seeking them, looking for the Sleeth, for anything, but the field was empty.

Reflexively, she reached up for Chutzpah again, but he was gone. She knew he was gone. But she had to deal with it all over again. And then the tears came properly. How could he be gone. A deep sob racked her body and then another.

"Mahra, are you okay? What just happened? They just disappeared. Mahra?" It was Timon's voice.

Haltingly, the words came out. "Yes. I'm okay," she said. "They're gone. They really are gone. So are the Sirona…for good, I think."

She reached out, looking for the trails in the void that would mark their direction, but there was nothing there, nothing but blankness superimposed upon the stars. But as she reached, a new realisation came to her. There were other traces there. She frowned. All of a sudden, she could feel other things, other places, destinations, end points. Her head was full of them. So many. So, so many. Her inner senses lit up with a multitude of possibilities. A galaxy of destinations. She drew in her breath.

She understood then what the Sleeth had done, what that vast rushing against her consciousness had been.

"Oh," she said.

She reached out again.

"Oh, my…."

"Mahra, what is it?"

"I think we are going to have some work to do, Jayeer," she said. "You're not going to believe it."

It would never make up for Chutz, ever, but it was something. She thought that they were going to be very, very busy for a long time.

Benevolent

"What do you think about…," she said reaching up to her shoulder, but then she realised once again that he was no longer there, and she bit her lip, swallowed back another sob, and closed her eyes.

"What was that?" said Timon.

"No," she said, steadying her voice. "It will keep till we get back."

"And the Sirona? They are really gone."

"Oh yes. And now we have to make sure that they don't come back. It's up to us."

"If you're sure…."

"Oh, I'm sure," she said. Let's go. We can let the others clean up the rest. We've got more work to do back there. A lot more work."

Chapter Thirty-Nine

Ramada

All over Ramada, the factories and production lines bustled. The vast stony deserts and underlying strata were mineral rich and had provided a ready source of materials for the industry that grew up there, expanded and in the end, dominated. Ramada was responsible for the production of all sorts of goods, but at the product end of the spectrum, relying on other, more technically focussed worlds for their supply of parts. That remained true, even for the vast plants producing vehicles, not only groundcars, aircraft, but space-going vessels as well. The demand for aircraft was mainly local, as the logistical problems with shipping such vast items, unless broken down into parts was problematic, and then, what would be the point? Ananda Luck had made himself a fortune by dint of his vast network of facilities and the products they shipped to market. That had enabled him to expand into shipyards, freighters in the first instance, and then later on into more martial applications, whether for mercenary forces or for planetary defence fleets. It didn't matter which; both paid equally well.

Ananda Luck was not on planet when the first of the CoCee ships appeared in the Ramadan skies. He was away on one of his country estates. Investment in the jump drive had allowed him to flit easily between his holdings and it

Benevolent

meant that life overseeing his vast estates and production facilities, had, become overall less demanding. As it was, he hated distant travel and the drive had proven to be a boon he had not expected.

He did not see the CoCee ships descend from the russet skies, landing at each of his shipyards on Ramada. He did not see those ships disgorge a number of uniformed troops who immediately took charge of each of those facilities and put them instantly into a state of lockdown.

The first inkling that he had about the state of play, was when a CoCee ship appeared above his own back gardens and descended, planting itself firmly on top of his prize carthalias.

He stood there, mouth open, wine glass in hand, not really comprehending what was happening.

Chapter Forty

New Helvetica

The Nameless set down quietly on a field in New Helvetica's outskirts. Valdor Carr was there to meet them. He stood, long grey coat slightly flapping, and his perfect hair being ruffled by the breeze generated by the ship's descent. The crew had not announced themselves to anyone and their meeting, hopefully for now, had defied observation. Traffic control had been under strict orders. Apart from Mahra, Timon and Jayeer, they carried a dozen uniformed and well-armed troops. As the ship settled, Mahra was already out of her couch and heading to the lock. She wasted no time opening it, certain that the others would be close behind.

One hand on the lock's frame, Mahra leaned out.

"Valdor," she said simply.

He nodded, waiting for her to step out properly and cross the grassy field to where he stood. His scrutiny as she approached was unashamed.

"Where's your little friend?" was the first thing he asked.

"Long story, Valdor. Not one I really want to go into at the moment." She could feel the catch in her throat, threatening more than that.

"Okay. And what about the others."

"Who?"

"The Benevolent," he said simply.

"Some of that's in progress right now. A couple already taken care of."

"Good. I would like this to be a surprise."

"Oh, I think they'll be surprised," she said and turned as Timon, Jayeer and the others stepped out of the ship and moved to join them. Valdor lifted one hand in greeting.

"Valdor Carr," said Timon. "Well, this whole thing doesn't seem to have done you much harm from what I can see."

Carr raised his eyebrows. "You'd be surprised," he said.

"Perhaps I would," said Timon. "Anyway. What is our plan."

"We can talk as we walk," said Valdor, setting off and waving for the others to follow. "I couldn't manage ground transport large enough without creating suspicion, but this spot is close enough to the buildings that we should be there in short order. Once there, I expect everything to get very frantic. Our main targets are Marina Samaris and Tsinda Bos, her sidekick. At least I think it was Bos. I only recently learned her other name," he almost muttered to himself with a little shake of his head.

"Marina Samaris, imagine that," said Timon. "Well, well."

Of course, he hadn't seen the recording. She was not one of the names that Mahra had mentioned and actually not one of the people she had recognised. She presumed it had been that woman in the white suit.

"We need to take down reception, gain control of the elevators. I am not sure where in the building she'll be, but I have a fair idea and I have access to that section through an ally of mine. Just before we get there, I'll get in touch with him and confirm. If, as you say, the others are being taken care of, I don't suppose there will be much communication back and forth, and hopefully, anything that does come through will be too confused. Either that, or they simply won't believe it. The Benevolent's arrogance knows no bounds."

Timon glanced at Mahra and raised his eyebrows. She kept her face blank. Her hand drifted towards her shoulder, but again he wasn't there, and she grimaced. He wouldn't be there ever again. She swallowed back the feeling.

They strode through some outlying buildings, drawing curious glances, but then faces turned away. The New Helvetian way of doing things was not to become involved. If any of the resort set had noticed them, they weren't in evidence. It was far too early in the day for most of them anyway. They turned a corner, and there in front of them was the ILGC building. They wasted no time, crossed the street at a rapid pace and stormed in the front. Confused faces looked up from behind reception desks. One of them looked a little less confused, more shocked and was reaching for something behind the desk. Mahra didn't wait, she charged across, blade already out.

"Stop what you're doing, now!"

The young man, lifted his hands, pushed his seat back.

"Good," said Mahra. She glanced around. The other desks had already been taken by the uniforms. Mahra turned her attention to Carr. He nodded, lowering a com device.

"There's a security station on the tenth, but my friends have already blinded that. They'll be a little confused and worried at the moment, and I suggest we send someone to deal with that."

Benevolent

Timon gestured to two of the uniforms who nodded and crossed to the elevators. They were looking around blankly for some way to operate them.

"You," Timon pointed. "Get them working. Tenth floor."

A pale looking young woman, nodded, bit her lip, and reached for something on the desk all the time under the close scrutiny of the uniform guarding her. The uniformed troops stepped into the elevator and disappeared from view.

"Marina?"

Valdor nodded. "Where I expected. Twenty-fifth." He turned back to the young woman at the control desk, and she nodded rapidly, her eyes wide. Valdor turned towards the elevator. Timon spoke to a couple of the armed troops.

"You, you, with us." He strode towards the elevator bank closely behind Valdor. Mahra came next, with Jayeer slightly behind. On either side, the two uniforms flanked them. They stepped on board and the doors slid shut behind them. Valdor had his weapon out now, Timon as well. Mahra stood with blade in hand, her fighting stance adopted, willing the car to move more quickly.

Finally the doors slid open. Valdor stepped out first. The woman who had to be Marina looked up from a display on her lap. There was someone else hovering behind her that Mahra could not see properly with Valdor obstructing her view. And then Timon stepped out. Marina stood then.

"Well, well," she said. "Valdor Carr and Timon Pellis together. Who would have thought it? Well," she gave a short laugh. "We would have."

She stood and took a step forward, after placing the display down on the couch beside her. If the unscheduled entrance had surprised her, she showed none of it. "And you appear to have brought company. She sighed then. "Not good, Valdor. I would have expected more from you, lover. You had such a future and now you're going to throw that away. Our reach is more than you can possibly imagine."

"And I think you overstate yourself, Marina," said Valdor. "You're nothing more than a lacky, just like I was supposed to be. A puppet of your precious Benevolent."

"Tut, tut, Valdor. Are you really starting to care? Anyway, none of that matters. You can take me down. The others will see to it that it just becomes a footnote to our new history."

Valdor shook his head, raised his weapon. "I'm sorry, Marina, but I can't forgive you"

Just at that moment, something triggered Mahra's senses, behind Marina, the figure that had previously been obscured by the others stepped out and raised a weapon, about to fire. None of the others seemed to have noticed and in that instant, Mahra reacted instinctively. In one smooth motion, she lifted her arm and threw. Her blade flew across the intervening space, and took the woman in the chest, knocking her back, the weapon flying from her hand and skittering across the floor.

Marina turned and cried out. "Tsinda!"

Mahra didn't hesitate, she launched herself across the couch, landed in a crouch, reached for her blade still embedded in the woman's chest, bright blood welling and then stopped mid-action, her jaw dropping open.

"Jacinda," she said, falling back on her hands, the realisation sweeping over her. "No!" she said. "No!"

Jacinda turned, looked at her, the strength already flowing out of her. She grimaced. And then, Mahra barely heard the words.

Benevolent

"Mahra. I'm sorry. I am so sorry." And then she was gone.

Mahra leaned forward, everything else forgotten. She touched her, gently moved her. There was no pulse, no life. She could feel that she'd gone. She tried again.

Behind her, uniformed men took Marina into custody, led her towards the elevators. Timon approached her, but she didn't hear him. He crouched beside her, rested a hand on her shoulder, the shoulder where Chutzpah should have been. She shook her head.

"Mahra, come on. She's gone. There's nothing you can do."

Mahra sat where she was.

Timon shook her shoulder, gently and then a little more firmly.

"Mahra. We have to go."

She swallowed, bowed her head, and then reluctantly leaned forward and pulled her blade free. Distractedly, she looked around, then seeing nothing stood, her gaze averted from the young woman's body. Still seeing nothing, and wanting to think about anything else, she crossed to one of the chairs and wiped her blade on its arms, marring the white with streaks of deep red. She sheathed it then, turning and walking distractedly towards the elevator, Timon in tow, leaving the lifeless form of Jacinda behind her.

Chapter Forty-One

Towards Belshore

After they'd left the ILGC buildings, they split up. The uniforms left, escorting Marina Samaris to a local CoCee holding until someone had decided what to do with her. Valdor Carr, they left standing in the ILGC lobby, watching them through the glass fronts as they crossed the street on the way back to *The Nameless*. Mahra saw all of it but wasn't really processing any of it. Inside her sat a hard knot of grief. She pushed it down as she walked, biting her lip, and trying hard to concentrate on the way ahead.

As they entered the ship and moved to their positions, news was already starting to filter through about the other actions. Larit Fren had been apprehended trying to flee the compounds with a case full of artefacts and an extensive credit holding. Eleni Kraus went public immediately, claiming that it was an affront to her standing and that she held immunity from anything because of her status. Mahra suspected they'd all be tied up in various legal battles across assorted systems for some time to come. Karl Abbas had fought, and in the end, took his own life.

"Huh, imagine that," said Timon from the bridge when that news came through.

Benevolent

Any information about Dareth Garin, however, failed to emerge, as did anything about the other shadowy figure from the distant cast whose image had remained obscured. It was bound to be a concern, as was the fact that they really had no idea how far The Benevolent had extended its reach deep within the CoCee itself. Mahra listened to the reports with half an ear, her mind elsewhere, back in the past, thinking about loss, thinking about consequences, seeing images of large silver ships sweeping down and delivering destruction to her world and to everything she had known. Much later they were to learn that Garin had parleyed a position where he would assist the CoCee rooting out the operatives in their midst.

While they had been occupied in the ILGC buildings, at the same time, all over New Helvetica, troops had been sent in to take control of the enhanced facilities and shut down that equipment for good. What would happen to the enhanced themselves, Mahra didn't know, but she thought that the CoCee would probably find them useful roles, where they could contribute, but not be a threat. Eventually they would meld with society as a whole, the engineered enhancements perhaps filtering into the race, but in a far diluted form. The enhancement program itself would be no more. Hopefully never to emerge again.

For a while, Mahra was able to concentrate on nothing really but the navigation tasks required to get them back to Belshore. She was still shaken up by the confrontation on New Helvetica, the unexpected meeting and what had turned into a dual loss. There was no way she could have foreseen that she would lose both Chutzpah and Jacinda, or should she say Tsinda. In a way it was more than that, for in reality she had now effectively lost Jacinda twice. All the way back to Belshore, she thought about that, wondering why circumstance would treat her so cruelly. There was no lesson to learn there, none at all. But just like everything else, she'd get over it. Out of habit, she reached for Chutz's comforting presence, but just like everything else, he was gone too. Instead, she used the hand to rub her neck and in so doing, her knuckles brushed against the hilt of her blade. Just briefly, she ran through the scene in the ILGC offices, feeling the hollow inside her form again, but at the same time dispassionately observing her actions, realising that she had been sloppy and out of form. It could have turned out much worse than it did. She'd been lucky. It was time for her to get back into training, to sharpen those reflexes and those senses. It was time to move on again, to find something she could do.

"Jay," she said as they popped into Belshore space again. "You ready to start work."

"Of course I am," he said. "What do you think, Mahra? But aren't you going to need some time?"

Again she reached for where Chutzpah should be. She could feel his absence almost as a presence.

"I don't think so, Jay," she said. "There's a lot to do."

"Besides," said Timon. "Our Mahra is made of stronger stuff than that."

"That she is," said Jayeer.

The Nameless levelled off and started the steady descent to the surface.

"What about Carr?" said Timon.

Mahra thought about that for a moment. "Oh I think he's earned a little time to himself don't you? Once he's had a bit more time to reflect, to consolidate, I think he could be quite useful. After all, we need to do something about the development of a proper navigation tool. Eventually, I'm going to get tired of that always being me."

Timon laughed at that.

"Oh," said Jayeer. "Yes I think Carr Holding or ILGC or whatever he's going to end up calling himself this time could indeed be quite useful. Add in a bit of the Bathyscaphe people and well…."

Jay was clearly off again. Mahra smiled to herself. And the choices they would have to make…well, who knew what they would turn out to be.

There was plenty of time to sort all that out now. Plenty of time. She knew however that it was going to be with both of them, Timon Pellis and Jayeer Sind. She'd finally found her family and in the end, her crew.

And unless they did something really stupid, now there was the opportunity. All they had to do, all humanity had to do, all of them, was to make it.

She concentrated her will then focussed her thoughts and sent them out with a single message. She didn't know whether it would reach him or not, but at least she could try.

"I hope we'll make you proud, Chutz. I hope we do, wherever you are."

She turned her attention back to watch the approaching landing field and the other jump ships already clustered there.

Thus ends the third and final volume of
The Sirona Cycle

About The Author
Anthony James

Anthony James writes science fiction, though sometimes he thinks that the science fiction writes him. He grew up on speculative fiction of all sorts, though it was the greats, Asimov, Herbert, Dick, Clarke, Wolfe, Heinlein that shaped his perception. In his real life, he does other things, apart from writing, following the principle laid down by Robert A. Heinlein, that specialization is for insects. So, he strives not to be an insect.

You can find him at www.ajameswrites.com

Books In This Series
The Sirona Cycle

Mahra Kaitan, her zimonette companion and the CoCee crew struggle against the deep and growing threat of the alien Sirona.

The Jump Point

Dragged from her homeworld, young Mahra Kaitan must discover the key to fighting an insidious alien threat. The Sirona promise to subvert and control humanity, but it is Mahra alone who holds the solution. She just needs to find out what it is before it's too late.

Daughter of Atrocity

Back from their encounter with the Sirona, Mahra and her team must employ their newfound knowledge to counter the ongoing threat. After the Sirona start showing their hand, the time to act is upon them. Mahra must find out more about her new abilities, and also discover the source of the mystery that is starting to follow her. It is now becoming much more than revenge. It's about all of their futures.

Benevolent

Mahra Kaitan has a new challenge now that she has separated from the crew. The Sirona present an ongoing threat, but who or what are the Sleeth. They are like nothing they've ever seen before. And what is Chutzpah's role? On new worlds and with a new company, Mahra finally finds the clues that will eventually lead to the truth.

Standalone Novel

The Serpent Road

Aliens, ancient civilisations, and the ultimate road trip. No one knows where the Seelee came from or where they went. All Tohil knows, is that he and his companions must find a way to stop them. His journey of discovery raises as many questions as it has answers. The clues to the alien technology that threatens them lie deep within himself.